BROKEN PROMISES

MICHAELA GREY

1

"Safeword." The Dom's voice was gritty with exhaustion and something close to fear.

It took several long, agonizing moments for the command to filter through the haze in Kellen's brain, wrapped as he was in cotton wool. His tongue refused to cooperate, in any case, so he just shook his head mutely, the movement making the chain hanging from his nipples sway and sending sparks of agony through his chest.

"Goddammit," the Dom snarled, and threw the whip down. "Red, I'm done. You're too fucked up for me." He unbuckled the cuffs, letting Kellen's arms fall roughly, and Kellen bit back a whimper at the jarring of the clamps. He slumped forward, one weak hand catching himself before he went facedown on the whipping bench, as the Dom unbuckled his ankles with the same harsh touch, and then stood. "Find someone else to fulfill your death wish, boy," he grated, and stalked from the room.

Kellen sat still for a few minutes, coming back from the edge in gradual stages, focusing on his breathing in slow, even repetitions, until the room swam back into focus, resolving in front of his tear-wet eyes. He looked around. *Five things I can see.* The black crushed velvet curtains hanging in a graceful arc at the end of the bed they hadn't even gotten to use. The whipping bench, marred with a streak of—Kellen touched it curiously and his finger came away red. Probably his. The picture on the wall, of a black-leather-suited Domme, bending over her sub and tracing a line up his ribs with the edge of her knife. Kellen glanced away. His clothes, folded neatly and set on the floor on top of his shoes. He couldn't remember how he'd gotten to the room, what time it was, or even the name of the Dom who'd brought him here.

He forced the panic down and looked for the last thing. His own reflection in a mirror on the wall caught his eye. Kellen saw haunted dark brown eyes in a pale face with a pointed chin, fair hair standing up in tufts as if it had been pulled. He jerked his gaze away.

Four things I can hear. His own breathing, stertuous in his ears. The thump of the bass from the club's main room, permeating the floor and walls with its insistent beat. Footsteps, walking past his room. And a man's voice, crying out in pleasure-soaked pain.

Kellen squeezed his eyes shut briefly. *Three things I can touch.* He smoothed a hand across the vinyl of the whipping bench, avoiding the bloodstain. Ran fingers through his own hair, concentrating on the way the strands curled against his skin as he tamed them. The movement disturbed the clamps again and Kellen gasped, jerked out of his routine. He had to take them off, and it was going to *hurt*.

Setting his jaw, he watched himself in the mirror, fingers long and thin and streaked with blood, as he unscrewed the first clamp. The pain hit him in a fiery bolt as it fell free and he curled forward with a choked noise. The Dom—whose name he still couldn't remember—hadn't taken it easy on him. He'd wear these bruises for a week.

After a few minutes, Kellen sat up and fumbled for the other clamp. He let it and the chain tumble to the floor as he hunched in on himself, breathing harsh and fast through his nose as his abused nipples woke to angry, scorching life.

Two—he whimpered aloud and forced himself to concentrate. *Two things I can smell.* Blood, coppery and sharp in his nostrils, hit him first. Close behind was the smell of latex and leather and sweat, combined into one gut-punch of sensory overload.

Kellen fought the panic that threatened to drown him. *You're safe*, he told himself. "Safe," he said aloud, voice sounding croaky.

He breathed in through his nose and out through his mouth until the fear receded, leaving him drained and shaky but calmer.

One thing I can taste. Kellen licked his lips. Salt, his own tears and sweat mingled.

There was a knock on the door, and Kellen straightened, alarm zinging up his spine.

"Who—" He swallowed and tried again. "I'll be out in a minute."

"It's Martha," a concerned voice said.

Kellen didn't answer, focused on getting to his feet and staying there.

"The Dungeon Master?" Martha said. "I need to make sure you're okay. Can you open the door, please, Kellen?"

Kellen stiffened. "Just—just a minute." He reached his clothes and sat heavily on the end of the bed to pull his underwear and pants on as the doorknob turned. Kellen recoiled, clutching his shirt to his chest. "I *said* just a minute!"

Martha was a sturdy woman with a perfect Afro and high cheekbones, dressed head-to-toe in white leather, wide white wrist cuffs stark against dark satin skin. Her eyes were worried. "Philip blew out of here looking equal parts scared and angry. Took me awhile to calm him down or I'd've been here sooner." Her voice was musical and low, with a hint of a Southern accent in it. "I need to check your injuries, Kellen, and bandage anything that needs it."

"I'm fine," Kellen said automatically. "And how do you know my name?"

Martha narrowed her dark eyes. "You told me when you came in here. Do you not remember meeting me?"

I don't remember anything. Kellen stifled a slightly hysterical laugh. "I'm—look, let me just get dressed and I'll go and you'll never see me again."

"Doesn't work that way," Martha said. "You're under my protection and supervision when you're in this place, which means I'm responsible for your well-being. Stop being difficult and let me look you over, goddammit!"

Kellen opened and closed his mouth and sagged against the bedpost, suddenly so exhausted he couldn't muster the strength to argue.

"Facedown on the bed," Martha told him, her voice gentle but uncompromising, and Kellen rolled over in a sullen heap, ending up with his cheek pressed to the comforter. The satin was almost rough against his nipples and they flared to angry life again, but he couldn't find the strength to reposition himself.

Martha's fingers were gentle as she eased his pants back down and off his ankles. She sucked in a breath and Kellen wondered vaguely what she saw.

"Be right back," she said, and left the room.

Alone, Kellen drifted into a light doze. The room was warm and the bed was soft, and all too soon, he was going to be back out in the cold, praying it wouldn't rain so he could sleep in the park on the grass under his favorite tree, the one with the lacy fronds that let him see the stars in stolen glimpses when the wind stirred them. And then he'd have to go back to—

He didn't hear the door open again, but it must have, because someone was there beside him in the bed, hands icy cold on his burning back, and Kellen jackknifed away, flinging himself sideways off the mattress to land with a bone-jarring thump on the floor.

The impact sent ripples of agony through him but he ignored them, struggling to his feet to face his attacker—Martha, kneeling on the bed with her hands up, as if she was afraid to move.

"Kellen?" Her voice was tentative, as if she was *worried* about him.

Kellen swallowed hard and straightened, rolling his shoulders and pulling his air of bravado back into place. "Can I go yet?"

Martha shook her head, hair swaying. "Not until I dress your wounds."

"So I'm a prisoner?" Kellen flung at her.

"No," Martha said. "You can go, but—"

Kellen ignored her, scrambling for his clothes as his world dipped and swung dangerously. He was dressed in record time and out the door before Martha could say anything else to stop him.

<hr>

"THE CROISSANTS ARE ABOUT TO BURN," Senna said without looking up from the dough she was shaping on the floury counter.

"Fuck, *shit*." Vee spun for the oven and yanked it open. "Hotpads, hotpads, where—" Senna threw one overhand at him and he caught it on the fly, grabbing the tray one-handed and dropping it on the granite countertop.

Senna leaned over, hands still buried to the wrists in dough, and wrinkled her nose.

"Melissa will make you throw them out."

"What? *Why?* I got to them before they burned!"

Senna gestured with her chin. "They dried out. She won't let us serve those to patrons."

Vee groaned, sagging against the counter.

"Oh, don't be so dramatic," Senna said. "Just toss them and start over. There's another batch proofing in the fridge."

Vee scowled at her but pushed upright and grabbed a bag. He shoved the hot pastries into them, muttering under his breath, and let the door to the alley slam behind him on his way to the dumpster. He was winding up to throw the bag when what he'd thought was a bundle of rags moved, and Vee lost his balance and nearly fell over.

A young man raised his head, dark brown eyes sharp and wary under hair so blond it was almost silver. There was a ring of bruises around his throat and matching ones on his skinny wrists. Vee opened his mouth to ask if he was okay, but the young man spoke first.

"Fuck off."

Vee's eyebrows went up. "Uh, you're in *my* alley."

The boy sneered. "You own it, huh?"

Vee bristled. "I have more right to be here than *you* do, since I work here."

The boy rolled his eyes and pushed himself to his feet. "I'm leaving, unbunch your panties."

"Wait," Vee said. He held out the bag of still-steaming croissants, but the boy just looked at them and back up at him. Vee hesitated and set it on the pavement. "There's nothing wrong with them," he said, knowing he sounded defensive, and turned to go back inside. He was nearly to the door when a croissant hit him between the shoulder blades.

Vee spun and the boy tipped his chin up defiantly, mouth set in a mulish line. Whatever angry words Vee was going to say died on his lips at the sight of the purple and green bruises mottling the young man's pale skin.

He cleared his throat and gestured vaguely. "You should… um. Get those looked at." He escaped inside before another croissant was hurled at him.

VEE SPENT the rest of the day on autopilot, thinking about the encounter and the stranger's dark brown eyes. He nearly burned the puff pastry, which made Senna yell at him, and then dropped a tray of scones halfway to the oven when he bounced off a wall, not paying attention to where he was going.

"My office," Melissa said, appearing in the doorway.

Vee looked up from where he was picking up scone triangles off the floor as Senna covered her face at the counter above him. "Um. Sure."

He sidled into her office, wiping his floury hands on his apron. Melissa was behind her desk, typing something. Her dark eyes gave nothing away as she folded her hands and nodded toward the empty chair.

Vee flopped into it gracelessly and something like amusement flickered through Melissa's eyes. She was tall even sitting down, dark-skinned with cheekbones that could cut glass, and she terrified Vee, although he'd die before admitting that.

"How's the baby?" he blurted.

Melissa almost smiled. "She took her first steps yesterday."

"Wow, that's great!" Vee hesitated. "Is it great? I mean, I don't know how old she is. Is she early or late or…?"

Melissa's lips twitched. "She's right on time. What's going on with you?"

Vee squirmed. "Like, in general?"

"I was thinking more today," Melissa said. "You seem distracted. Anything I can do to help?"

Vee thought about it for a minute. "Why do we throw away the burned food?" he finally said.

"Instead of—"

"Well, some of it's still perfectly edible, just not *perfect*, you know?" Vee said. "Why couldn't we give it to the homeless? People who need it? Wouldn't that be better than letting it go to waste?"

Melissa nodded. "Believe me, I'd love to do that. Unfortunately, the lawyers on Dominic's staff are sharks, and bloodthirsty ones at that. I'm specifically barred from giving away food from the bakery because they say it's a liability issue and I could open us up to a lawsuit."

Vee slumped, deflated.

"However." Melissa picked up a pen and spun it between long fingers, seemingly focused on it alone. "If someone were to buy the food from me, at a deeply discounted rate, perhaps, I would have no say in how that person distributed his baked goods, and the sharks would have no reason to complain."

Vee perked up and an actual smile flickered across Melissa's lips.

"Can I—um. I'd like to buy your overstock, ma'am," he finally said, and Melissa inclined her head.

"Get with Senna at the end of the day. She'll get it sorted out."

Vee nodded. Melissa was already turning back to her computer. Vee dithered and finally stood, nearly knocking the chair over, bobbed his head, and bolted.

When he got back to the kitchen, Senna was filling a basket.

"Order for the top floor," she said, adding croissants and sausage rolls. "I can't leave the brioche, so you're up."

Vee took his apron off, swiping at his face to remove any errant flour, and accepted the basket.

"It's for Dominic," Senna said, grabbing a pomegranate soda from the fridge and shoving it into Vee's arms next to the basket. "Farid called it in. *Do not embarrass me.*"

Vee scowled, affronted, and stalked for the elevators. He rode them up to the top floor and stepped out into lush carpet, wide hallways and huge paintings in muted swirls of blues, grays, and creams on the walls. Down the hall to the left—a small brass nameplate above a door proclaimed it Farid Qadir's office, in front of the inner sanctum that was Cory's domain, the holy ground no one set foot on without invitation. Which meant that to Vee's right, directly opposite, was Dominic's workroom.

He'd heard the wild rumors about what had gone down eight months ago, of course. Everyone had. They ranged from 'Farid had taken money to betray Dominic's secrets to a rival company but had backed out, giving himself up to keep Dominic safe', to 'Farid had been contracted to put a hit on Dominic and possibly Cory as well but had a change of heart at the last second'.

In any case, at the end of it all, Dominic had left the country, Farid had gone into seclusion, and everyone at Spectral had done their best to get on with life, buzzing with gossip whenever they met in the halls.

But then Dominic had come back, with Farid right beside him, and called an employee meeting where he'd told them that Cory was stepping into his position as CEO, Farid would be taking over as Cory's personal assistant, and Dominic was moving into a more behind-the-scenes position where he would be free to work on his code and not be bothered.

As Dominic had stood before them, his hands trembling before he shoved them in his pockets, Vee had remembered that Dominic hated public speaking. But Farid had stepped closer, as if offering his presence as reassurance, and Dominic's posture had eased, just a fraction. Vee had watched them, the way they looked at each other, the way they both seemed calmer next to each other, and had wondered what it would be like to be someone's anchor that way, to trust someone that deeply.

Dominic's door opened and Farid looked at him, one eyebrow raised. He was a slim man, neatly built, with dark hair and eyes, a bold nose, and a distractingly sweet mouth.

"Planning on standing out there all day?" he inquired, his soft, husky voice amused.

"Sorry," Vee said, and shoved the basket at him just as Dominic appeared behind Farid.

Vee had never spoken to Dominic before. He'd been hired by Melissa, and kept in the bakery most of his time. Senna usually made the deliveries to the top floor.

Dominic was intimidatingly tall, with brown hair that fell in shining waves around his face and dark gray eyes. He looked politely interested but also somewhat irritated at being interrupted.

Vee gulped and held out the basket again.

"Oh, you must be Vee," Dominic said, as Farid took pity on Vee and accepted the baked goods. "I've heard a lot about you from Lily."

Despite himself, Vee groaned. "Whatever she told you, it's not true, I swear."

Dominic grinned. He had a nice smile, Vee thought helplessly. "So you didn't tell a police officer he was raised by a pig, which was why he made such a good cop?"

Vee winced. "I, um. That's not an exact translation, but…." He floundered as Dominic and Farid waited expectantly, matching looks of curiosity on their faces. "I don't keep halal?" Vee offered feebly.

Dominic burst out laughing as Farid rubbed his face, unable to hide the twitching of his mouth.

"I like you," Dominic said when he'd sobered. "It was nice to meet you, Vee. Tell Senna thanks for the pastries." He disappeared back into the office as Farid lingered, dark eyes amused.

Vee remembered the pomegranate soda and held it out hastily, kicking himself, but Farid just accepted it with a nod.

"Get in here, 'Rid," Dominic called, his voice dark with promise, and Farid gave Vee a smile and slipped back into the office, closing the door behind him.

Alone, Vee wondered briefly if he could die from embarrassment, or if retiring to become a monk in a secluded monastery was a more feasible alternative. He wandered back toward the elevator, thinking about the young man behind the dumpster again. Would he still be out there when Vee was off work? Probably not, and even if he was, Vee was likely to just get another pastry hurled at him for his efforts.

Sure enough, when he clocked out and stepped through the back door with a box of baked goods, the young man was nowhere in sight.

He walked around to the front of Spectral, a towering glass and steel structure, and stopped at the sight of a group of people gathered by the doors. They were holding up signs. One said "LEVITICUS 18:22", and Vee made a mental note to look it up later. Another said "KEEP QUEERS OUT OF OUR SOFTWARE." Vee scowled at that. A third sign simply said "SPEC-TRAL = SIN".

One of the protestors spotted Vee. "Excuse me, sir, do you work here?" he called. He was a tall man, thin and pale with blond hair fading to gray and stooped, rounded shoulders.

Vee tipped his chin up. "So what if I do?"

The man held out a pamphlet and Vee took it warily. "HOMOSEXUALITY IS SIN", it told him in bright, cheerful letters, and underneath, an address for the Church on the Hill.

Vee dropped the pamphlet on the ground and wiped his hand on his shirt. "You people are sick," he said, clutching the box of pastries to his chest.

"Oh no," the tall man said earnestly. "Gay people are the sick ones. We're trying to *save* them. That's our mission from God."

"They don't *need* 'saving'," Vee hissed. "*We* don't need saving. Take your hate elsewhere. Why are you even protesting here?"

The man's eyes clouded with anger and distaste and he took a step back. "One of the largest software development companies in north America, and it was founded by a pair of faggots," he spat.

Vee flinched. "Dominic and Cory are better people than you'll ever be," he said.

The man sneered and Vee shook himself. Why was he even engaging?

"This has been fun, but I have to go give food to the homeless and then have sex with my boyfriend," he said brightly, and relished the look of horror on the man's face as he spun and walked away. Safely out of sight around the corner, he hailed a taxi. "Nearest homeless shelter, please," he told the driver.

HE GOT home over two hours later, covered in croissant crumbs but feeling proud of himself for his idea. The homeless shelter had also regretfully refused the bread, citing the same issue Melissa had, so Vee had taken to the streets, handing out each pastry individually until the box was empty. He'd watched for silver-blond hair and pale skin, but he'd seen no sign of the croissant-hurler.

He pushed open the door and kicked off his shoes. "Sean?"

"Kitchen."

Vee padded through the tiny apartment and found his boyfriend standing at the stove. It smelled like spaghetti, which Sean was stirring. Vee wound his arms around Sean's waist, resting his chin on his shoulder, and sighed.

"How was your day?"

He felt tense, Vee realized too late. He straightened as Sean dropped the spoon and shrugged.

"My day was fine. I was *hoping* to have dinner with my boyfriend, but I guess you were too busy to spend time with me."

Guilt stabbed Vee. "Fuck, I texted you, didn't you get it?" It had said *read* after he sent it, but Vee could already tell it wasn't the time to bring that up.

"Oh, I got it," Sean snapped, and turned off the heat. He stepped away from Vee's arms, turning to face him. He was shorter than Vee, who tried to downplay his lanky 6'1 frame, with a pug-nose and freckles, and usually his green eyes held a smile.

"I was trying to do something nice," Vee said, knowing it sounded like an excuse, and Sean's eyes narrowed.

"You could do something nice for me and be

here on time for dinner. Isn't that what boyfriends are supposed to do? Spend time together?"

Vee ran a hand through his hair, blowing out the frustration. "I'm sorry," he said, and took a step closer. "Let me make it up to you."

Sean didn't move, expression suspicious, and Vee took another step, until they were chest to chest. He ran his hands down Sean's arms, smiling at the goosebumps that raised under his touch, and leaned in to press a kiss to his throat.

"Let me show you how good I can make you feel," he murmured.

Sean closed his eyes, those thick, pretty lashes sweeping down, and nodded.

THIRTY MINUTES LATER, Sean yanked the front door open. "You fucking *freak!*" he shouted, as if Vee hadn't heard him the first twenty times, and shoved his suitcases into the hall. The door shut behind him with an explosive bang and Vee flinched, rolling onto his side on the couch.

He fumbled for his phone, eyes blurry with unshed tears, and hit Lily's number.

"'Sup, bro?" she greeted him cheerfully.

"Can you—" Vee stopped to swallow.

"What is it?" Lily said, voice sharpening to concern. "What happened?"

"Can you come over?" Vee said desperately.

"On my way."

"Bring alcohol," Vee said, and hung up.

Fifteen minutes later, Lily walked in the front door, a bottle of vodka in her hand. Vee was curled on the couch, staring sightlessly at the wall, and Lily knelt in front of him.

"Hey," she said softly.

Vee almost managed a smile. Lily was his favorite cousin, with her mohawk and silver jewelry and the black leather she loved to wear. "I fucked up," he whispered.

"Sean?" Lily asked.

Vee nodded. "I, um—" He pushed himself upright and reached for the vodka, but Lily held it out of reach.

"Shot glasses," she said, and disappeared into the kitchen. In a minute she was back and pouring their first round.

Vee knocked it back, letting the alcohol scorch a path to his stomach, and dropped his head back against the couch cushion with a sigh. "Sean dumped me."

"Is that good? Bad?" Lily shrugged at Vee's look. "I never really liked him, bhai, but I'll be whatever you want me to be right now. Are we mad? Upset? Hurt? Heartbroken?" Her eyes narrowed. "You weren't in love with him, were you?"

"God, no," Vee said, shuddering. "No, nothing like that. But... I liked him. I thought... I thought maybe he'd like...."

"Are you about to tell me kinky sex stuff?" Lily said, pouring another shot for each of them. "Because if you are, I need more alcohol in my system."

"It's just always the *same*," Vee said, turning the shot glass in his hands. "Every once in awhile we'd mix it up and do doggy-style, but it was always just… one kiss, two touches, three pumps, done."

Lily stared at him and Vee downed his shot, feeling suddenly defensive.

"He liked a routine," he said, holding out his glass again. "He got upset when it changed, which fine, I understand, but he *hated* it when I tried to switch things up a bit. I wanted *more*, Lil, I wanted to try stuff, figure out what I liked, I wanted—" He flopped back against the cushions and glared at the ceiling. "He called me a fucking freak."

"He *what?*" Lily sounded angry for the first time. "*Why?*"

Vee stared at his glass.

Lily refilled it.

Vee drank it, held it out, waited for the liquid courage to loosen his tongue. "I told you, I wanted —" He squeezed his eyes shut. "I asked him if I could tie him up and spank him." Mortification burned in his stomach with the alcohol.

"Is that *it?*" Lily said, and Vee's eyes shot open.

"That's not enough?"

Lily refilled his glass, scowling. "That's *nothing*, Vee. That's like… kiddie wheels shit. Like… floaty wings in a pool. Like—"

"I get it!" Vee said loudly, and downed his shot. "Thank you, I have no idea what I'm doing."

"Maybe not, but he had no right to react that way," Lily said, tone reasonable. She was matching him drink for drink, but while Vee's head was beginning to feel loose and possibly disconnected, her movements and speech were as assured as ever. "It's okay to want different things, bhai. It's *not* okay to make someone else feel like shit for not wanting what you want. Sean's an asshole, okay?"

Vee closed his eyes. "Does it make me…." He groped for the word but it wouldn't form.

"Make you what? Fucked up? Dangerous? Abusive?"

Tears pricked Vee's eyes and he nodded mutely.

"*No*," Lily said. She put a hand on his knee and waited for Vee to meet his eyes. "Listen, I think you need to talk to someone."

"Like a doctor or psychiatrist?" Vee said, struggling upright.

Lily grinned. "Not exactly."

2

"Hɪ," Farid said when Vee opened the door. He'd changed into soft, faded jeans and a T-shirt that looked even softer, his hair falling free from its careful coif.

Vee stared at him, the alcohol making his head spin. "Lily, I'm going to *murder*—"

Lily popped up beside him, grabbing Farid's arm and pulling him inside. "Hey, 'Rid, good to see you. How's my boy Dom?"

"You mean your *boss*, Dominic?" Farid asked, allowing himself to be towed into the living room. "He's well. Sends his regards."

Lily grinned. "He's not really my boss anymore. Cory signs my checks, Dom just hides in his office and writes his code." She disappeared into the kitchen as Farid sat down on the couch.

Vee hovered in the middle of the room, not sure what to do.

Farid patted the cushion beside him. "Sit. You're too drunk to be upright, I think."

Vee sank onto the other end of the couch and resisted the urge to wrap his arms around his knees as Lily came back with another glass.

"Hope you like cheap vodka," she said cheerfully.

Farid sighed. "Halal, Lily," he reminded her.

Lily smacked her forehead. "Grape juice? I think there's some behind the moldy cheese Vee keeps saying he's going to throw out."

"*Lily*," Vee hissed.

"That's fine," Farid said. "And then maybe you could give me and your cousin some privacy?"

HE TURNED BACK to Vee once the door was shut behind Lily.

"Sorry," Vee mumbled to his lap. "I don't even know why you're here."

"I learned a while ago there's no point in trying to resist Lily when she's set her mind to something," Farid said. "She thinks I can help with… whatever's going on, so that's why I'm here."

"Do you always drop everything to help out random strangers?" Vee asked.

Farid's eyes creased in a smile. "I do when it's a friend asking. So why don't you tell me what's going on?"

Vee tried to sink into the couch cushions. "It's really not a big deal."

"Your cousin thought it was worrisome enough that she asked me to come halfway across town to talk to you, which tells me two things.

One—it *is* a big deal, or at least something that needs to be addressed. And two—she thinks I can help. Meaning it's something I have experience with. And since I don't think your current crisis has anything to do with being a personal assistant, that means it's the *other* thing I'm an expert in."

Vee blinked, trying to follow. "I'm—I don't—what?"

"What happened tonight?" Farid asked.

"My boyfriend broke up with me," Vee said miserably. "Because I'm a freak."

Farid's eyebrows lifted. "Is that so? How, exactly?"

Vee squirmed. Farid waited.

"I didn't—" The alcohol soaking Vee's brain made it hard for him to find words. "I didn't want to hurt him."

"Didn't you?" Farid asked gently. "Or is it that you *did* want to hurt him that's got you so worked up?"

Vee covered his face. "I *know* I'm a bad person," he said into his palms. "Can you just—please just go away? I know I need therapy and probably medication, can you *please* leave it?"

Farid stood and Vee dropped his hands, but Farid was just gathering the glasses and taking them to the kitchen. He came back in a few minutes and sat down again.

"You know what BDSM is, Vee?"

"'Course," Vee mumbled. "Everyone does."

"Describe it to me, then. What is it?"

Vee blew his hair off his forehead, scowling. "It's—I don't remember what the letters stand for, but like, um—something about sadism and masochism. People liking to hurt other people, and other people liking to *be* hurt. Whips and latex and chains and candle wax."

Farid looked amused. "Candle wax can be fun, but it gets messy. And I've never really seen the point of latex."

It took a minute for that to sink in. Vee's mouth fell open. "*You?*"

"Me," Farid agreed calmly, and sipped his juice.

"But—" Vee struggled to push himself upright. "But you—"

"But I what?"

"You—you were Dominic's assistant. *He* told *you* what to do."

"In the office, yes," Farid said. "Out of the office…." He trailed off and smiled as Vee gaped at him.

"You're shitting me."

"I assure you I'm not."

"You—you tie Dominic up and whip him? You *hurt* him? And he *likes* it?"

"Well, no," Farid said. He set his glass down. "Dominic doesn't get off on pain. What he likes is the D in the acronym—domination. He has anxiety, you know that?"

Vee nodded blankly, mind spinning.

"Dominating him gives him an opportunity to turn his brain off. He goes away in his mind. He can stop worrying, stop fretting, and just *be*. I take control, so he can let go."

"I'm not drunk enough for this," Vee muttered.

"I think you've had enough," Farid said,

sounding amused. "So you wanted to dominate your boyfriend, right?"

Vee stared at the ceiling.

"Look," Farid said. "I know you don't know me. And I know it's hard to talk about this kind of thing in general. But it's nothing to be ashamed of, okay?"

"I wanted to *hurt* him," Vee snarled. "Tell me why I shouldn't be ashamed of that."

"Did you choose to be gay?" Farid asked.

"What? *No!* I just... I just *am*."

"And are you ashamed of it?"

"No," Vee muttered, crossing his arms. "But *hurting* someone is different."

"Even if they want to be hurt?"

"No one wants to be hurt," Vee snapped. "Not *normal* people."

Farid's eyebrows lifted. "One of my best friends is a masochist. He loves pain. He gets off on it. He begs to be hurt, because it makes him fly, okay? And yeah, no one would accuse him of being normal, but he's stable, his career is really taking off, he has a boyfriend who adores him, and I think he'd be pretty offended at your suggestion that he's fucked up just because he likes things outside the 'norm.'"

Vee opened and closed his mouth. "What do you mean, fly?"

"It's also called subspace. It's hard to explain to someone who hasn't experienced it, but it's a sense of euphoria, bliss that allows the person to fully let go and surrender to whoever's controlling the scene. And it's addicting. Once someone's experienced it, it's hard to go without it, and one of the ways to hit subspace is for the Dom to inflict pain."

"But—" Even amidst the confusion and alcohol clouding his mind, Vee couldn't stop the twitch of his dick. God, he *wanted* that, he wanted to be in control and make someone fly, make them feel better than they ever had....

Farid leaned forward. "There's nothing to be ashamed of," he said, holding Vee's eyes. "It's not abuse, and you're not a bad person."

Vee shook his head silently, not even sure what he was arguing about. "I don't know what to think," he finally admitted.

"It's a lot," Farid agreed. "Look, just... promise me something?"

Vee made a noncommittal noise.

"Promise me you'll take the time to learn about this kind of thing before you jump in and try to do it without any experience or guidance and end up getting someone hurt?" Farid reached into his pocket and pulled out a card and a pen. He scribbled on the back and then handed it over. "Here. Start with these websites. That's my cell. Call or text me anytime."

Vee accepted it, unsure what to say.

Farid tilted his head and smiled. "You seem like a nice kid, Vee."

"I'm twenty-five," Vee said, stung.

Farid's smile widened. "Drink some water for that hangover. I'll let myself out."

<hr>

KELLEN ATE TWO-THIRDS of the croissants before

he was out of the alley, even scooping up the one he'd thrown at the distractingly attractive Indian man before he bolted, half-afraid the man would change his mind and demand his baked goods back.

But he didn't reappear, and Kellen made his escape, tucking the last three croissants inside his jacket and heading into downtown Seattle.

It was a Thursday, so Cuffs wasn't very busy. Kellen nodded at the bouncer, who frowned at the sight of him but didn't stop him.

Inside, Kellen ducked left into the bathrooms. A few wet wipes took care of the body odor problem, and he tied his ragged T-shirt at his midriff, hiding the worst of the holes, before swiping on some eyeliner from his pocket.

He stared at himself critically in the mirror. *Too skinny, too angry, too fucked-up.* He shook his hair forward over his face, hiding the worst of the shadows in his eyes, and left the bathroom. Cuffs was a decent-sized establishment, featuring a main room on several levels that descended in wide, shallow steps with comfortable leather seats ringing each level. In front of each seat was a metal bar at waist-height. Kellen was intimately familiar with those bars—he'd been chained to them on more than one occasion.

He trotted down the levels until he was at the bottom, skirting the raised dais at the center of the room to make for the bar and the sturdy Hispanic woman behind it.

"Hey," he said in greeting.

Lucero raised a cool eyebrow. "Back again, are you?"

Kellen tried for a cheeky grin. "Insatiable, I guess. Got anything for me to do?"

Lucero jerked her square chin toward the tray at the end of the bar. "Start bussing. It's gonna be busy soon."

Kellen grabbed the tray and went to work. Bussing was easy, and it gave him an opportunity to scope out the Doms who'd come looking for an unattached sub to play with. He didn't want the ones who played it safe, who insisted on safewords and that stupid traffic-light system—God, he hated that system. He wanted someone who'd take him to the edge and throw him off it, let him fly, let him *soar*. Set him free.

He found him during the second rush of patrons, about three hours into the night. Lucero was grudgingly teaching him how to mix drinks in her spare time, and she'd finally unbent enough to say, "Guess even you can't fuck up drawing a beer. House first, brand name only if they ask. Remember what the wristbands mean?"

Kellen nodded. "Red for subs who have scened, nothing but juice or soda for them. Yellow for anyone planning to scene—only one beer for them. House brand, of course."

Lucero nodded, satisfied, and went back to mixing drinks.

A man settled at the bar, his shirt open almost to his navel and showing thick, curly hair on his barrel chest. His wrists were broad, a yellow band circling one of them, and there was an avid light in his eyes when he looked at Kellen.

"New here, sugar?" Kellen said, sliding a beer down to a waiting patron.

The man made a noise that could have meant anything. "What's your name?"

"Kellen. You?"

The man's eyes tightened. "You don't ask me questions."

Kellen suppressed the zing of fear and excitement that zipped up his spine and nodded.

"Beer," the man said. He waited until Kellen had drawn the house beer and handed it to him, then shoved it back across the bar, hard enough that beer slopped over the side in a foamy wave. "The good stuff, not this horse piss."

Kellen ducked his head and obeyed. He kept drawing beer for other patrons, watching the man at the end of the counter, and was ready when he stood and turned away without waiting to see if Kellen would follow.

Kellen yanked the apron off and dropped it in the hamper. "Lucero, can I have my pay for the night?"

Lucero looked at him, then past him toward the man who was walking toward the stairs that led to the private rooms. "You sure you know what you're doing?"

"Of course," Kellen said, nearly bouncing on his toes. "Please, my pay?"

Lucero sighed and opened the register.

UPSTAIRS, Kellen had to stop and figure out what room the Dom was in. He caught the Dungeon Master's eye—not Martha this time, thankfully, but an older man with silvering hair and shrewd eyes.

"Did a guy take a private room just now?" Kellen asked him. "Stocky, balding, mid-thirties?"

The Master studied him and then nodded, jerking a thumb at the room behind him.

Kellen flashed him a grateful smile and went past him to knock on the door. He didn't wait for a response, slipping inside and shutting it behind him.

The Dom caught him by the throat and slammed him against the wall. Kellen's head bounced off the hard surface and he went limp with a choked gasp.

"You're late," the Dom growled.

***

VEE WOKE UP ALONE, pushing the covers off and stretching in the sunlight that streamed through his windows. It was his day off, and he'd intended to spend it with Sean—going to the pier, maybe, picking up some fresh fish so Vee could cook something delicious for dinner.

He didn't have the hangover he'd expected, and vaguely remembered Farid telling him to drink water. He must have obeyed. He rolled onto his back and stared at the ceiling.

Sean was gone. Left him for wanting something more… adventurous in bed. Vee scowled at the cornice. Was it really so wrong to be interested in more than just missionary or doggy-style? *Was he perverted? A freak?*

He shook his head. If he was, then so was Farid, and Vee refused to believe that of him.

Sitting up abruptly, he leaned over and grabbed his laptop. Time to do some research.

An hour later, his eyes were burning and he was half-hard, buzzing with frustrated energy that didn't have an outlet. He'd read about Dom/mes, safewords, subspace, munches, edge play, how to spot a good Dom and how to avoid a bad one, RACK and SSC, and his head was spinning with terms and descriptions and phrases.

Finally, he closed the tab and opened another, to his favorite porn site. Typing in "BDSM" brought back a dizzying amount of results, seemingly all of them featuring black leather and some rather alarming bondage gear.

He clicked on one, with only two guys in it and no leather. The sub was tied to a rack shaped like a large wooden X, arms and legs outstretched. He struggled occasionally, testing his bonds, as the Dom paced around him, holding a whip with several soft leather straps trailing from the end. Judging from the state of the sub's back, the Dom had been whipping him for awhile. The sub's pale skin was flushed an angry red in an overlapping pattern of stripes, from mid-ribs to mid-thighs.

As Vee watched, the Dom brought the whip down again. The sub jerked and Vee caught his breath, going from half-hard to fully erect. He fumbled his pajama pants down with one hand and set the laptop beside him.

The whip smacked, the sound obscenely loud, and the sub moaned, pulling at the bonds. Vee watched, spellbound, as the Dom whipped him methodically, each stroke even and perfectly placed.

"Please," the sub begged, twisting, and the Dom took his chin in one hand and kissed him, slow and tender and full of affection as Vee squeezed his eyes shut and came in hot, pulsing throbs on his belly.

KELLEN WOKE up in a pool of blood. The grass was cold beneath his cheek, and when he lifted his head, several strands stuck to his face. He got one hand underneath himself but halfway up, what little strength he had evaporated and he sagged back onto his stomach. Panting rapidly, he lay still and took stock. He had no idea how he'd gotten to the park. Had he somehow gotten out of Cuffs under his own power? No—the Dom wouldn't have risked leaving him there. He'd never be allowed back if Kellen had been found like this. Which meant he'd been dumped.

There was a terrible ache in his right shoulder, deep in the bone, and Kellen had a vague memory of the Dom wrenching his arm violently up behind his back and tying it there. *It might be broken*, he thought dizzily.

Time enough to worry about that later. He'd been beaten with either a crop or some other sort of narrow whip, judging by the feel of the welts on his back and upper thighs. His ass ached dully, and Kellen flinched, remembering how the Dom had used only spit.

I wanted this. It was hard to keep that thought

in his head sometimes, when the pain was especially bad, when he ached in every fiber, when he knew that his sustained injuries would keep him from working for several days, which meant he wouldn't eat. Which meant he'd heal more slowly. Days of agony, hunger, and the itch slowly swelling under his skin until he thought he'd go mad with it.

Kellen closed his eyes and took a deep, steadying breath. For some reason, the face of the young Indian man the day before swam into his mind's eye, worried dark eyes and soft mouth. Would he help? Could Kellen even make it to the bakery?

Probably not. His shoulder wasn't the only thing that ached with a deep, grievous hurt. He didn't think his ankle was broken, but it was sprained, certainly.

"Oh my god." The voice was soft and horrified. "Are you alive?"

Kellen lifted his head enough to see a curvy Black girl standing on the path at the base of the tree, her eyes huge with worry.

"'M fine," Kellen slurred. "Go 'way."

Instead, she climbed the small hill and knelt beside him. She had a dog on a leash, Kellen realized fuzzily when the dog tried to lick his face. He recoiled, putting an elbow up, and the girl swore and pulled the dog away.

"9-1-1?" she said into her phone, and Kellen jolted upright in horror, ignoring his body's protests. "I need an ambulance."

"*No,*" Kellen said, reaching for the phone, but she sidestepped his wavering arm easily.

"He's been beaten really badly, he's covered in blood. I don't know—hang on." She stooped and looked into Kellen's eyes, lifting a hand. "How many fingers am I holding up?" she asked.

"Fuck off," Kellen snapped.

"Just hurry," the girl said to the operator, and gave directions to the park. Then she sank to her knees, pulling her small, furry dog into her lap and staring at Kellen.

"Stop looking at me," Kellen said through his teeth, and got his good arm under himself to push himself upright. He had to get out of the park before the ambulance arrived. But his arm buckled and he nearly face-planted again.

"Don't move, you might start the bleeding again. What's your name?"

"Go away."

"I'm Star," the girl said. She was wearing neon bright leggings and a navy blue sweater with tiny stars embroidered all over it. "Do you have somewhere to go?"

"Would I be *here* if I did?" Kellen tried again to get up and failed just as quickly. Star put out a hand but pulled it back when he snarled.

"Do you want a granola bar?" she asked next.

Kellen's stomach growled but he didn't answer.

Star held it out and Kellen hesitated but then snatched it. It hurt to chew, he realized quickly, but that didn't stop him from demolishing it in two bites and shoving the wrapper in his pocket.

He ducked his head, wincing at the motion. "Thanks." The word felt sour on his tongue but Star smiled at him, petting her dog absently as she watched him.

They both heard the siren at the same time and Kellen stiffened.

"They'll help," Star said softly.

Kellen couldn't stop the bitter laugh. "No one can help."

HE LET the paramedics check him over, but refused to tell them what had happened. At the hospital, the nurse made sympathetic noises as she cleaned his wounds, but Kellen kept his mouth stubbornly shut as she asked him gently probing questions.

"Do you have anyone to call?"

Kellen stared at the opposite wall.

The nurse sighed and patted his knee carefully. "Doctor will be in soon. Don't go anywhere."

Kellen waited until the ward was busiest, and when a code blue sounded and nurses went pounding by, all their attention on the patient who needed them, he carefully untangled himself from the monitors. His ankle was sore, but the rest and fluids had helped, and he was able to walk silently from the room and down the stairs to the staff's lockers, where he swiped a set of scrubs. On his way out, he saw a dark brown hoodie hanging on a hook by the door. He hesitated briefly and then grabbed it and pulled it on, the voluminous folds enveloping him as he tugged the hood up. Then he left the hospital without looking back.

3

Kellen headed for the underpass, taking it slow so his ankle didn't protest too much. The cool autumn wind chilled his skin under the thin scrubs and he shivered, huddling inside the too-big hoodie. He was late, and Jacob wouldn't be happy.

Sure enough, Kellen spotted Jacob's thin, stooped figure pacing as he got closer to the underpass, and his heart thumped painfully in his chest. Jacob looked up and saw him, and Kellen hid the flinch as he strode forward and caught Kellen's chin in a viselike grip.

"Where have you been?"

His fingers were tight, squeezing Kellen's jaw until it ached, and Kellen stood very still.

"I'm sorry," he managed.

Jacob's grip somehow tightened, making Kellen's eyes water, and then he let him go, turning away as if in disgust and stalking back toward his usual perch, a concrete ledge under the overpass.

"I didn't mean to be gone so long," Kellen said, following him. His ankle was protesting and he hid the flinch. "I'm—I'm sorry."

Jacob sat down and looked Kellen over, his thin face pinched with anger. *Because he cares about me*, Kellen reminded himself.

"Do you know how I worry?" Jacob said.

Kellen nodded, shoving his hands deep in the hoodie. "I don't mean to make it harder on you."

Jacob sighed. "So? You do without trying. Where were you?"

"I—" Kellen wavered, strength rapidly fading, and sat down on the cold concrete before he collapsed, his body protesting the motion. "I was… at the club, and then after, I guess I was sleeping it off in the park, and some girl called an ambulance, I tried to make her go away but she wouldn't, and the EMTs took me to the hospital." He swallowed hard. "I left as quick as I could."

Jacob's eyes narrowed. "'Some girl'? Are you telling me someone stopped out of, what, the goodness of their heart?" He barked a laugh. "That's endearingly naive. Just another liberal looking to cross off their do-gooders to-do list for the month. She didn't care about you."

Kellen hunched his shoulders. "I know," he whispered.

Jacob leaned forward and took Kellen's chin, his grip gentler this time. "I'm the only one who cares about you," he said.

"I know," Kellen repeated. He was so tired.

"How much did you make last night?"

Kellen flinched and Jacob's eyes narrowed. "Well?"

"About seventy-five dollars, but—" Kellen hesitated. "They cut my clothes off at the hospital and burned them. They said I could have the money back when I was discharged. I'm—I had to leave without it."

Thunder rumbled and died in Jacob's eyes. "So you're telling me you were gone that entire time, made me worry all night long, only to show up with *nothing*?"

"I'm sorry," Kellen whispered, ducking his head. " I didn't mean to—"

"Your *stupid* fucking addiction is the reason we're in this state," Jacob spat, and Kellen absorbed the words, letting them flay him open. Jacob was right. It *was* his fault. "I've been patient, I've tried to understand, but I am *sick* of you constantly fucking up and leaving me to clean the mess. *God.*"

Kellen lowered his head further, until his chin was on his chest. "I'm sorry," he repeated. "Please…. I'm—" He rubbed his arms. "I know I don't deserve it, but… would you hold me?"

Jacob regarded him silently and finally shook his head. "No. But you can use my bedroll." He pointed.

"Okay." Kellen dragged himself to his feet. "Thank you, Jacob." He curled up on the thin mattress that smelled like Jacob, dragging the tattered blanket up over himself and tucking his arms close to his body, knees to his chest.

VEE WENT RUNNING the next morning, still thinking about the world Farid and his computer had opened up for him. His feet pounded the pavement, sending little jolts through his body, his motions free and easy. He loved running before the sun rose, when the world was cool and dark and the city was just starting to wake up. It was a misty, chilly morning, a hint of fall's sharpness hanging in the breeze, and Vee took a deep lungful and sped up, letting the rhythm of the music in his earbuds and the pounding of his feet chase the cobwebs from his head.

Could he hurt a sexual partner? Could he take someone he cared about and willingly inflict pain on them? He couldn't deny that the thought sent a frisson down his spine. Did that make him bad? He still couldn't quite separate out the feeling that hurting someone else was abuse, even if the other person wanted it, begged for it. And yet—

He cleared his throat and forced his mind away from the topic. Running with a hard-on was… uncomfortable. He slowed his pace, looking around. The sun was peeking over the hill he was currently climbing, sending questing golden rays through the trees. This part of Seattle was popular with equestrians and joggers alike for the wide, smooth paths that formed a tangled web over several square miles, allowing people to explore the forest when it wasn't raining. And sometimes when it was—Vee usually jogged no matter the weather, and he knew most of the regulars who frequented the paths, by face if not by name.

Hoofbeats sounded on the path behind him and Vee automatically swerved to the edge and slowed down, glancing over his shoulder. But the horse that appeared, intimidatingly large and moving too fast, didn't have a rider, the reins swinging loose and the saddle empty.

Vee acted on instinct, lunging forward to grab the rein closest to him. He got both hands around the strap as the horse skittered sideways, yanking Vee off his feet. He landed hard on his knees but the impact stopped the horse's forward trajectory, turning it into an orbit around Vee where he was struggling to catch his breath and not get tangled in the leather.

"Fuck—hold still, *whoa*," Vee gasped, bending to let the rein go over his head as the horse passed behind him, and then scrambling to his feet. Those hooves were huge and *much* too close for comfort.

Upright, Vee tightened his grip on the rein, even as the horse threw its head, snorting loudly, and tried to back away. It bumped into a tree and jolted forward again, eyes ringed with white. Vee looked around for help. He had absolutely no idea what to do with what felt like two thousand pounds of excitable equine attached to him by a thin leather strap.

"Okay, easy," he said, trying for his most soothing voice. The horse—big and brown, with a white stripe down its face—did not appear convinced. Vee took a step closer, holding the bridle as if it were radioactive, as running footsteps pounded behind him.

"Oh thank God," a girl panted as she came around the curve. She was short, Black, and wide-eyed with terror, helmet covering her hair, tight riding pants ripped at the knee and blood trickling down her leg. "You caught her, is she okay?"

"Is *she* okay?" Vee repeated. "Are *you* okay? You're bleeding!"

The girl glanced down at her knee and shrugged. "I can walk. What about her?"

Vee made a gesture that could have meant anything. "I mean, I don't see any blood?"

The girl limped closer and held her hand out for the rein, which Vee willingly surrendered. "How did you catch her, anyway?"

"Um, I sort of… grabbed the… whatever that is you're holding as she went by," Vee said, bending to dust off his own knees.

The girl spun to stare at him, making the horse throw her head up with a snort. "You caught her while she was *running*? Are you *insane*? You could have been killed! You could have hurt *her*!" Her voice told him which was clearly the more horrifying of those possibilities, and Vee bristled.

"So I should have just let her go so she could trample a toddler or something?"

"No, but you can't grab a horse by the mouth when they're *running*, you could rip their mouth up, it's so dangerous." She turned back to the horse, crooning to her, and cupped the horse's muzzle in her hands to examine it.

"Fine," Vee said, straightening. "You're welcome or whatever."

The girl turned back to him, contrition on her pretty face. "I'm sorry. I'm Star. This is Kitt. Thank you for saving her, if she'd gotten out into traffic she really could have been hurt."

Somewhat mollified, Vee shrugged. "S'not a big deal. I'm Vee. Kit as in Kit-Kat?"

Star smiled, dimples flashing. "As in Eartha." Her smile faded and she winced as she shifted her weight. "I'm not going to be able to get back on her, I think I twisted my knee when I fell."

"How *did* you fall?" Vee asked, edging nearer in spite of himself.

"She spooked at a bike pulling a baby carriage," Star said, rubbing Kitt's nose. The horse snorted but her ears flicked forward, the ring of white around her eyes fading. "Yeah, those things are scary, aren't they, baby?" Star continued, clearly to Kitt. "Well, let's get walking." She smiled at Vee. "Thanks again."

"Wait, are you sure you can make it back? How far do you have to go?"

"It's about a mile back that way," Star said, pointing behind them.

"But you sprained your knee," Vee said. "You shouldn't walk."

"Well, I can't get back on her," Star said, shrugging. "And I don't think it's a good idea to ride her right now anyway, she's still too tense. She spooks again with me on her back and she'll end up in Canada." She pulled her helmet off and shook out her hair.

"I'll go with you," Vee offered on impulse.

Star stared at him. "That's not necessary."

"But what if she *does* spook again?" Vee pointed out. "You're injured, you're not going to be able to catch her. Plus you can lean on me, take some of the weight off your knee."

Star considered him as Kitt stretched her nose

out to investigate the fern growing on the edge of the path. "Are you sure?"

"Yeah," Vee said. "You can tell me why you named your horse after Eartha Kitt, and why you obviously still love her even though she dumped you like that."

Star laughed out loud and accepted the arm Vee offered. "Because she didn't *mean* to." They started walking and to Vee's relief, Kitt fell placidly into place on Star's right, head at her shoulder. "She's young and a little silly sometimes. She's an OTTB, so I'm still showing her the world."

"A what?"

"Off the track Thoroughbred," Star clarified as they turned the corner and moved haltingly down the path.

"Like Secretariat?"

"Sure," Star said, laughing and then wincing as she put too much weight on her knee. "Only not quite as famous. She's only four years old, and I shouldn't have hacked her alone, Monica told me to wait, but no one else was at the barn and Kitt's so sick of the arena, so I thought… what's the harm?"

"I guess you found out," Vee said dryly, and Star laughed again.

"Monica's going to have my head. She says Kitt's her best shot at getting some ribbons for her wall next summer. If she'd gotten hurt…." She shuddered.

"Wait, you don't own her?"

"No, I do. But Monica's my trainer, and when I win at shows, then it looks good for her. Brings in more students, more boarders, all that good stuff."

"So, like advertising." They came to a gate off the side of the path that Star pointed to.

"That's us. And yes, exactly like advertising."

Vee opened the gate and let them through. The fenced path stretched before them, grassland hemmed in by trees all around.

"Close it behind you," Star said. "First rule of being on any kind of farm—leave gates the way you found them."

Vee obediently closed the gate and offered his arm again. Star's movements were slowing down, her smile slipping as the limp became more pronounced.

"How much farther?" he asked.

"Half a mile," Star said through her teeth.

"Can I—I don't know, take Kitt ahead and come back with a car or something for you?"

"You have no idea how to handle her," Star pointed out.

"Yes, but—" Vee gestured to the fenced in path, the rolling pastures on either side. "Does it lead directly to the barn?"

"Well, yes," Star admitted.

"So even if she got away from me, all that would happen is she'd either come back this way to you, or she'd end up at the barn on her own, right?"

Star scowled. "When you put it like that…." She spied a tree stump and hopped toward it, Kitt right behind her. "Look. Hold the reins like this. Loosely. If she pulls away, let her go, *don't* try to stop her." She demonstrated. "Do *not* yank on her mouth, she has a bit in and if you hurt her I swear to God I'll skin you. If she spooks or tries to bolt, just let her go, okay?"

Vee gingerly took the reins, eyeing Kitt, who eyed him right back.

"Just—" Star eased herself onto the stump and sighed with relief. "Walk straight down the path until you get to the stable. If you don't see Monica, put Kitt in the round pen that's just to the right of the arena. Take her reins off—see the buckles?" She pointed to them and Vee nodded dutifully. "Then just leave her and find Monica. She has a golf cart, she can come get me."

"Okay." Vee made a clucking noise at Kitt, who looked at him suspiciously. "Um. Walk?"

Star rolled her eyes. "*Honestly*. Just start walking, she'll follow you."

Vee took a step and nearly jumped out of his skin when Kitt mirrored it. He took another, and another, and Kitt stayed close to his side, her head lowered and her eyes dark brown again, no white showing.

"Nice horsey," Vee said as they walked. Kitt flicked an ear. "Nice, *big* horsey." He couldn't help admitting that she smelled surprisingly good, like grass or hay and something wild and sweet, and when he cautiously reached out to touch her shoulder, her skin was satin-soft under his fingers. Kitt blew a breath and bumped his arm with her forehead, and Vee found himself grinning. "You're not so terrible, are you?"

The path curved, taking them under a tree that drooped over the path, and wound its way up through several more pastures, with horses grazing in them. One whinnied at Kitt, who answered in a surprisingly deep voice, her ribs shaking with the force of it.

"Holy shit, that's what a horse sounds like in real life?" Vee said. "The things I'm learning today." He petted Kitt's shoulder again as they rounded another bend and the barn was revealed before them, a huge white structure with dark green accents, massive double doors standing open at both ends, a large rectangular arena beside it, and between them, a smaller, perfectly circular pen.

A white woman was sitting on a riding mower, tinkering with something between her feet. She sat up as Vee and Kitt came into view, eyes narrowing, and swung fluidly off the mower to stride toward them.

"Who are you? Where's Star? Is she okay? Is Kitt okay?"

"Um. Vee. Star's back that way. She twisted her knee but she's fine, I think. Kitt's fine too, at least Star says she is. Can you—" Vee gestured with the hand holding the reins, and the woman took them. "Are you Monica?"

Monica nodded, inspecting Kitt quickly. She was short and solid, wispy blonde hair curling around her temples and faded blue eyes that nonetheless were sharp and clearly missed nothing. "I have to go get Star. Can you put her away?"

"I don't know *how*," Vee confessed. "Star said to put her in the round pen and take the reins off?"

Monica nodded and passed the reins back to him. "Yes, do that. I'll be right back." She strode in the direction of the golf cart parked by the barn doors and Vee looked at Kitt, who had spotted a clump of grass and was eyeing it hopefully.

He led her to the round pen, misjudging how far open he needed to open the gate and making Kitt snort and startle when the stirrup on her saddle hit the metal, but he managed to get her inside and close the gate behind them somehow, juggling reins and impatient horse until it was latched.

Then he turned back. Star had said take the reins off, but surely he could remove the saddle too. It didn't look *too* difficult, and Kitt would probably be more comfortable without it on.

He ran his fingers over the leather flap below the seat. The—whatever it was that held the saddle on—seemed to run up beneath the flap. He lifted it and discovered two buckles. "Aha!"

Kitt yawned and cocked a hip.

"Am I boring you?" Vee said, fingers busy on the buckles. He popped them both free and Kitt sighed happily as the leather slid free, leaving a sweaty mark on her belly just behind her front legs. Vee considered. "Do I just pull the whole thing off?" he asked her.

Kitt didn't answer.

"Thanks," Vee told her, and tugged at the saddle. It slipped off surprisingly easily and he staggered backward, reins still over one arm. Kitt followed him to the railing and Vee draped the entire thing over the top, the stirrups bouncing against the leather. Then he turned to Kitt again. "I'm not sure how the bridle works," he admitted.

There was a strap that buckled at her cheek on

the left, he noticed, and he went around to inspect the other side. No buckle on that side. Vee returned to Kitt's left and reached up to trace the band around her ears. Kitt immediately dropped her head, butting into Vee's hand as her eyes half-closed.

"Oh, you like that?" Vee grinned and rubbed the base of her ears as Kitt's head drooped lower. "Okay, let's see if I can get this off." He unbuckled the cheek strap and stopped to reassess. "I can't see how to unbuckle the ear thingy. How do they do this in the movies?" Memories of an old Western floated up. "They just pull it off, don't they?"

He put his fingers behind Kitt's ears and lifted the leather, slipping it forward until it was off her ears and lowering his hands. He was temporarily stymied by the bit still between her teeth for a moment, until Kitt opened her mouth and daintily spat it out, covered in green saliva.

"Ew," Vee told her.

Kitt snorted and trotted away to explore the small area. Vee stood where he was, watching her and wondering what he should do with the saddle and bridle, but the golf cart reappeared just then, and he went to meet it, careful to close the round pen gate behind him.

Star was sweating, her jaw set with pain, and from the look on her face, Monica hadn't held back on her opinions, but she greeted Vee with a smile.

"Oh my god, you got her tack off! Where's her saddle?"

"On the fence," Vee said, pointing. "I didn't want to put it in the dirt."

"I love your face," Star said fervently. "Getting sand out of the cracks of an Antares is a bitch."

"I don't know what that is, but okay," Vee said, and Star laughed as Monica rounded the golf cart to help her out.

"It's my saddle. Second-hand, but still expensive."

Vee handed the bridle over and Star accepted it with another brilliant smile.

"You're a lifesaver," she told him. "Mon, can we offer him some free riding lessons for saving my ass?"

Monica scowled. "*One* lesson free. The rest full price."

"Oh, I don't—thanks, but I'm okay," Vee said, startled.

"Come on," Star wheedled. "I need someone to keep me company. Monica's mean when it's just me."

Vee glanced at Monica, whose lips were twitching as she headed for the round pen. "Don't you have other students?" he asked.

"Sure, but they're mostly rich, preppy white girls," Star said. "Fun to look at but boring as hell when they get going about Daddy's latest investment, you know what I mean?"

Vee couldn't help the laugh. "I can't believe I'm even considering this. You want me to actually come ride with you. A *horse*. Something I never even touched before this morning?"

Star tilted her head and smiled at him. "You're good with Kitt. You've got soft hands and you don't shout or move suddenly. And you untacked her without hurting her or yourself, and with no instruction, I mean come on. That was pretty good."

"I'll think about it," Vee said, smiling back at her.

———

HE CALLED Farid on his way home, walking along the path as the sun cleared the tops of the trees and crept into the sky.

"Hello, Vee," Farid said. "You're up early."

"Oh shit, I didn't wake you up, did I?" Vee asked, briefly horrified.

Farid laughed quietly. "No, I've been up for awhile. What can I do for you?"

"Um." Now that it was in front of him, Vee found himself hesitating. "Would you—do you think you could teach me?"

"Teach you?"

"How to do what you do," Vee said in a rush.

"You want me to teach you how to be a personal assistant? Ow!" There was a clunking noise and muffled voices, and then Farid was back. "Sorry, Vee. Dom didn't appreciate me teasing you."

Vee sighed. "Forget it."

"No!" Farid said, sounding suddenly serious. "I apologize, Vee. It's just—look, this stuff can get heavy fast. I've found it's safest to keep your heart light when you approach it. Don't take yourself too seriously, you know?"

Vee fumbled for his house keys and trotted up the steps to his front door. "Yeah, I get what you're saying. So, uh—"

"I can give you some basics," Farid said. "But the best way for you to learn is by scening. And I can't do that with you."

"Why not? Oh. Dominic?"

"Yes," Farid said simply. "However, I know someone who can, and most likely would be delighted to initiate you into the world of domination. Do some more reading up on it, and meet me at Cuffs this coming Friday at 8 p.m. Bring a clean bill of health from your doctor."

"VEE, this is Sanyam Desai and Fox Reynard." Farid was impeccable and put together as ever, even in faded jeans and a T-shirt and leaning against the bar inside Cuffs. Beside him, Dominic was dressed similarly, eyes friendly, but Vee's attention was taken by Sanyam, holding out his hand.

Sanyam was desi, slanted eyes dark and sharp but not unfriendly as they inspected Vee from head to toe. He had a short beard and high cheekbones and Vee was briefly distracted by just how attractive he was as he accepted the hand Sanyam was offering.

"The baby Dom," the white man beside Sanyam drawled. Fox. Vee narrowed his eyes and looked him over. Fox was taller than Sanyam by about an inch, willowy where Sanyam was sturdy, with disdainful green eyes and silky brown hair swept back from a high forehead.

Sanyam elbowed Fox in the ribs. "Be nice," he chided. "Vee, this is my boyfriend, Fox. I understand you're interested in learning about domination and submission?"

Vee nodded and Farid leaned forward.

"San and Fox are from Vancouver," he told Vee. "San headlines at a very popular BDSM club up there."

"Oh—you didn't come down here for me, did you?" Vee asked, suddenly worried.

"Don't flatter yourself," Fox said, tossing his head.

Sanyam gave him a look and turned back to Vee. "This trip was already planned. When Farid called, I said I'd be happy to talk to you while we were down here."

"Let's go to a private room," Farid suggested.

"Excellent idea," Sanyam said. He turned and caught the eye of a Black woman in red leather passing by, her impressive breasts strapped into a tight bustier. "Martha, is there a room available?"

Martha smiled at him. "I reserved it for you when Farid told me you were coming. It's the Ivory Room, end of the hall."

Vee trailed behind as they made their way upstairs, anticipation stringing his nerves tight. The room was spacious and comfortable, several chairs and a loveseat lining one wall facing a bench and a large, upright wooden X. Beside them stood a bed and a huge armoire, doors open, and Vee went over to inspect the contents. Every type of whip imaginable lay before him, from cat o'nine tails to soft leather floggers to wide paddles, both flat and studded. There were handcuffs, some smooth and others with spikes facing inward. Every shape and size of butt-plugs and dildos paraded across the velvet, and a row of blindfolds and masks were tucked neatly between, including a mask shaped like a horse's head, and Vee had to stifle a slightly hysterical laugh, thinking of Star and Kitt.

Fox stepped up beside him and hummed appreciatively, running a hand over the leather flogger. "Not as nice as San's collection, but not bad."

Behind them, Dominic and Farid were sitting on the loveseat, Dominic sprawled against Farid's chest, head on his shoulder.

"San, you have the floor," Farid said, stroking Dominic's chest in a slow, hypnotic pattern. "I'm just here to observe, unless you need me."

Sanyam nodded. "First things first. I'm assuming this scene will be of a sexual nature?"

Vee blinked. "There's... nonsexual BDSM?"

Fox snickered. "God, you really are an infant."

"That's enough, kit." Sanyam's voice was sharp, and Fox's mouth snapped shut. Sanyam looked at Vee, eyes sympathetic. "We're here to help you learn. Don't be ashamed of not knowing something. Yes, BDSM can be nonsexual, although it evokes deep emotions and physical feelings that typically lead to sex for many people. Fox and I are willing to scene with you—or rather, I should say *Fox* is willing to let you Dom him. If that includes some form of sex, that is... acceptable to us. Is it to you?"

Vee floundered briefly. "I—yes. I mean... I don't know what I want. To like, do?"

"That's okay too," Sanyam said. "We'll play it

by ear. Now, Fox and I are clean, but we will insist on condoms during any type of sex."

Vee fumbled with the piece of paper from his doctor and held it out. Sanyam accepted it and looked it over, then nodded and handed it back. In return, he offered Vee two similar sheets—his and Fox's results. Vee scanned them, not sure what he was looking for, and finally nodded, returning them.

"Fox, present." The easy calm was gone from Sanyam's voice, replaced with an almost military sharpness, and Fox stiffened, beside Vee.

He shot Vee an insolent smile and sauntered to the middle of the room, clasping his hands behind his back and subtly squaring his shoulders as he lifted his chin, tilting his head slightly to the side.

Sanyam circled him, looking him up and down. "If you want to show off your sub to others, this is a pose you might have him take," he said, running a finger down Fox's spine. "You can also put him on his knees." He tapped Fox's shoulder and Fox dropped gracefully to the floor, hands still behind his back.

Vee nodded, but there was hesitation in it. He didn't think he wanted to show off a sub, although he could see the appeal in it. *Here to learn*, he reminded himself.

"Fox," Sanyam said, and his voice was a caress. "Will you allow Vee to dominate you?"

Vee nearly choked on his tongue as Fox turned to look at him, eyes calculating.

"He can try," he finally said, mouth curling up.

"What's your safeword?" Sanyam asked him.

"Calypso," Fox said, still looking at Vee.

"And yours?" Sanyam asked, and it took Vee a minute to realize he was asking him.

"I—oh, uh. I don't really have one yet?"

"Some Doms prefer to use the traffic light system," Sanyam said. "The safeword is really more for the sub, but it's important you have something in place to protect you both, in case you need to redirect or end a scene. For now, let's use red, yellow, and green. I do recommend you choose one, though, before contracting with a regular sub. For now, check in with Fox often, since you don't know him well yet. Assess his color as you go. Fox, strip and get up against the X."

Fox stood fluidly and pulled his clothes off, revealing a pale, perfect ass and creamy skin as he padded across the floor and stopped in front of the wooden X.

"That's the last order I'm going to give him," Sanyam said to Vee. "You're taking over now."

Vee swallowed hard, and Sanyam jerked his chin toward Fox.

"Strap him in."

Vee obeyed, taking one of Fox's slender wrists and pulling it up toward the cuff above him. Fox allowed it, but his eyes were amused, and Vee scowled and tightened the cuff, breaking his gaze and reaching for Fox's other arm.

"Ooh, bossy," Fox said, sounding far too collected for a man standing naked tied to a wooden X.

Vee set his jaw and strapped his other arm in, drawing it up taut.

Sanyam was sitting in one of the chairs, his legs crossed. He beckoned and Vee went to him.

"The first and most important thing you have to understand is this," Sanyam said. "The sub controls the scene. If you don't respect the sub's limits, then you'll never have true submission. No matter *what* you are doing, in the middle of the most intense scene of your life, if your sub safewords, *you stop*. Do you understand me?"

Vee nodded.

"He's going to test you," Sanyam said. "Needle you. Get under your skin. Can you handle it?"

Vee nodded again, fully hard and buzzing with nerves.

Sanyam gestured. "Go ahead."

"What—" Vee cleared his throat. "What does he like?"

Sanyam's eyes creased with amusement. "You'll have to find out, won't you?"

***

VEE TURNED and went back to Fox, standing docilely in place with his back to the room. Farid had coached him on this part.

"What are your limits?" he asked.

Fox shot him a sultry look over his shoulder. "No watersports, electricity, or penetration unless it's San. Anything else is fair game."

"Okay," Vee said. "And, uh… what do you want?"

"For you to get on with it, mostly," Fox said, rolling his eyes.

Vee took a step back, chewing on his lip. His

hesitation must have showed, because Farid disentangled himself from Dominic suddenly and crossed to him.

"Start with a spanking," he suggested, his tone low.

"Using *what?*" Vee asked wildly.

Fox sighed and pulled on the cuffs. "Sometime this year?"

Farid turned Vee toward the armoire. "How about the flogger?"

Vee lifted it out, feeling the soft leather between his fingers, and snapped it a couple of times.

"Finally," Fox said, and Vee set his jaw and brought the whip down across Fox's ass.

Fox jerked but didn't make a noise as a red welt rose across his skin. Vee hesitated as shock set in. *He'd* done that. He'd created that mark.

"Oh, come *on,*" Fox said, twisting in his bonds.

Farid went back to Dominic as Vee repositioned himself and tried again. But the angle or the way he was holding the flogger was wrong, and the next three blows landed with almost no force.

Fox sighed again and gave Sanyam a pointed look that said *how long do I have to put up with this?*

Sanyam said nothing. Vee fought the rush of embarrassment and irritation and went back to the armoire. This time, he selected a smooth leather paddle. Surely he could handle that without humiliating himself.

Fox gave him an unimpressed look when Vee took up his stance again.

"Round two already?" he said. "We'd barely started round one."

"Do you ever shut up?" Vee snapped before he thought better of it.

"It's my superpower," Fox said, unperturbed. "I can even snark during sex."

Vee gritted his teeth and swung. The paddle connected with a loud *pop* and Fox swayed in the cuffs, still without a noise. Vee hit him again, and then again, swinging until his arm ached and sweat trickled down his forehead.

Finally, he let his arm drop, muscles burning, and dragged in air. Worry hit him like a fist. Had he gone too far? Pushed Fox too hard? He was opening his mouth to ask when Fox *yawned*.

"Let me know when things get interesting," he said.

Fury swamped Vee, making it hard for him to breathe. He was doing his best, and this insolent fucker had the *nerve*—he reared back, raising the paddle to bring it down with every ounce of strength he had—and was stopped by Sanyam's hand clamping down on his wrist, squeezing so hard Vee dropped the paddle.

Sanyam's eyes were chips of black ice, his grip uncompromising. "*Never* touch a sub in anger," he hissed.

Fox glanced over his shoulder. "Especially not *his* sub," he sang.

The fury in Sanyam's eyes fled and he sighed, dropping Vee's wrist. "I know just how irritating he can be, believe me," he said. "But the second you react in anger, it stops being domination and becomes abuse. This is not about how strong you are, or beating him into submission. He has to *want* to submit to you."

Shame and humiliation warred inside Vee's chest and he clamped his mouth shut to keep them in, nodding tightly.

"I'm—" He cleared his throat. "Sorry. I'm sorry. It won't happen again. Fox—" He waited until Fox looked at him, raising a cool eyebrow. "I'm sorry. It was stupid and dangerous and—I'm sorry."

Fox considered him for a long minute and then glanced at Sanyam. Whatever he said was a silent communication, but Sanyam nodded and moved to the armoire, where he selected a plug with a flared base and a bottle of lube. He drizzled some over the plug, rubbing it in with his fingers, and then went back to Fox.

He put one hand between Fox's shoulder blades, pushing him forward so that Fox bent at the waist, and with the other hand, he slid the plug home.

Fox made a guttural noise, head falling back, and Sanyam kissed his throat briefly.

"Keep it in until we're ready for you again," he ordered, and unbuckled the cuffs.

Fox took a step back, rubbing his wrist, and Sanyam pointed to the floor by the loveseat. "On your knees there, kit." He waited until Fox had obeyed before turning back to Vee. "I think we need to switch it up slightly."

Vee met his eyes warily. "How so?"

Sanyam's smile was predatory. "I think *you* need to submit first."

Vee recoiled. "You *what?* But—I'm not—I—"

I can't, he thought wildly. The thought of submitting to someone else, even someone Farid knew and trusted, horrified him.

"San, may I?" Farid asked. He'd stood again and was beside them, concern and sympathy on his face. He waited for Sanyam's nod before continuing. "Vee, San helped train me, did you know that?"

Vee shook his head dumbly. "I don't think I can—"

Farid moved closer, putting a hand on Vee's wrist. "One of the first things a good dominant learns is how to submit themselves, because if you don't know what it's like, you'll never be able to safely put a sub in that space." His hand was warm and reassuring against Vee's skin. "You can trust Sanyam," he said quietly.

"Did you—"

Farid's eyes creased with amusement. "Of course I did."

"How—how was it?"

Farid's smile bloomed across his face. "It was amazing. I can see why people get addicted to it."

Vee fought back the bubble of fear that threatened to burst within his chest. *Could* he trust Sanyam, though? Farid did. Unreservedly, apparently. And if Farid did…. He took a deep breath and nodded. Farid squeezed his wrist.

"Good man," he said quietly. "Choose a safeword, then; he'll want you to use one."

Vee nodded again, groping for words. "I… I know he's here because you asked him to come."

Farid lifted his eyebrows, listening.

"I don't want to embarrass you," Vee blurted, and Farid's eyes softened.

"You won't," he said. "You're doing great." He stepped in close, so near their bodies brushed, and lowered his voice. "Listen; Fox—he's testing you. Don't let him see that he's gotten to you. Smile at him. Throw *him* off-balance. And watch his body, not his face. He won't be able to hide it when you get through to him. Also blindfolds really help put him in the right space mentally."

"Okay," Vee said. "Thanks."

"Strip," Sanyam said behind him, and Vee jolted. Farid gave him a sympathetic smile and went back to Dominic, pulling him into his lap again.

Vee fumbled with his pants, hands shaking suddenly, but finally got them pushed down over his hips. He dragged his shirt up off his head and stood bare in front of Sanyam.

Sanyam didn't give him time to think. "Safe-word," he said.

"Croissant," Vee said, and did his best to ignore Fox's snicker, across the room.

Sanyam didn't challenge it. "Mine is Crawford. On the bench, facedown."

Vee moved to the bench and straddled it, lowering himself until his chest was pressed to the cool vinyl. Sanyam bent and caught one arm, pulling it back to Vee's thigh and tying it there with a length of soft rope Vee hadn't even seen. Then he went to the other side and repeated the process, so that Vee was effectively hogtied across the bench, helpless and exposed.

He *hated* it, he realized immediately. Shame

crawled up his throat, stinging his skin, and he pressed his face to the bench so he wouldn't catch sight of the people in the room who were witnessing his humiliation. He could hear Sanyam rummaging in the armoire, and then footsteps coming back.

Black silk settled over Vee's eyes and he caught his breath.

"Color," Sanyam said.

Vee struggled to think. Was it better or worse, not being able to see? He honestly didn't know. "Yellow—no, green."

Sanyam waited but Vee kept his mouth shut.

"Alright," Sanyam said, and stroked Vee's spine, a featherlight touch that made him shiver.

The first blow jolted Vee almost upright, driving him up the bench as he cried out in shock.

Sanyam ran a hand over the mark and Vee shuddered. It *stung*, a sharp pain that lingered even when Sanyam lifted his hand away.

"Let go," Sanyam said.

"W-what?"

"Let go," Sanyam repeated. "Stop trying to control what we're doing. Be *in* it. Let me be in charge. All you have to do is feel."

Vee shook his head wordlessly but Sanyam hit him again and the words dissolved. He moaned, muscles tensing, and waited for the next one.

"You're overthinking it," Sanyam said above him, his voice calm and unchanged. "Stop anticipating and just let it happen." He struck him again and then again, over and over, layering each blow so that they overlapped each other by a few inches.

When he stopped, Vee lay quivering, tears

soaking the blindfold. *Let go.* He hated this, hated it with every fiber of his being. *He* should be in control, not the one hogtied and helpless, but he couldn't deny there was a certain seductive quality to not being able to predict what happened.

Sanyam hit him again and Vee went limp against the vinyl, eyes sliding shut.

"There you go," he heard Sanyam say as if from very far away, and then the blows fell again, one after another without pause or respite. Vee spun free of his moorings, floating in the black. He was untethered by reality, barely aware of what was happening to his body as his mind soared.

Sanyam flogged him for what felt like hours and Vee sank into it, letting each blow drive him further into subspace.

Finally, Sanyam stopped. "Color, Vee," he ordered, his voice sounding thick.

Vee's tongue wouldn't form words. He swam through the fog in his mind that threatened to overwhelm him and pull him back down again as Sanyam rubbed his shoulder with one gentle hand.

"G-green," he finally managed.

"Very good," Sanyam murmured, and the pride in his voice made tears prick Vee's eyes behind the blindfold. "You're doing so well, Vee. Do you want some more?"

Vee nodded dreamily, his cheek sticking to the vinyl, and sighed with relief as the blows began to rain down again.

Finally, Sanyam stopped and the whip clattered to the floor. His hands were gentle as he untied Vee from the bench, removed the blindfold, and helped him upright.

"On the bed," he said, and Vee struggled to obey, but his feet and legs wouldn't cooperate. Sanyam scooped him up, careful to avoid Vee's burning ass and spine, and carried him to the bed, where he deposited him gently on the mattress.

"I'll stay with him," Farid said as Vee rolled onto his side and Sanyam pulled a blanket up over him. The bed dipped and a warm body slid in behind Vee's, one wiry arm going around his waist. At the same time, someone clambered on the other side, and Vee managed to open his eyes just enough to recognize Dominic's thigh next to his face. "Rest," Farid said in his ear.

Vee's eyes slipped shut again and he obeyed.

4

He came to in stages, awareness filtering in slowly like sunlight through deep water. Farid and Dominic were talking in low tones above his head. Vee made an effort to focus on the words and realized that Farid was telling Dominic about a television show he'd watched a few years before as Dominic asked occasional questions.

Vee lay quietly, Farid's husky voice soft and calming and his arm a comforting weight across Vee's stomach, and tried to remember what had happened. Sanyam had tied him up and… whipped him. He'd hated it, the feeling of vulnerability and helplessness, but when he'd surrendered, there'd been peace, a sea of it so huge it swallowed him entirely and left him relaxed and whole.

He stretched and Farid stopped talking.

"*That's* what it's like?" Vee asked through a yawn, and Dominic laughed as Farid helped Vee sit up, steadying him with a hand on his shoulder.

"Yeah," Dominic said, smiling at him. "Pretty cool, huh?"

"How are you feeling?" Farid asked.

Dominic leaned over to pull a bottle of water from the mini-fridge beside him as Vee assessed.

"My ass hurts," he confessed, and Farid's lips twitched.

"And mentally?"

"Good, I think," Vee said. "Sort of… clearer?"

Dominic handed him the water. "A good scene will do that to you, and San is one of the best."

Vee drank thirstily and looked around the room. "Where did they go?"

"San took Fox away to give you some privacy, and I suspect to possibly burn off some energy," Farid said.

The door opened and Sanyam put his head in. "Ah, you're back." He swung the door wide and Fox skulked in behind him, still naked but considerably more flushed and disheveled than before. And, unless Vee was imagining it, *much* harder, his cock a deep, angry red and leaking in slow, steady drops. Vee's own dick twitched and he took another quick drink and slid off the edge of the bed to walk right up to Fox, whose eyes widened as Vee approached.

Sanyam took a step back, subtly ceding the floor.

"Hands behind your back," Vee ordered, and Fox's eyes narrowed again but he obeyed.

Vee reached up and caught Fox's hair in an iron grip, dragging his head sideways. Fox's nostrils flared but he didn't fight it, eyes hot with need and challenge as Vee met his gaze.

Still holding his eyes, Vee clasped Fox's cock, stroking it hard and rough until Fox bucked in his grip and nearly fell against Vee's body, arms still behind him.

Vee let go of his hair and caught him with an arm around his waist, still stroking. Fox was heavier than he looked, his fair skin rosy with exertion and denied pleasure, ribs heaving. He smelled like sweat and pine needles and juniper, sharp and wild and sweet, and Vee could see teeth marks on his shoulder. That made him laugh, and he turned his head and muffled it against Fox's damp skin, unable to resist nipping at his neck.

He knew Sanyam, Farid, and Dominic were all still in the room, watching everything he did, but suddenly it no longer mattered. All he could think about was making Fox twist and cry out and beg, and he stepped back, letting go so fast Fox stumbled and nearly went down.

"Up against the X," Vee ordered.

Fox's eyes were wild, and his throat bobbed as he swallowed, but he didn't move.

Vee slapped him. Fox's head snapped back as a handprint bloomed on his cheek and Vee caught himself, horrified. Had he gone too far? He resisted the impulse to look at Sanyam and focused on Fox instead.

"Color," he said.

Fox *did* look at Sanyam, over Vee's shoulder, and then back at Vee. His voice was rusty when he opened his mouth. "Green."

"Good," Vee said, relief like cool water against his skin. "Against the X now."

Fox obeyed as if on autopilot and once his back was turned, Vee glanced at the others.

Dominic and Farid were still on the bed, Farid's eyes wide, Dominic's mouth hanging slightly open, and Sanyam's eyebrows nearly in his hairline. But he nodded when Vee met his eyes, gesturing toward Fox's waiting form.

It was different this time. Vee still didn't know what he was doing, but somehow it didn't matter, because Fox was watching him, breathing hard but otherwise completely still, tracking Vee's movements with his eyes. Vee took his wrist and pulled it up to the cuff, and Fox said nothing.

"No smart remarks this time?" Vee murmured, repeating the process on the other side. He smiled as Fox opened and closed his mouth, finally settling for shaking his head.

Vee turned to the armoire. He wanted to try the flogger again, but he'd need to practice until he was good with it. He had a feeling Fox could go either way, whether toppling into outright submission or regressing into rebellion, and Vee didn't want to push him the wrong way. He chose a paddle with small, round nubs adorning the surface and then picked up a blindfold.

He settled it over Fox's eyes and watched the tension drain from his body in a wave.

"God," he murmured, running a hand over the curve of Fox's ass. "I see it now."

He struck before Fox could speak, layering the blows in a rapid pattern across the meat of Fox's buttocks and down his outer thighs in quick, sharp blows, until Fox was jerking with each one, noises falling from his throat in a stream he seemed to be unaware of, head falling forward on his chest.

Vee was so engrossed in what he was doing that Sanyam appeared as if out of nowhere. His eyes were hot, fixed on Fox's trembling body, but he caught Vee's wrist before he could hit Fox again.

"He's under," he said in a low voice. "Look."

Vee obeyed. Fox was hanging in the restraints, his body limp, and when Sanyam touched his back with one gentle finger, he only moaned, low in his chest.

"You have to be careful here," Sanyam said. "If you're too rough or abrupt, you'll jerk him back out, which is very disorienting. But you also have to gauge how much he can take in this state, because his body will lie to him. Right now he wants whatever you'll give him, even if it's more than he'd willingly accept in his right mind. It's up to you to monitor his limits and not go too far."

Vee nodded.

"Again," Sanyam said. "He's coming out of it."

Vee gripped the paddle tighter and went back to work.

Fox in subspace was a beautiful thing. His body was immensely reactive, shuddering under Vee's touch, swaying toward him as if trying to get more, turning to blindly track Vee's movements. The trust Fox was putting in him was heady and terrifying. So much could go wrong. Anything could happen, and it was on Vee's shoulders—he was responsible for putting Fox in this place and bringing him back out of it safely.

"Please," Fox whimpered, twisting in his bonds.

"You want to come?" Vee asked, rubbing a welt. The plug was still in place, he saw, impressed with Fox's determination. He wanted to push Fox over the edge, but he hesitated. Something wasn't right. Fox wasn't *his*, even though he'd submitted to him so beautifully. Vee wanted his own sub, someone who belonged to *him*.

Fox was nodding and Vee glanced at Sanyam, watching hungrily.

"He's all yours," he said.

Astonishment filled Sanyam's face but he was on his feet instantly.

Vee stepped back and turned to look for his clothes. He didn't watch Sanyam and Fox, although he couldn't help hearing the noises, but he pulled his pants on and tucked himself away with gritted teeth as Farid slid off the bed and came to stand by him.

"That was pretty impressive," he said quietly.

Vee glanced at him as he tucked in his shirt. "I just used a paddle on him."

"Not that," Farid said. "Giving him back to San like that. I don't know many seasoned Doms who'd have that much self-control."

Vee shrugged, uncomfortable. "It didn't feel right."

"That's how I know you're going to be a good Dom," Farid said, patting his shoulder. He glanced in the corner at Fox and Sanyam. "I'll make your excuses, since they may be busy for awhile. You should… take care of that." He glanced at the bulge in Vee's pants, lips twitching.

Vee couldn't help his laugh. "Thanks, 'Rid. This was amazing. Do you think… can we do it again sometime?"

"Hell yes," Farid said, grinning at him. "Be seeing you, Vee."

Vee made his way out of the club, avoiding the clutch of patrons in the main room and climbing the stairs to street-level. Halfway there, he caught a glimpse of white-blond hair in the crowd and he stiffened briefly, but whoever it belonged to was gone before Vee could get close.

Stupid, he told himself. No reason to think that the homeless kid from behind the bakery would be *here,* after all. Plenty of people had light blond hair.

———

KELLEN MADE it out of the club that night under his own power, which he decided was a win. He'd caught sight of Martha in the hall and the confusion and concern that had creased her brow, and he'd ducked away down a side corridor, eventually finding his way back out into the Seattle night. Everything hurt, the skin on his back raw and abused, and he could feel his shirt stuck to him in several places. Peeling it off was going to be a bitch, and Jacob would be furious that Kellen had ruined another outfit.

I should just disappear, he thought as he limped down the pavement. *Jacob will find someone else to help him run his cons. What if I just… vanished?*

It wasn't the first time he'd had that thought, but he didn't stop walking. Jacob would find him.

He had before and he would again, if Kellen tried to run. He put his head down and tugged his thin jacket closer around him. There was no escape. Only temporary respite.

———

HE MANAGED to wait almost two weeks before he slipped away again. Jacob would be angry, he knew. He hated it when Jacob was angry, not just because he tended to express himself with his fists but also because he got that cloudy look in his eyes and Kellen would know he'd disappointed him yet again. But he couldn't help it. The itch was swelling under his skin, making it hard for him to breathe, hard to think. He'd tried hurting himself, pinching and even cutting his skin, but it never brought him the euphoria, the soaring feeling that took him out of his body and catapulted him to a different realm completely. He *needed* it, couldn't live without it.

So when Jacob got into an argument with a street vendor over a piece of turf, Kellen took his chance and ran. He'd healed quickly over the past weeks, his ankle strong and only his shoulder still tweaking him occasionally when he forgot and used it too much.

He headed downtown as quickly as he could, dodging pedestrians with only one goal in mind— the floating neon handcuffs that blinked above the door to the club. When they came into sight, Kellen's chest eased a fraction. He was close. He'd be able to fly soon.

The bouncer took one look at him and his lips tightened into a flat line. "No," he said.

Kellen stopped abruptly, feeling like he'd been punched. "What?"

"Boss gave orders. You're not allowed in."

"But—" Kellen swallowed hard. He looked around desperately. "I've never hurt anyone," he said urgently. "C'mon, man, please? Please, I need this."

The bouncer shook his head but his eyes were sympathetic. "You're going to get yourself killed," he said, his voice low.

"I'm *not*," Kellen said. "I—look, I just… *please*." He blinked back the unwelcome tears that prickled suddenly. "Please?"

The bouncer looked at him for a long moment. Finally he shook his head, but it was resigned. "I didn't see you."

Kellen was suddenly so light he thought he'd float off the pavement. He went up on his tiptoes and dropped a kiss on the bouncer's cheek. "I owe you," he said, and ducked inside the club.

He stopped in the bathroom to inspect his appearance quickly. He'd scored a shower at the homeless shelter that morning, so he was clean, in newish clothes with only a few threadbare patches, and his hair fell softly over his face in pale, shining waves. He applied some eyeliner and pressed his lips together hard to bring some color into them, then slipped back out and into the crowd.

He was later than usual, and the club was already mostly full, the music thumping over the din of patrons talking. Kellen sidestepped a server wearing a mesh shirt that did nothing to hide his rouged nipples and headed down the steps toward the bar.

But Lucero shook her head hard when she caught sight of him, and Kellen changed direction smoothly, settling onto an empty corner of the nearest sofa. Onstage, a Domme was working over her sub, her hand perfectly steady as she marked his back with cruel precision. Kellen scanned the crowd for an unattached Dom. He didn't see the one he'd been with several weeks before, and he didn't know if he was relieved or disappointed.

But everyone he saw either avoided his eye or outright turned their back on him, pointedly engaging others in conversation. Kellen fought back the bewilderment and kept looking. There had to be *someone* who would take him for the night.

He sidled closer to a man standing near the bar. Short and stocky, he had a thin, cruel mouth and hard eyes. *Perfect.* But when Kellen opened his mouth, the man shook his head.

"You're blackballed, kid," he said flatly. "Save your breath and get your kicks elsewhere." He strode away before Kellen could reply, leaving him staring after him.

On the stage, the Domme was untying her sub. He sagged against her and she steadied him with a gentle hand as she undid his other wrist and helped him off the stage.

Kellen was moving before he thought better of it, grabbing the microphone from its stand and planting himself in the center floodlight.

The song ended and the club went silent, all eyes fixed on Kellen.

He spread his arms and turned in a circle, heart thumping madly against his breastbone. "I need a Dom," he said, the mic making his voice startlingly loud. He swallowed and tried again. "Come on, I'm a great sub. You can do anything to me—*anything*."

The silence was loud in Kellen's ears. He searched the crowd, but no one would meet his eyes. He clutched the microphone tighter. "Are you all cowards? I'm right here. I'm *offering* myself. I don't care what you do to me. Who here has the balls to take me on?"

No one spoke. Kellen scanned the faces, desperation and terror churning in his stomach. The bouncer was coming down the steps toward him, he realized, and he took a step back, shaking his head.

"No, *no*. Come on, what's wrong with you people? You spineless, worthless, useless—"

"Get off the stage!" someone shouted.

Kellen throttled back the nausea. He was so close. He couldn't have it snatched away, not like this. "*Please*," he managed, his voice cracking.

"You've got a fucking death wish!" someone else called.

Someone shot to his feet, several rows up, just as the bouncer reached the stage. "I'll take him," he shouted.

A hush fell once more. The bouncer paused, turning, as Kellen shielded his eyes against the lights and strained to see who had spoken. From where he was, all he could see was a thin, lanky frame and broad shoulders, backlit so no details were visible.

The bouncer turned back, looking over Kellen's head toward someone in the balcony behind him, and Kellen turned too, peering upward.

Martha and a man Kellen didn't recognize stood there, talking quietly, pointing at Kellen and then to the speaker in the audience. Finally, the man sighed and threw his hands in the air, and the woman pointed at Kellen and beckoned, then to the man in the seats.

The bouncer nodded and took the microphone from Kellen, pointing with a meaty fist toward a door set off the side of the stage. Kellen headed that direction, face and hands numb. Inside the door, he hesitated and then began climbing the narrow concrete steps. At the top, he stopped, unsure what he should do. There was a door right in front of him. Should he knock? Wait to be invited?

"Come in, Kellen," a gentle voice called, and Kellen opened the door to see the couple who'd been arguing. The man was tall and thin, thinner than anyone Kellen had ever seen, his wristbones protruding and his fingers knobbly and long. He was Hispanic, with muddy brown hair and sharp brown eyes, and he scowled as Kellen entered.

"Sit down," Martha said. It wasn't a suggestion. Kellen's heart thumped harder.

Oh god, I'm so fucked.

He sank onto the chair Martha gestured to, clutching his knees, as someone knocked and the bouncer opened the door.

"Martha, this is Vee."

"Thank you, Vic," Martha said. "Vee, please come in."

The young man from the bakery stepped through the door, his brows dark slashes above wary brown eyes, and Kellen shot to his feet.

"*You?*"

Vee met his gaze. He looked nervous but unsurprised. "Me," he agreed.

"Vee, my name is Martha, and this is my husband, Carlos." Martha looked serene, sitting in a plush red velvet chair that resembled a throne and perfectly highlighted her dark skin. "I take it you two know each other?"

"We've exchanged croissants," Vee said, and Kellen laughed, hysterical and wild, before he could stop himself.

Martha's eyes narrowed, but she didn't ask for clarification. "Have a seat, Vee. We have some things to discuss." Kellen opened his mouth and Martha pointed at him without looking. "You are not to speak until invited, Kellen." Her voice was hard, and Kellen snapped his mouth shut, glowering, and sank back to the seat.

Vee sat down close to Kellen, their thighs almost but not quite touching. This close, he smelled intoxicating, spicy and sharp with a hint of sweetness underlying it, and Kellen caught himself before leaning closer and taking a surreptitious breath.

"I need you to understand the situation," Martha was saying to Vee. "Kellen here is… dangerous."

"I am *not*—"

Martha's voice cracked like a whip. "One more

word and you'll be gagged until it's time to talk to you."

Kellen swallowed his fury and frustration. Was he not even allowed to defend himself? Martha was still speaking.

"He is dangerous because he has no limits. Do you understand what that means, Vee?"

Vee nodded slowly. "I think so. You mean he won't safeword even when he's in danger?"

"Exactly," Martha said. Carlos got up and stalked to the wetbar to pour himself a drink, muttering under his breath. "I will not allow that type of behavior in my institution. It's bad for business, you see, and also for some reason I like this young man and have no wish to see him dead or permanently disabled."

Kellen hunched his shoulders, avoiding her gaze.

Martha continued. "He's an addict, Vee. Not to needles or pills. To pain. To subspace. He can't live without it."

"I've tried," Kellen whispered, and clapped both hands over his mouth, horrified.

Martha didn't seem to notice, fixed on Vee. "You see my dilemma."

Vee looked at Kellen, eyes cautious and assessing. "He needs this," he said, holding Kellen's gaze but speaking to Martha. "But it's going to get him killed if he keeps giving himself to unsafe Doms."

Kellen shook his head, hands still over his mouth, as a tear slid down his cheek. He could feel his escape slipping further away with every second that ticked by. He had to get out of there. He'd find someone on the street, someone who'd beat him until he was numb again. But as he tensed to stand, Vee reached out and wiped the tear off Kellen's face with his thumb. Kellen froze.

"I'll take him," Vee said to Martha, still looking into Kellen's eyes.

Kellen couldn't move, spellbound. The corner of Vee's mouth twitched up and Kellen dropped his eyes to his lap.

"I won't have this at my club," Martha said. There was sympathy in her voice, but steel as well. "You'll both sign a waiver releasing this institution of any liability, and you—Vee? You'll do whatever it is you're going to do *off* my premises."

Carlos slapped the paper down in front of Vee, who picked it up. Released from his gaze, Kellen sucked in air, but he still couldn't move, watching helplessly as Vee signed the form in smooth, looping letters, and then slid it across the coffee table to Kellen.

"Sign it," he said quietly, for Kellen's ears alone. "And let me take you out of here."

Kellen fumbled for the pen with numb fingers.

5

KELLEN FOLLOWED Vee out of the club, feeling as if he were floating just above his body as Vee strode down the pavement. Kellen tried to keep up, unsure what to say. Why had he agreed to this? Jacob would be furious. He had to go. He hesitated, tensing to bolt.

Vee caught him by the shoulders and shoved him into the alley they were passing. Kellen stumbled, breath catching, but Vee steadied him even as he pushed him up against the wall, one hand on Kellen's chest and the other cupping the back of his head before it hit the bricks. His dark eyes were fierce.

"Do you want this?" he asked.

Kellen gulped, hands fluttering.

"You can touch me," Vee said.

But Kellen couldn't quite bring himself to. He turned his head away and stared at the grimy pavement.

"I asked you a question." Vee's voice was uncompromising.

"Yes." It was little more than a whisper, but it was all Kellen could get out.

Vee's grip eased, and something in Kellen's chest fluttered. *Don't let go, don't let me fall*—but Vee was bringing a hand up to brush Kellen's hair out of his face, his touch gentle, almost wondering.

"My place isn't far," he said quietly. He stepped back and Kellen followed him from the alley and back onto the busy sidewalk.

They didn't speak again until Vee stopped in front of a clapboard house.

"This is me," he said, digging in his pocket for keys. "It's a farmhouse. This used to be farmland, you know. The city just—" He gestured vaguely. "Swallowed it up."

He's nervous too, Kellen realized, and somehow the thought was comforting. He stayed close to Vee's heels as they climbed the steps, and inside the hall, Vee took the stairs on the right-hand side.

"I've got the top floor," he said over his shoulder. "Which sounds fancy but mostly consists of a bedroom, tiny kitchen, bathroom, and a sort of alcove that doubles for a living room if you squint." He stopped on the landing and found the right key, finally pushing the door open with a *tada* motion.

Kellen stepped forward into the space, looking around. It *was* tiny, the living room walls almost close enough to touch if he stretched out both arms, widening into a bedroom dominated by a large bed. To his right was a kitchen and just past it was a door that he supposed led to the bathroom.

He hugged himself, unsure what to say. Vee had kicked off his shoes just inside the door and gestured for Kellen to do the same. Kellen blinked and Vee hunched his shoulders and laughed.

"Asian thing," he said. "Humor me."

Kellen stepped out of his shoes and set them neatly by the front door.

"Are you hungry?"

Kellen shook his head silently.

"Okay, I know you *can* speak," Vee said, sounding briefly impatient for the first time. "So why the silent treatment?"

Kellen opened his mouth and closed it again. "I shouldn't be here," he finally said.

Vee cocked his head. "Why not?"

Kellen shrugged. "You—you're not… this was a mistake."

"Why don't you give it—me—a chance?" Vee said.

"This isn't a relationship," Kellen flung at him, suddenly angry. "We're not dating. I don't have to give you *shit*."

Vee's eyes tightened and he moved before Kellen could react, crowding him up against the door, hands on either side of his shoulders and trapping him in place. "But you *want* to, don't you?"

Kellen gasped at the heat, the press of Vee's firm body up against his, warm breath on his face, and nodded helplessly, squeezing his eyes shut. Something whisper-soft brushed his temple and Kellen opened his eyes to Vee stepping back.

"First things first," he said, and pointed at the door beyond the kitchen. "Shower. I'll bring you some clothes."

"I don't stink," Kellen protested.

Vee's eyes warmed. "Maybe I just want you to smell like me."

Heat shot through Kellen's groin and he stifled a groan.

"Take as long as you need," Vee said. "I'll be here."

VEE WAITED until Kellen was safely inside the bathroom with the shower running before dragging out his phone and dialing Farid's number.

Farid picked up on the first ring. "Vee, it's late. What's wrong?"

"What's wrong?" Vee hissed, clutching the phone to his ear and pacing from one side of his tiny living room to the other. "What's wrong is I have a sub in my bathroom right now, 'Rid, a *sub*, and not just any sub, one who's *seriously* fucked up, *I don't know what to do.*"

"Okay, breathe," Farid said, immediately serious. "What happened?"

"I was at the club, just watching stuff," Vee said. The shower was loud and he knew Kellen couldn't hear him, but he still lowered his voice. "He was there. He got up onstage, 'Rid, he *begged* a Dom to take him, any Dom, he said. No one would touch him. He was desperate, I could see it all over him, he was going to do something stupid —so I said I'd take him."

"And you took him *home?*"

"I didn't have a choice!" Vee snapped, and dropped his voice again. "Martha said we couldn't scene on the premises, that Kellen's too dangerous and she didn't want to risk it. So I— he's showering. He's... oh my god, what do I *do?*"

"The first thing you do is you get him tested," Farid said flatly. "If he's that unhinged, who the fuck knows what he's been exposed to. Be *careful.* I wouldn't even kiss him until I knew for sure."

Vee closed his eyes. "No one's open for a blood screen this time of night, 'Rid."

"Then you don't scene tonight. This isn't negotiable, Vee, and you know it."

"No, I know," Vee said. "But I'm afraid he's going to bolt. He's only here because I promised I'd help him fly, and if I tell him we're not scening, he's going to run and not look back."

"Figure out how to make him want to stay," Farid said. "Vee, look, I know you want to help him, but you don't have to fix him. This isn't your problem. Give him a twenty, take him to a shelter. You're not responsible for him."

"You didn't see the look in his eyes," Vee whispered.

Farid sighed and Dominic asked a low question in the background.

"How do I handle him?" Vee asked, as the water turned off. "What if I make things worse?"

"Insist on a safeword, first of all. And remember how you handled Fox. Listen to his body, not his words. He may lie to you but his body won't. Above all, don't let him see that you're not sure of yourself. If he loses faith in you, he *will* bolt."

"Great," Vee muttered. "I gotta go."

"Let me know what happens," Farid said.

Vee hung up and shoved the phone in his pocket as Kellen emerged from the bathroom, a towel around his waist and beads of water still clinging to his chest and damp hair a tangle around his face.

"Clothes," Vee said aloud, and dove for his bedroom.

When he came back with sweats and a frayed, soft T-shirt, though, Kellen had dropped the towel and was kneeling on the floor, hands clasped behind his back and head bowed.

Vee stopped dead, air stolen from his lungs. Kellen's back was covered in scars, thin and ragged, thick and ropy, twisting up his ribs in white ridges. They stood out in sharp relief against his pale skin, a chilling reminder of what he'd been through and the depths to which he'd sunk in his desperation. He was at once a fragile, fey creature and battle-weary soldier, and Vee wanted nothing more than to protect him, soothe away the wounds and bring a measure of peace into those haunted eyes.

Kellen finally glanced up. "I don't need those," he said softly.

Vee jerked, recalled to himself and the clothes in his arms. "We're doing this on my terms, not yours," he said, and something like relief flashed across Kellen's face, there and gone again almost too quickly to identify. Vee tossed the clothes on the floor in front of him. "Put them on."

Kellen's mouth worked but he picked up the

shirt and dragged it on over his head, then stood in a quick, fluid motion to tug the pants up over his skinny hips. "Now what?" he challenged.

"Now you tell me your safeword," Vee said.

"I don't have one."

Vee pointed. "There's the door."

Kellen's eyes widened and he shifted his weight but he didn't move.

It was a calculated risk. Kellen might well take the invitation and walk out. Vee held his breath as Kellen looked at him, at the door, and back at him.

"Don't make me," Kellen said, voice almost pleading.

"I'm not making you do anything," Vee said, keeping his tone even. "I told you we're doing this on my terms. This is part of them. Choose a safeword, and promise you'll use it if anything we do is too much."

He realized his mistake too late, as Kellen nodded eagerly.

"If it's too much, I will. I will, I promise."

Vee kept his expression blank with an effort. "So what is it?"

"Um. Satin," Kellen said. "Please, I need—"

"Hard limits?"

"I don't have any," Kellen said, too fast.

"Blood, fecal, electricity play?" Vee said, moving forward to circle him.

"I don't care, I don't—" Kellen's breath hitched in his chest as Vee ran a finger along his shoulder blade. "Do anything to me," he said, and it sounded like a plea.

"You want me to fuck you?" Vee asked, sliding

his hand down Kellen's back and feeling the scars under the shirt as Kellen shivered.

"*Yes*," Kellen said.

"You want to fuck me?"

Kellen twisted away so quickly he stumbled and nearly fell. His eyes were wide when they met Vee's. "No," he said, shaking his head. "No, I d-don't—"

"Really?" Vee said, surprised at the vehement response. "Topping is a lot of fun."

Kellen shook his head again, wariness in every line of his body. "I'm not—"

He was losing him, Vee realized, and he switched tactics. "What do you like?"

"Anything you want," Kellen said immediately.

"No," Vee said. "I asked what *you* like. I know you'll do whatever I want. That's not what I want to know. What do you *like* to do?"

Panic flickered across Kellen's face and he backed up a step, glancing at the door and up at Vee again.

Vee gritted his teeth. "We're not done discussing this," he warned. He took a step back and sat down on the tiny loveseat crammed under the window. "Facedown." He patted his thighs.

Kellen hesitated and then took a step forward. Another brought him to Vee's feet, and he lowered himself slowly, without the grace he'd displayed so far, until he was balanced awkwardly across Vee's lap, body rigid and tense.

Vee stroked his back. "Relax," he ordered.

He struck the first blow and Kellen bucked, muffling a noise against the cushion. Need thrummed through his body, drawing him taut as a bow, and Vee hit him again and again, keeping his hand flat as he pulled the noises from Kellen's throat.

He didn't stop until his hand was stinging and his arm aching. Kellen was hard against his thigh, rutting in tiny, helpless motions. Vee couldn't help pulling the sweats down to reveal the curve of his ass. It was rosy-red and perfect, Vee's handprints marking the porcelain skin, and he probed the crack of Kellen's ass with one finger, finding the flexing knot of muscle and pressing curiously.

Kellen arched back into it, making an inarticulate noise.

"Did I find something you like?" Vee asked, pushing until his finger slipped inside, up to the first knuckle.

Kellen squirmed, whimpering.

"Answer me," Vee ordered.

"*Yes*," Kellen said, hips bucking. "P-please—"

Vee pulled his finger out, making Kellen sob with frustration, dragged the pants down more, and started hitting him again. He liked it without the barrier of fabric between them, he decided. He could paint Kellen's skin a bright, flushed red this way, making each blow sting until Kellen was writhing helplessly.

Finally he stopped again.

"No," Kellen moaned.

Vee smacked him hard, just to watch the skin flash white and then pink, and pushed him gently off his lap.

Kellen hit the floor in a sprawl of limbs, pants still caught around his thighs, his cock hard and leaking against his stomach as he stared up at Vee.

"Do you want more?" Vee asked, pressing his hand to his own aching length. Just the brush of contact had him biting his lip, struggling to keep from coming as Kellen nodded. "You'll get it," Vee promised. "Tomorrow."

Kellen's mouth fell open and he rolled to his knees, catching blindly at his too-big pants. "Why?" he demanded.

"Because—" Vee stopped himself. *Because you've pushed yourself too hard for too long and you've become desensitized. Because you have to learn to enjoy the smallest of pleasures before being taken further. Because you're in so much danger to yourself.* "Because I said so," he finally said.

Kellen surged to his feet. "No." He shook his head, hand clutching the pants to keep them from falling off again. "No, you *can't* make me wait. I'll —I'll leave. I'll walk out the door and find someone else, someone who'll—"

Vee lunged upright and caught Kellen's throat in one hand, shoving him backward until his shoulders hit the wall. "Say the word. Say it, and I'll let you leave." He leaned in until their chests were pressed together and Kellen's breath rasped in his ear, quick and panicky. "Say it," Vee repeated. "You know the word."

"I—" Kellen licked his lips and Vee followed the motion, wanting desperately to taste and holding onto his willpower by a thread.

He slipped his free hand between them and cupped the bulge in Kellen's pants. "If you don't say it, I'm going to assume it's because you want to stay," he warned.

Kellen let his head fall back against the wall with a thump as he closed his mouth.

Vee bent and pressed his face to the curve of his neck, tasting sweat-dampened skin. "All you have to do is say one word," he whispered. "Or you can be quiet and I promise I'll give you what you need. I promise—I'll make you fly."

Kellen was trembling, but he said nothing. His eyes were wide and unfocused when Vee lifted his head.

"Bedroom," Vee said.

Kellen didn't move. Vee caught his wrist and pulled sharply, knocking Kellen off-balance so that he stumbled behind him into the bedroom.

"On your back on the bed," he ordered. Thank *God* he had an actual four-poster bed, a gift from his parents when he'd gotten his own apartment. He didn't look to see if Kellen had obeyed as he rummaged in the box he kept by the nightstand. He hadn't planned this, hadn't had time to stock up the way he would have liked, but he'd bought some soft rope and a leather flogger a few days before, a blind impulse more than anything.

When he turned to the bed, Kellen was flat on his back, watching him raptly.

"You're so good," Vee breathed, and lashed one wrist and then the other to the headboard. "Try to get out of them," he said.

Kellen pulled, tendons standing out in his neck as he did his best to break free. When he sagged back to the bed, Vee caressed his stomach, smiling at him.

"You know what to say," he said.

Kellen was silent, eyes intent.

The urge to kiss him was becoming over-whelming, so Vee turned away and left the bedroom. He went to the bathroom, brushed his teeth, used the toilet, and texted Farid. *So far so good I think.*

Then he went back to the bedroom and slid onto the mattress beside Kellen's tense form, sitting up briefly to pull the blanket at the end of the bed over both of them.

"Goodnight," he said, and closed his eyes.

6

KELLEN LAY ON HIS BACK, staring at Vee beside him in the bed. The curtains were open and moonlight glanced off the shell of Vee's ear, haloing his black hair in silver and leaving his face in shadow. Was he asleep? His breathing was even and regular and he seemed relaxed, as if he hadn't just tied a total stranger to the headboard and then gotten into bed beside him.

What the fuck had just happened? Vee had barely done *anything* to him, but Kellen ached for more, for Vee's hands all over him. God, he was so beautiful, with those dark eyes and slashing eyebrows that made him seem so fierce until he dropped his guard. Kellen turned on his side, as much as the ropes would let him, and inched a foot across the bed until his toes nudged Vee's shin.

Vee's breathing changed briefly and he sighed deep in his chest, snuffling against his pillow.

Kellen caressed his leg, watching Vee's face.

The spanking had helped, but the need was swelling under his skin again, making it hard to breathe. He squirmed in place as he hardened, imagining Vee sinking into him, pinning him down with hands and keeping him there, hot and forceful and taking all choice from Kellen until he was mindless with it, begging for more.

He rolled his hips up, desperate for friction that wasn't there, and Vee lifted his head.

"What are you doing?" He didn't sound sleepy.

"I'm sorry, please, I just need—" Kellen bit his lip so hard he tasted blood. "You promised," he whispered. "I need—"

Vee rolled fluidly to his knees and straddled him in one quick move. Kellen bucked up against his weight, pulling uselessly on the ropes.

"I promised you'd fly tomorrow," Vee said, leaning down. His face was in shadow, but moonlight glinted off his eyes as he looked at Kellen. "Do you not believe me?"

"I do, I just—" Kellen pulled on the ropes again. "I…."

"You're an addict," Vee said quietly. "And you need a fix, don't you?"

Kellen squeezed his eyes shut against the judgment he knew he'd see in Vee's.

Vee went up on his knees and patted Kellen's flank. "Roll over. There's enough leeway in the ropes to let you cross your arms."

Kellen opened his eyes, startled, but obeyed, squirming around under Vee's body until he was facedown on the mattress, arms crossed above his head.

"Comfortable?" Vee asked, sliding down so he was sitting on Kellen's thighs.

Kellen buried his face in the pillow and didn't answer. He didn't *want* to be comfortable. He wanted the burn and ache and the agony, sharp as a knife, that would take him away.

Vee hooked his thumbs in Kellen's pants and pulled them down around his thighs. Then he leaned over and Kellen heard a drawer open and close.

"What do I do?" he asked helplessly.

Vee resettled his weight and stroked Kellen's back. "You take it. And you don't come without my permission."

Fingers probed his ass, slick with lube. Vee pushed two in without giving Kellen time to adjust, pressing all the way inside in a tight, hot slide. Kellen gasped against the pillow, canting his hips to give Vee a better angle. It felt *good*, nerves firing and sparks of pleasure rippling under his skin as his body stretched to let Vee in.

"Will you fuck me?" he managed and then moaned in protest when Vee stopped moving.

There was silence for a moment as if Vee was considering, and then he pumped in and out again, setting a steady rhythm.

"No," he said. "Not yet."

"But—don't you have condoms?"

The spank was unexpected, making him yelp. Vee hadn't held back—the palmprint burned against Kellen's skin, making him whimper.

"Who said you could argue with me?"

Kellen gulped air and pushed his face back into the pillow.

After a minute, Vee resumed. His fingers were relentless in their slide and stretch. He didn't vary the speed, pressing in and pulling out in the same slow, steady motion. It was delicious and agonizing, nowhere near enough but somehow still taming the fire in Kellen's bones so that he went limp against the bed, letting Vee work.

"There," Vee murmured. "God, you're so lovely when you submit."

Kellen closed his eyes and fell into space as Vee fucked him with his fingers, long and slow strokes that never sped up or slowed down, in and out, in and out. He floated in the dark, bliss gathering in his stomach, and time slowed and stretched, twisting like warm taffy through his fingers.

He wasn't close to orgasm but he didn't care. It felt so good to be held, pinned down and taken over. It was enough. Then Vee added another finger and changed his angle, and Kellen arched up off the bed, clawing for purchase on the headboard as Vee drove deep and nailed his prostate in hard, punishing thrusts.

"No, *no*," Kellen gasped, pulling uselessly on the ropes. "No, please, I'm going to—"

Vee pressed Kellen back to the mattress with a hand between his shoulder blades. "Not until I say." His voice was like iron, fingers probing deep and ruthless, and Kellen sobbed out loud.

"I can't, I *can't*—" He was going to come, he knew he was, and Vee would be angry at him for failing his first test, he couldn't bear that—Kellen turned his head and bit down hard on his forearm, pain blooming bright behind his eyes as he tasted copper on his tongue. The orgasm receded and Vee faltered, swearing under his breath, but Kellen pushed back against him. *Don't stop, please don't stop.*

Vee spread his fingers across Kellen's spine and pushed deep again with his other hand. Kellen sighed against his forearm. He barely felt the sting in his arm as Vee propelled him back to the edge again, but this time Kellen was able to hold it back, letting Vee take over his senses as his cock dragged wetly against the mattress beneath him.

"I can't wait to fuck you," Vee said, his voice thick, and grabbed Kellen's hip, pulling him up onto his knees so he could slam deeper.

Kellen let Vee manhandle him into place, focused on keeping the bliss from overwhelming him, until Vee crooked his fingers again and fireworks exploded behind Kellen's eyes.

"Come for me," Vee ordered, fingers bruisingly tight on Kellen's hip, and Kellen fell gratefully over the edge, cock pulsing and jerking as he came untouched, pleasure cleaving him in two. He clenched around Vee's fingers, hips stuttering, and Vee hissed and eased him through it in slowing strokes until Kellen collapsed back to the bed. Vee pulled out gently and leaned down to press a soft kiss to his shoulder blade.

"You were so good," he whispered.

Kellen's eyes wouldn't stay open. He was barely aware when Vee left the bed. When he came back, he put a hand on Kellen's shoulder.

"This is going to sting."

Kellen hummed, unconcerned, but the cold antiseptic hitting his broken skin had him jolting upright, ropes stopping him from getting away.

He writhed as Vee caught his arm and held it steady.

"Burns, it *burns*—"

"I know," Vee said. His grip was uncompromising, but his voice was gentle. "You broke the skin. I have to clean it. Almost done, I promise."

Kellen rolled sideways as much as he could, butting his head against Vee's ribs, and Vee cupped his face, smoothing a thumb over Kellen's cheekbone.

The burning eased after a few minutes and Kellen sucked in air, coming back to awareness. He pulled away, tucking his face into the pillow again so he didn't have to see Vee's expression.

Vee said nothing, but his fingers were gentle as he put a bandage over the bite and smoothed the tape in place, then pulled his pants up.

"Do you think you can sleep now?" he asked quietly.

Kellen nodded, face still buried, and Vee patted his shoulder and slid off the bed again. When he came back, he tucked a towel under Kellen's hips and then pulled the blanket up over both of them.

"What about you?" Kellen whispered as Vee got comfortable.

Vee laughed under his breath. "You think I could see something that hot and *not* come? Go to sleep."

Instead, Kellen lifted his head. "Can I—you said... can I still fly, tomorrow?"

Vee's eyes were somehow sad in the moonlight, but he smiled. "Yeah," he murmured. "Now sleep."

Kellen relaxed back against the pillows and obeyed.

HE WOKE up alone in the bed. Kellen fought back the instinctive rush of fear and tried to sit up. The ropes weren't cruelly tight but they wouldn't let him move, and he sagged back to the mattress. Vee wouldn't have left him, surely. He couldn't quite stop the noise that fell from his mouth, though, and Vee appeared around the corner as if called, hair rumpled and a smile on his face.

"Hey, you're awake." His eyes sharpened as he took in Kellen's state. "What is it?"

Kellen shook his head, feeling stupid. "Nothing, it's—I have to…. Bathroom?"

"Of course," Vee said. He made quick work of the knots, but when Kellen tried to sit up, Vee took his wrist, rubbing the rope marks gently.

"Feeling okay?" he asked.

"Yeah," Kellen said, pulling away.

"Hungry?" Vee asked, letting him go.

Kellen shrugged and stood up, catching the pants before they fell off, and shuffled for the bathroom. When he came out, Vee was flipping eggs in the skillet on the stove. He pointed to the couch.

"Sorry I don't have a real table. Sit there and I'll bring you food."

Kellen obeyed, crossing his legs as Vee whistled snatches of a vaguely familiar tune and slid eggs onto a plate. The toaster popped and Kellen jumped, schooling his expression immediately, but

Vee didn't seem to notice. He buttered the slices and drizzled honey over them, then brought the plate to Kellen with a smile.

Kellen ate in gulps, barely tasting the food, as Vee sat down beside him.

"I've been thinking," he began, and Kellen froze. He put the plate down on the coffee table and tensed to stand, but Vee held out a hand. "Please, just—hear me out?"

Kellen sank back onto the cushions, still poised to flee.

Vee rubbed his face. "I like you."

Kellen blinked. What was he supposed to say?

"Last night—it was good, right? You liked it?"

Kellen nodded warily.

"Would you like… more?"

Kellen nodded again, looking for the trap.

"Look, I know I'm probably doing this all wrong," Vee said, fixing Kellen with a serious look. "I'm sure you've figured out that I'm pretty new to the scene." Kellen didn't respond to that, and Vee huffed a quiet laugh. "Yeah, okay. So what I'm trying to say is, I talked to a friend. He's been doing this a lot longer and he had some advice for me." Vee blew out a breath. "Um. I'd like to offer you a contract."

Kellen stared at him.

"Say something," Vee said, half-despairing. "Anything, tell me I'm an idiot and leave if you have to, but *something*—"

"Why?" Kellen interrupted.

It was Vee's turn to blink. "Because—" He lifted his hands, looking baffled. "Because you submitting to me was… beautiful. Because *you* are beautiful. And I don't think I'm imagining this connection between us, am I?" He looked suddenly worried. "Am I? Is this all in my head?"

Kellen almost smiled. "No," he said quietly. "But I don't… you heard Martha. I'm… damaged. I'm not safe. You should have a good sub, one that's right for you."

"Oh, *fuck it*," Vee said, caught Kellen's face in his hands, and kissed him.

Kellen's breath stopped, his head spinning. Vee's hands were warm and solid, cradling his face, and his mouth was sweet, tongue soft as he teased along the seam of Kellen's lips. Kellen opened his mouth and Vee hummed and slipped inside, tasting Kellen's tongue. When he broke away, he didn't let go, still cupping Kellen's jaw and nosing along his cheek, breath puffing warm against his skin.

"Will you at least look at it?" he whispered.

It took Kellen a minute to collect his wits and realize Vee was talking about the contract. He hesitated. He shouldn't. He should leave, thank Vee for the night before and go back to Jacob.

But the thought of leaving, of Jacob and his heavy fists and the permanent disappointment in his eyes, made Kellen's stomach cramp.

"You don't know me," he managed. "I could— I could be bad news. I *am* bad news. How do you know I won't steal your things and run?"

Vee sat back, laughter creasing his eyes. "Do you see anything worth stealing? About the only thing in here worth anything is the bed, and you can't fit that in your back pocket."

Kellen ducked his head and Vee reached out, taking hold of his chin and lifting it.

"Hey," he said quietly. "I know it's fast. And maybe we won't suit, and we'll drive each other nuts. That's okay. If you want to leave, I won't stop you. But if you want to try... I'm offering."

"What—" Kellen cleared his throat. "What would it entail?"

"Well, I work at a bakery, so I have early hours and I'm usually home by three. I'd like to spend my afternoons with you. Do you—God, I don't know anything about you. Do you have a job? A home? Do you *want* to—"

"Yes," Kellen interrupted, and joy lit Vee's eyes, making Kellen's chest hurt. "Yes, I want to, but—" He looked down at his lap. "I don't have a job. Or a place to live. I'm sorry. I can't pay for food or... anything."

Vee took his hand. "We'll figure it out. Hey, I wonder if Dom would give you a job."

"Who?"

"He created Spectral. I just work in the bakery, but I know his—um. Boyfriend. We're friends. I can talk to him, if you want."

"I'm not good at anything," Kellen warned, and Vee laughed out loud.

"*That's* not true, but okay. Here." He picked up a manila envelope Kellen hadn't even noticed off the coffee table and handed it to him. "I asked Farid to help, he couriered it over this morning while you were asleep."

Kellen drew out a sheaf of papers.

"It's a standard Dom/sub contract," Vee said.

"Look, there are places for hard limits, soft limits, length of the contract, and everything."

Kellen read it over slowly. He'd heard of contracts, of course, but he'd never been with a Dom who'd wanted him to sign one.

"I don't—" He looked up, hair in his eyes. "I don't have anything valuable. If I break the contract, you won't get anything from me."

Vee brushed the hair off Kellen's forehead. He couldn't seem to stop touching him, not that Kellen minded. "It's not legally binding. It's just so we both know upfront what we're getting into. No surprises, right?"

"Sure," Kellen said, looking back at the papers. Vee had already filled in the hard limits on his own page—watersports, fecal play, and… Kellen looked closer. "Roleplay?"

Vee looked embarrassed. "Squicks me out. Can't explain it."

Kellen shrugged. "Heard weirder." He kept reading. The contract was for three months, at the end of which time they would reevaluate and decide if they wanted to sign for longer.

He put the pages down and bent forward as the reality of the situation swamped him, making his head spin. Vee *wanted* him. Wanted him to stay, to sub for him. Kellen couldn't breathe, the room spinning around him, as Vee touched his head.

"Hey, it's okay," he said, as Kellen labored for air. "We haven't even really scened yet. You don't have to sign it now. You can—you can leave if you want, go, um… wherever it is you go, and come back when you're ready. If you decide you want it, I mean. Um."

Kellen lifted his head. "I do, I told you that. I want… this. I just—" He swallowed hard. "You're going to regret it."

"Let me be the judge of that," Vee said. "There's only one real stipulation I have, and I understand if it's a deal-breaker."

Kellen waited, wary.

Vee fidgeted. "I… would want to be monogamous."

"Oh." Kellen considered that. "Alright."

"Really?" Emotion flitted across Vee's face, too quick to be identified.

Kellen raised a shoulder. "If you can—give me what I need, I don't have to look elsewhere."

Relief filled Vee's eyes. "Okay," he said. "Okay. Now, put your street clothes back on. We're going out."

"Out?" Kellen leaned back, alarmed. "Why?"

Vee tilted his head, a smile creeping across his face. "Because if you want to fly, we're going to get tested right now, so I can do everything to you I've been wanting to do since I saw you standing on that stage."

FARID HAD SENT him the address of the closest clinic that did rush STD screening, and Kellen spent several hours submitting to mouth swabs and blood draws, then waiting for the results. He said nothing, sitting quietly beside Vee and gazing at the poster on the wall opposite with the earnest young man urging safe sex. If it hadn't been for the jiggling of his knee, Vee would have thought him completely relaxed.

He didn't push, though. Instead, he scooted down in his seat, just enough that his leg pressed up against Kellen's.

Kellen stilled, looking at him sideways under his shaggy hair, and Vee pretended not to notice, crossing his arms and relaxing.

The silence eased, and after a few minutes, Kellen's frame slowly unwound.

They waited without speaking until they got his results. All clear. Vee couldn't help catching Kellen's face and pulling him into a jubilant kiss.

Kellen huffed what sounded like amusement against Vee's mouth but kissed him back willingly.

"So I'm usually home by three," Vee said, out on the street.

Kellen slanted another look at him and said nothing.

"I just meant, for your own schedule," Vee said, feeling ridiculous. "If you want to, like… come over after work, spend the evenings with me, then go, I'm okay with that. I don't want you to feel trapped or pushed into anything."

"That sounds good," Kellen said. "Every day?"

"Um. Any time you want?" Vee offered. "It can be every day if you need it that often. But if you can go longer, that's okay too."

"Just sex, right?" Kellen asked.

Vee faltered. "Well… yeah. You said you didn't want more."

Kellen nodded, mouth firming. "Just sex."

Vee swallowed something like disappointment and smiled at him. "Perfect. Are you hungry?"

Kellen shook his head. "I want—" His eyes were hungry and ashamed when he snuck a glance at Vee.

Heat flashed through Vee. "You'll get it," he promised. "But I'm hungry. Let's get food."

"Can we eat at your place?" Kellen asked, and Vee laughed out loud.

"I see what you're doing, but fine. We can eat at my place."

Kellen ducked his head as a smile flashed across his face, there and gone.

WHEN THEY GOT BACK to the house, there was a box addressed to Vee on the doorstep. He handed the food to Kellen and picked up the box, grunting at the weight.

"What on earth…."

"What is it?"

"No idea," Vee said, struggling to balance the box and fish his keys from his pocket. "But it's got my name on it."

Upstairs, he set the box on the floor as Kellen stood in the middle of the tiny living room, looking uncertain and hopeful. Vee found a sharp knife to open the box. Inside was a note.

Vee. Thought some of these would come in handy. Remember, listen to his body.

—Farid

Vee lifted out the first item and promptly dropped it when he realized he was holding a huge pink dildo. "Oh my *god*!" He wiped his hand on his shirt and looked up at Kellen, who was *laughing*. His cheeks were flushed, eyes sparkling, and Vee forgot how to breathe.

Kellen sobered as Vee gaped up at him, and Vee shook himself.

"I can't believe Farid. I'm going to have words with him."

"Your friend bought you sex toys?" Kellen asked, folding himself onto the floor beside him and picking up the dildo. He ran thin fingers over it curiously and Vee swallowed hard and turned back to the box, dumping the contents out on the floor.

Silence fell as they stared.

"Wow," Kellen murmured after a minute.

"Yeah," Vee said, running a hand through his hair. There was a pile of rope, soft and supple. Handcuffs, both padded and hard steel. Several vibrators of varying shapes and size. Vee picked up a small golden tube, turning it curiously in his hand. "What the hell…."

"It's a cock cage," Kellen said helpfully.

Vee stared at him and back at the object in his hand. "Do you… *like*…?"

Kellen shrugged, pawing through the stuff on the carpet. "They can be fun. By which I mean they're torture, but sometimes that's what I need, you know?"

"Sure," Vee said, setting the cock cage down very carefully and picking up the rope.

Kellen's eyes caught and snagged on his hand and his pupils dilated, his throat bobbing.

Vee stroked the rope, watching Kellen, who looked spellbound.

"You want to be tied up again?" he asked.

Kellen swallowed again and nodded silently.

"Then eat," Vee said, gesturing at the food with his chin.

Kellen nearly knocked the bag over grabbing it. He pulled out one of the cheeseburgers and ate in quick gulps as Vee leaned back against the couch, running the rope through his fingers and hardening in his pants. Kellen's eyes darted from the rope to Vee's face to his crotch as if unable to decide where to look. He finished the burger and wadded up the paper with hands that shook a little.

Vee took pity on him. "Take your clothes off."

Kellen scrambled upright to shed his clothes. Vee allowed himself a minute to enjoy the sight of him, naked and vulnerable. His silvery hair fell over his brown eyes, collarbones standing stark under his satiny skin. Vee stretched, moving the rope so the tent in his pants was obvious as he continued to look. There were scars on Kellen's ribs, but not as many as on his back. The hair at his groin was a little darker than his head, but not much, and his cock was long and slender, thickening fast as he shifted his weight and let Vee look his fill.

"Lie down on your back on the coffee table," Vee said.

Kellen stepped over the pile of toys and sat on the edge of the table. He lowered himself on his elbows in stages until he was flat on his back, legs hanging over the side and feet on the floor.

Vee stood and picked up the rope. "What's your safeword?"

Kellen didn't even seem to hear him, staring at the ceiling and gripping the sides of the table.

Vee turned on his heel and went to the bedroom. He retrieved the leather flogger, lube from the nightstand, and the rest of the rope, and went back to the living room. Kellen's head thumped back to the table at the sight of him and he couldn't quite hide the sigh of relief.

Vee secured the rope to the table leg and began wrapping it around Kellen's chest, starting at his shoulders and working his way down. Kellen shifted against the restraints, making a soft noise, and Vee bent to kiss him as he fed the rope under the table and back around again. Kellen kissed back eagerly and Vee groaned.

"God, you're beautiful. Are you comfortable?"

Kellen made a noise that could have meant anything. Vee slipped a finger under the ropes on his chest and deemed them good. He kept going, strapping Kellen's hips to the table but avoiding his cock where it lay on his belly, twitching as Kellen squirmed.

Next were his feet. Vee took one of the shorter pieces and tied Kellen's right ankle to the leg of the table, then repeated the process on the left.

Finally he stood up to admire his work.

Kellen lay spread out for the taking in front of him, legs wide and pale skin stark against the mahogany wood and flushed where the ropes cut in. His cock was already red and straining, leaking steadily, and his pulse beat rapidly in his throat.

"First things first," Vee said, and rummaged through the pile of toys until he found a plug that looked suitable. Squat and short, it flared at the base, perfect for stretching Kellen's hole until he was ready for him.

He took it to the bathroom and washed it, taking his time and listening for any noise from Kellen. When he came back, Kellen's head was up, his eyes anxious but his mouth firmly shut.

Vee smiled at him and squeezed lube onto the plug. He touched it to Kellen's entrance and felt the shiver that rippled through him. Vee couldn't help the teasing, pushing in a fraction and then retreating, mesmerized by the way Kellen's body stretched to accept the intrusion even as he thrashed and moaned. Finally, though, he pressed it all the way inside until it settled in place, stroking the soft skin of Kellen's inner thigh with his free hand until Kellen relaxed.

"Beautiful," Vee repeated. "What's your safeword?"

Kellen blinked as if he couldn't remember words.

Vee stooped and picked up the flogger. He brought it down with a stinging snap on Kellen's thigh, making him jerk and cry out.

"Safeword," he repeated.

Kellen's mouth worked. "I—"

"Tell me," Vee demanded. "Promise you'll use it if it gets too intense."

"S-satin," Kellen managed, and licked his lips. "P-please—"

It would have to do for now. Vee had been practicing with the flogger, and he put it to good use, striping Kellen's thighs until they were bright red under the rope. Kellen took everything Vee gave him, hips rolling in tiny, clearly unconscious movements, eyes fixed on Vee as he moved around him.

Vee stopped briefly and stroked Kellen's cock. Kellen bucked against his grip, moaning, and Vee smiled and let go.

This time, he brought the leather strips down on Kellen's stomach. Kellen curled forward against the blow with a choked groan, but Vee didn't stop. He flogged Kellen's chest and stomach in quick, hard snaps of his wrist, until Kellen was shaking and sobbing, twisting in the rope.

"Please, no, please—"

Vee hesitated. Had he gone too far? But a closer look at Kellen's face revealed the truth—he'd fallen into subspace, his eyes open but unaware, mouth shaping pleas he didn't seem aware of. Vee straightened and kept going, layering his blows up and down Kellen's chest and thighs until he was dripping with sweat and his arm ached.

Finally he dropped the flogger and clasped Kellen's cock, stroking it rough and careless. Kellen struggled against the ropes, begging incoherently.

"You like that?" Vee asked. He bent and sucked a bruise into the skin over Kellen's collarbone, hand still moving.

Kellen twisted, his reactions slow and distorted, and Vee couldn't help leaning down and taking another kiss from him.

His mouth was sweet and languid, no urgency

to it despite the erection that strained in Vee's hand, and Vee took his time exploring, memorizing the taste and feel of Kellen's lips for several minutes before pulling away to pepper kisses along his jaw.

Then he stood and yanked his shirt off over his head. His pants and underwear followed, and he settled himself between Kellen's thighs quickly, one hand on Kellen's knee and the other on his own cock. He hissed at the contact and gave himself several quick strokes to take the edge off before leaning over and checking Kellen's face.

His eyes were still open, lips moving slowly, utter peace saturating his body. He was soaring, Vee realized, probably only barely aware of what Vee was doing.

He lubed himself up and took hold of the plug. Kellen made a protesting noise as Vee pulled it free.

"Shh," Vee soothed him, petting his thigh. "I've got you." He lined up, teasing himself as much as Kellen by rubbing the head of his cock against Kellen's hole as it flexed. Then he pressed forward. Kellen opened sweetly to him, back arching and eyes closing, and Vee slid home, gritting his teeth to keep from coming at the molten heat that surrounded his dick. "*Fuck,*" he whispered.

This wasn't going to take long. He drew almost all the way out and pushed back in, fighting the sensations threatening to drown him as Kellen's body swallowed his length, silken walls tight around him.

Vee leaned forward and braced himself with a

hand on either side of Kellen's shoulders and started fucking him in earnest, slamming home in sharp, hard thrusts. Kellen gasped broken encouragement, pinned and immobile and the hottest thing Vee had ever experienced, his eyes glassy and unfocused, blurred with ecstasy.

Vee could feel his orgasm swelling beneath his skin and he held on by his fingernails, shifting his angle until Kellen arched sharply against him and cried out. Then he wrapped a hand around Kellen's cock again, stroking in counterpoint to his thrusts.

There were tears on Kellen's face, his face contorted as mindless pleas fell from his mouth. Vee twisted his wrist on an upstroke and Kellen sobbed brokenly and clenched around him, spilling in helpless spurts all over the ropes and his belly. The sight and sound of Kellen so undone was too much for Vee—he drove deep one last time and came, brain whiting out with bliss as he emptied deep inside Kellen's body.

Arms and legs shaking, he collapsed on top of Kellen's helpless form, heaving for air. Kellen had gone utterly still, and Vee pushed himself upright, worry slicing through the afterglow.

"Kellen?"

Kellen's head lolled, eyes closed. He'd passed out, Vee realized, but his breathing was steady and so was his heartbeat, if rapid.

Vee withdrew gently and paused to watch the come seep from Kellen's hole. *God.* He rubbed a thumb against the muscle and his dick twitched. Kellen didn't stir. Eventually, Vee managed to haul himself to his feet, legs rubbery, and stumble for the bathroom and a warm cloth. When he came back, Kellen was coming around, blinking slow and unfocused.

"I'm here," Vee said, fumbling for the end of the rope. "Hold on, let me get you untied and cleaned up." His fingers were shaky but eventually he got it untied and began the process of unwinding the pieces until Kellen was free. "How are you?" he asked, gently pulling him into a sitting position.

Kellen didn't answer, but he leaned sideways, into Vee's body. Vee slipped an arm around him.

"Come on, let's get you into bed. Do you think you can walk?"

Whatever came out of Kellen's mouth wasn't words, his head drooping as he slurred something. Vee took his arm and draped it over his shoulders.

"You're gonna have to help me, gorgeous," he said, and stood, gently hauling Kellen upright.

They staggered into the bedroom, one halting step at a time, Vee supporting almost all Kellen's weight as he guided him to the bed and eased him down onto it.

Kellen curled onto his side and Vee hesitated. Farid had coached him on aftercare, but would Kellen welcome Vee's touch? He waffled for a moment, but the need for intimacy won out, and he slid onto the bed, molding his body up against Kellen's. Kellen reached back and draped an arm over Vee's hips, and Vee swallowed around the lump in his throat and pressed a kiss to the nape of his neck.

KELLEN CAME TO IN SLOW, almost imperceptible stages. He was floating in the vast, fathomless black, and then he wasn't, the room around him solidifying in increments until he could make out Vee's lamp on the bedside table, the print on the wall swimming into focus.

Five things I can see. The lamp. The picture. A watermark on the wallpaper in the corner, shaped like a ragged heart. He looked down. The green and blue blanket pulled up over his shoulders. Was it knit or crochet? He didn't know, but it looked handmade. Vee's hand, resting over Kellen's heart.

Kellen took a careful breath. *Four things I can hear.* Traffic on the street outside, a honking horn. Vee's breath in his ear. His own heartbeat, thumping slow and steady in his ears.

Three things I can touch. The blanket was soft under his fingertips, the pillow satiny against his cheek, and Vee's skin warm, the tiny hairs on his arm crisp when Kellen ran his palm over them.

Two things I can—

Vee lifted his head. "Hey," he said, voice blurred with sleep. "How are you feeling?"

Crisp linen in his nose vied with Vee's scent, warm and rich and comforting. Kellen turned over, wriggling around until they were facing.

Vee looked as exhausted as Kellen felt, but he smiled, running a hand over Kellen's shoulder and down his arm. "Was it good?"

Kellen scooted closer and kissed him. *One thing I can taste.* Vee tasted as good as he smelled, sweet and wet and willing against Kellen's mouth, lips curving. Kellen pulled away, frowning.

"What?"

Vee's smile widened. "That's the first time you've kissed me."

Kellen tucked his chin, embarrassed. He *knew* better than to let his own desires show. What had he been thinking?

But Vee just cupped his face. "Feeling okay?"

Kellen nodded. "What time is it?"

"A little after four," Vee said.

"Fuck, I should go." Kellen sat up, throwing the blanket off, and Vee followed him upright, smile sliding off his face.

"Already? Are you—um, okay. Do you need anything?"

Kellen slanted a look at him. "No?" He slid to the edge of the bed, finally registering that he was naked and his stomach and thighs were covered in red stripes. He touched one with a fingertip and hissed through his teeth.

"I can put some cream on before you leave," Vee offered.

"I'm fine," Kellen said. He stood, praying the wobble in his legs wouldn't give the lie to that statement. "I—can I use your shower?"

"Yes, of course." Vee's eyes were troubled, and Kellen looked away.

He found his street clothes folded neatly on the arm of the sofa, and carried them into the bathroom.

When he emerged, Vee was dressed and sitting in the living room, the sex toys all put away and his hands in his lap. He stood when Kellen appeared.

"Hey, so—"

Kellen cut him off. "I don't know when I can come back, but if you still want me to sign, I will."

Relief flooded Vee's expressive face and he nodded quickly. "It's up to you when you want to come back," he said, digging around beside the sofa until he came up with the manila envelope. "I won't hold you to a schedule or anything. Just— whenever you want to come over, I'm… I'd love to see you."

Kellen took the contract from him, avoiding his eyes, and scrawled his name across the last page. Then he shoved it back into Vee's hands and took a step sideways, shaking his hair out of his face.

"I have to—"

"Okay," Vee said softly, and the tenderness on his face made Kellen's chest hurt.

"Bye," he said, and turned away before he did something stupid, like kiss Vee breathless or push him onto the lumpy sofa and ride his dick until they both came screaming again.

The door banged shut behind him and he clattered down the stairs and out the front entrance, doing his best not to think about what had just happened. The subdrop was going to be brutal, but worse—Jacob was going to be *furious*.

7

Jacob greeted him with a fist.

Kellen went down hard, cupping his throbbing jaw, and scrambled backward as Jacob advanced.

"Where the *fuck* have you been?" he snarled.

"I'm sorry," Kellen panted, still scooting away from Jacob's boots. "I—I was trying to—" He searched for words. "I know we need money, I was —looking for work, please don't be mad, Jacob, I was trying to help—"

Jacob glared at him, heavy brows drawn over his nose. "And did you find any?"

"N-not yet," Kellen said, getting himself up on his elbows. "But—" *Maybe Dom would give you a job.* Vee's voice, echoing through his mind. "I might have a line on one."

Jacob's fist lowered a fraction and Kellen pressed his advantage.

"If—if I get it, I could… I could bring you a

regular paycheck, every week. You wouldn't have to con people, you could—"

Jacob gave him no warning before he let fly with a boot, connecting with Kellen's ribs. Kellen curled around the agony, breath hitching.

"You think what I do is *con* people?" Jacob hissed. "It's not my fault that startup didn't work out, and now you sit here and accuse me of *cheating* people?"

Kellen pushed away the memories of standing in front of an ATM with an "OUT OF SERVICE" sign, taking money from unsuspecting customers, and dragged in a halting breath.

"I'm sorry," he managed. "I j-just want to help, I—"

Jacob stooped and Kellen cowered backward, but Jacob caught his shoulders and dragged him upright with terrifying ease. He stared into Kellen's face, brows still furrowed and mouth set in a bitter line.

"If you'd just *talk* to me," he growled, and pulled Kellen into a rough hug.

Kellen stifled the pained noise as his bruised ribs hit Jacob's chest, but he couldn't help sagging against him, an arm sliding around his waist.

"You just make me *crazy*," Jacob muttered into Kellen's hair, holding him tighter.

Kellen blinked back tears. "I'm sorry, Jacob."

VEE HAD ALREADY BEEN at work for several hours when Farid and Dominic finally arrived, engrossed in coaxing the brioche into the right shape without tearing it and practicing his croissants.

Senna called his name and Vee looked up, blinking sweat from his eyes.

"Farid placed an order, he wants you to deliver it." She handed him the list and Vee took it.

He filled the basket quickly and drew two coffees, toting everything out to the elevators and upstairs. On the top level, he glanced sideways at Dominic's door, which was firmly shut. Farid's was open, though, and he was at his desk, typing busily.

"Come on in," he called, not looking away from the monitor.

Vee put the basket and coffees down on the edge of the desk as Farid hit Send and swiveled to face him.

"Um, is this for Dominic?" Vee asked, indicating the second coffee.

Farid shook his head. "It's for you. Sit. Tell me everything."

Vee sank into the chair but shot a look at Cory's closed office door.

"She's down the hall, talking to the board," Farid said. "We're alone. Now spill."

Vee took a long swallow of coffee. "So, um. We spent the night together—he wanted to stay but he didn't know how to say it. I did what you told me; I listened to his body. I gave him the opportunity to leave and told him if he stayed, I'd help him fly."

Farid nodded, leaning over to pick up his own cup of coffee. "What's his name again?"

"Kellen. We signed the contract."

"Good," Farid said. "Have you scened?"

"Yeah, twice," Vee said. "That first night, he—God, 'Rid, he really is an addict. It scares me. I tied him to the bed because I felt like he needed the… security, I guess? And it helped, but he woke me up begging for… more."

Farid pursed his mouth but didn't say anything.

"So I—you know. Gave him some, but didn't do anything unsafe, because he hadn't been tested, right? And then the next morning we went to the clinic and when we got home, your *gift* was there."

Farid grinned, bright and unrepentant. "Was it helpful?"

"Yes, and you suck," Vee muttered.

Farid laughed out loud.

"I tied him up properly that time," Vee continued. "He… I think he needs it."

"Makes him feel safe, probably," Farid said, nodding.

"That time I flogged him, and then we fucked. It was—" Vee passed a hand over his face, remembering. "It was good. Really good."

"What was your aftercare like?" Farid asked.

"I cleaned him up and then took him to bed and held him while he came down. When he woke up, he signed the contract but said he didn't know when he could come back." Vee leaned forward, elbows on his knees. "I don't know what I've gotten myself into, 'Rid."

Farid hummed agreement. "Lucky for you you're not alone."

"He *wants*—" Vee sighed. "He's starved for touch. When he doesn't realize he's doing it, he like… gravitates toward me. And then when he—it's like he realizes what he's doing and pulls away and it meant nothing. I can't get a read on him."

"What's his home life like?"

"I don't *know*," Vee said. "He's homeless, did I tell you that? I almost asked if he wanted to move in but—"

"Yeah, too soon," Farid agreed. He picked up a pen and spun it between his fingers. "No job?"

"No. That's actually something I wanted to ask you—or Dominic, I don't know—about."

Farid raised his eyebrows.

"Is there some sort of entry-level position here he could take?" Vee blurted.

Farid looked thoughtful. "I'm sure there's something. Let me talk to Brenda. Head of hiring," he clarified, at Vee's blank look. "I'll let you know."

"Talk to Brenda about what?" an unfamiliar voice said, and Vee twisted to see the CEO, Cory Somerland, breeze in the door. She was short, trim, and—*sleek* was the word that came to mind. From the perfectly tailored pale blue pantsuit to the dark red hair swept up into a perfect chignon, she was stunning and lovely. And terrifying, as she fixed her sharp eyes on Vee. "Hi. Who are you?"

Vee gulped but Farid beat him there.

"Didn't anyone ever tell you it's rude to eavesdrop?"

Cory rolled her eyes. "I'm allowed a little harmless voyeurism after the meeting I just had. Who *is* this, Farid?"

"This is Vijay Annapurna," Farid said. "He's

Lily's cousin and he works for your wife. He's a friend of mine."

Cory's smile was heartstopping as she held out a hand. "Hello, Vijay, it's lovely to meet you. Now if you don't mind, please go away. 'Rid, I need you in my office." She disappeared as quickly as she'd arrived and Farid grimaced apologetically at Vee.

"The board puts her in a bad mood. I have to go. Text me when you see Kellen again, alright?"

Vee nodded.

It was four days before Kellen came back. Vee was climbing the walls by then, wondering if he should go out and search the city or homeless shelters. He didn't even know where to *start*, where Kellen spent his time, who his friends were —anything.

He was going to fix that, he decided, if—*when* —Kellen returned.

On the fourth day, he trudged up to his house from the bus stop with leftovers from the workday tucked under his arm, feet leaden from being on them all day, and stopped dead at the sight of Kellen sitting on the top step, arms around his knees. He scrambled to his feet when Vee appeared and shifted his weight as if not sure what to say.

"Hi," Vee said, breathless, looking him over. Kellen was rumpled, hair a mess and shadows under his eyes, but he ducked his head and returned Vee's smile shyly.

Vee climbed the steps and unlocked the door,

watching Kellen the entire time, who followed him inside when the door opened. They climbed the stairs to the top floor in silence. Once inside, Vee put the keys on the hook and pulled his jacket off.

"Are you thirsty? Hungry?" He held up the paper bag in his hand. "I have sausage rolls, muffins, and a few cupcakes. I was going to take them out and give them away, but it was a really long day. So, um… they're yours if you want them?"

Kellen licked his lips but shook his head. His eyes looked haunted, and there was a shadow of a bruise over his right cheekbone.

Vee dropped the bag and crossed to him. Kellen held his ground, swallowing as Vee lifted a hand and brushed his thumb over Kellen's cheekbone.

"Are you okay?" he asked quietly.

Kellen nodded, swaying toward him.

Vee didn't miss it. But how to get Kellen to accept his touch in a nonsexual capacity? He chewed his lip for a minute and then made up his mind.

"I know you're just here for scening," he said, running a hand down Kellen's arm to his hand. "But I want… more than just sex."

Kellen's eyes narrowed with suspicion. "This isn't a relationship," he said, his voice soft and husky, as if he were just as affected by Vee's nearness as Vee was by his.

"I know," Vee said. He lifted Kellen's hand and kissed his fingertips, one by one. "I'm not asking you to be my boyfriend." He sucked the tip of one finger into his mouth and bit down lightly. "But —" He stopped to search for words. "I'm… tactile. You know what that means?"

A spark flared in Kellen's eyes. "I'm not stupid."

"I never thought you were," Vee hurried to say. "Just—can I—" He reached out, and Kellen let him gather him close as Vee wrapped his arms around Kellen's skinny frame.

There was a heartbeat of silence, and then Kellen tucked his face into Vee's neck and clutched at the back of his shirt. Vee closed his eyes, thanking any god listening, and held on.

They stood that way for several minutes until Kellen's grip loosened and he eased back. The shadows in his eyes had lightened a fraction, and Vee wanted to kiss him but restrained himself.

"Can I use your shower?" Kellen asked quietly.

"Of course," Vee said, letting him go. "I'll put the food away while you do that."

―――――

Ten minutes later, Kellen emerged from the bathroom completely naked, and Vee dropped the cupcake he'd just taken a bite out of. It bounced and rolled, leaving a smear of icing on the kitchen floor, but Vee barely noticed, eyes fixed on Kellen, damp and rosy from the hot water, veins translucent under his pale skin and hair a wet, tangled cloud around his elfin face.

He cleared his throat. "Um. Bedroom."

Kellen ducked his head as a smile flickered across his mouth, and brushed past Vee to enter the bedroom, where he stopped dead. Vee nearly bumped into him, grinning as Kellen turned to look at him.

"Been doing a little renovating," he said, affecting nonchalance. "Not much room, but I didn't need much. You like it?"

Kellen moved over to the big metal frame that Vee had fastened to the ceiling and floor, and ran a finger over the cuffs in the upper corners.

"They'll stretch a little," Vee said, moving up close behind him again. "But not much."

Kellen's eyes were huge, his pupils blown as he glanced at Vee and back at the frame. "Will you—"

"Do you want it?"

Kellen nodded quickly.

Vee squeezed his ass briefly and then slapped it. "Get in position then." He waited until Kellen had obeyed and then pulled his arms up one at a time and strapped them into the restraints. Then he bent and tugged Kellen's feet apart until he was teetering, held upright by the wrist cuffs, and buckled the ankle cuffs on. "Comfortable?"

"Stop asking me that," Kellen snapped, and then flinched as if realizing what he'd said. "I'm—I…."

Vee hesitated and Kellen tucked his chin to his chest.

"I'm not going to punish you for telling me how you feel," Vee said.

"That's the problem," Kellen blurted, turning his face away, and Vee sighed.

"Is it that bad?"

Kellen nodded miserably, and Vee stepped up close, molding his body to Kellen's.

"Alright," he murmured. "I'll take it away, okay?"

"Thank you," Kellen whispered. He was trembling, and Vee pressed a kiss to the nape of his neck and then stepped away.

The flogger to start, he decided. And once Kellen was nicely warmed up, he'd switch to the crop.

He took his time, working his way up and down Kellen's back and thighs until his skin was a bright, cherry red and Kellen was swaying with each blow, his cock hanging flushed and heavy between his legs.

"One of these days," Vee mused, running a hand over Kellen's hot skin, "I'm going to put you in a cock cage and *then* beat you until you're begging."

Kellen jerked, cock hardening even more, and made an unintelligible noise.

"You like that idea?" Vee said, landing another blow.

"No—*yes*," Kellen gasped.

Vee picked up the crop and swished it through the air. Kellen flinched.

"Don't anticipate," Vee said, hearing Sanyam's voice in his head. He touched the end to Kellen's shoulder blade, trailing it down his spine. "Accept each blow as the first. Just let it happen."

He struck him hard, and Kellen bucked in the cuffs. His skin went dead-white and then flushed angry red, and Vee couldn't resist scraping a fingernail over the stripe.

"More," Kellen begged.

"Mm," Vee said. "I think you need to earn it."

Kellen slanted a wary look at him over his shoulder.

"What's your favorite color?" Vee asked.

Kellen's brow knitted and he didn't answer.

Vee waited.

After a minute, Kellen broke. "B-brown."

Vee rewarded him with a quick, hard blow. "Why brown?"

Kellen twisted, but his answer came faster that time. "It's—so rich. W-warm. Comf—comforting?"

"Good," Vee said, and hit him twice. "Favorite movie."

Kellen dragged in air through his nose. "W-why…."

"Because I asked," Vee said. "Answer the question."

"Groundhog Day," Kellen said.

Vee blinked. "Interesting. Why?"

"B-because…." Kellen pulled on the cuffs. "Because I want… I like… he fucks up so much, and—"

"And you like the idea of being able to fix your mistakes?" Vee asked, and Kellen nodded.

"I can't fix anything," he whispered, head drooping.

That wouldn't do. Vee brought the crop down again and Kellen jerked.

"You're doing really well," Vee told him. "Do you have any family?"

Kellen said nothing.

Vee waited.

Kellen was utterly still, and unease crept through Vee's chest.

"Answer me," he said, putting more command than he felt into his voice.

Kellen shook his head, mouth stubbornly closed.

It was the first time Kellen had deliberately disobeyed him, and Vee was thrown. What was he supposed to do? He hesitated a moment and then switched topics.

"Favorite song."

It took Kellen a minute to answer, making Vee even more uneasy, but then he realized Kellen was trying to think of one.

"The… The Way," he finally said. "Fastball."

Vee rewarded him with three quick stripes, then stepped close, curving fingers over Kellen's hip and pressing his nose to his throat.

"Good," he murmured. "It's okay. I'm not angry."

Kellen turned his head, blindly seeking Vee's mouth. The kiss was hungry and desperate, full of things neither of them could say, and they were both breathing hard when they broke apart.

"*Please*," Kellen said.

"Okay," Vee said. He beat him in even, firm strokes, careful not to hit the same place twice in a row, until Kellen's buttocks and lower back were a mass of red and white welts and his head was hanging. Vee stopped to rest his arm, moving in close to grind his erection against Kellen's bare ass, knowing his clothes had to feel like sandpaper against the weals.

"You want me to fuck you?" he murmured into Kellen's ear.

Kellen's head lolled back against Vee's shoulder, his body sweetly limp with trust and surrender. It shook Vee to his core, the faith Kellen placed in him. He nipped lightly at the juncture of neck and shoulder, probing with one finger at Kellen's center.

"Don't want… prep—" Kellen slurred.

God. It was going to be so *tight*, and it would probably hurt. Vee kept it together with an almighty effort, gritting his teeth to keep from coming in his jeans as he pulled his finger out and Kellen moaned.

He was the perfect height, Vee thought as he stepped away to yank his clothes off and find the lube. Just a few inches shorter than him, so that Vee could fuck him standing up.

Slicked up, he got back in position and pressed inside with no warning, pushing in hard and deep and punishingly fast as Kellen writhed and cried out, impaled on his cock.

Vee caught his hips, pulling him down onto his dick, and set a rapid, steady rhythm, driving home in long, steady thrusts. Kellen flexed and struggled, pushing back and pulling away, and Vee caught his hair, dragging his head back and baring his throat.

"Mine," he growled against Kellen's skin, punctuating his words with snaps of his hips. "Mine. Say it. *Say it.*"

"Yours," Kellen sobbed, head flung back and eyes unfocused with bliss. "Please, can I—I need—"

Vee wrapped a hand around Kellen's cock and pressed his thumbnail against the slit. Kellen's cry was almost a scream as he came, every muscle locking up and squeezing Vee viciously tight inside him. That was all it took. Vee bit down hard on Kellen's neck and spilled inside him in needy, helpless jerks.

***

HE CAME BACK DOWN SLOWLY, the room swimming into focus, and gritted his teeth as he slid out of Kellen's body. Kellen's chin was on his chest, eyes open and completely unaware, and Vee couldn't help kissing the scar on his shoulder.

"God, what you do to me," he whispered.

It took him a few minutes to get Kellen out of the frame and onto the bed. Kellen seemed even more out of it than last time, but he curled into Vee's warmth with a contented noise, eyes falling shut as he relaxed into boneless oblivion and Vee held him.

He didn't sleep, but he rested, listening to Kellen's breathing and the traffic on the street. After awhile, he realized Kellen was whispering something to himself. Vee held his breath and tried to hear.

"Five… five things… f-five—"

"Five what?" Vee asked, keeping his voice low so he didn't startle him.

"I can see," Kellen slurred. "Five—"

"Five things you can see?" Vee asked gently, and Kellen nodded, slow and uncoordinated. *Grounding exercise*, Vee realized. Someone had taught Kellen how to come back to himself after an intense scene. "See the lamp?" Vee pointed. "That's one." He took Kellen's hand, folding all but his index finger down and using it to indicate the small carved jade cat beside it. "That was a gift from my cousin."

"Two," Kellen whispered.

"Good," Vee told him. "What else?"

"Lube… nightstand," Kellen managed, a hint of something like amusement in his voice.

Vee huffed a quiet laugh. "Yeah, I used that on you, didn't I?"

"Mm. Three."

"What's four?"

Instead of answering, Kellen wriggled around, clumsy and awkward, until he was on his side facing Vee. He touched the bedspread beneath them.

"Blanket," he whispered.

Vee kissed his nose for that. The awareness was slowly swimming into focus in Kellen's eyes. "My mother made that for me," he said. "Five?"

"You," Kellen said, tracing Vee's jaw with a butterfly-soft finger, his lips curving sweetly.

Vee's breath hitched in his chest. "What's next?"

"Four things… I can feel." He drew his finger down Vee's shoulder. "One."

Vee shivered. "What else?"

"My—I can feel… where you hit me," Kellen murmured.

"Does it hurt?"

Kellen nodded, a dreamy smile on his mouth.

"I'll put something on them later," Vee said. "That's two. What's three?"

Kellen stretched, sighing. "Muscles. They burn. Feels good."

"Okay," Vee said, caught by the sight of the long, pale throat bared to him. "Last one."

Kellen reached up and threaded his fingers through Vee's hair. "So soft," he murmured.

Vee held very still. "What's next?"

"Three things I can hear."

Vee waited, watching the play of shadows on Kellen's face.

"Traffic," he said after a minute.

"That's good," Vee said softly.

A robin whistled from the tree outside the window and a smile flickered across Kellen's face. "Bird."

"Last one?"

Kellen scooted forward until he could press his ear to Vee's chest. His breath was warm, and Vee's heart skipped a beat.

"Is there more to this, um… ritual?"

Kellen nodded and lifted his head. "Don't need it."

Vee touched the bruise on Kellen's cheek. "Where did this come from?" he asked.

Kellen's eyes shuttered and he tensed to pull away.

"Never mind," Vee said immediately. "Hey, guess what?"

Kellen looked wary.

"I talked to Farid. Spectral, even on entry-level positions, kind of requires a knowledge of code. Do you—can you code?"

"No," Kellen said, looking resigned.

"That's okay," Vee said, wanting to wipe the disappointment off his face. "How would you feel about working in the bakery with me?"

Kellen's eyes widened. "I can't cook."

"Neither could I, when Melissa hired me. Senna will teach you."

Kellen chewed on his lip. "I wouldn't be good at it."

Vee couldn't help his smile. "You should have seen me, my first few weeks. I was a *disaster*. Trust me, you can't be worse than that."

Kellen searched his face, and whatever he saw seemed to reassure him. "I can… try."

"I mean, it's not guaranteed—they can't just automatically give it to you—but you could at least apply…." Vee shrugged.

"I don't have anything to wear," Kellen pointed out, shame in his eyes.

"You can borrow my suit," Vee said, and couldn't help kissing his nose again. "It'll be a little loose on you, but it'll work."

Kellen burrowed closer until he could press his face to Vee's chest again. His breath was warm and tickly on Vee's bare skin, and Vee cupped the back of his skull.

"Can you interview tomorrow?" he asked into Kellen's hair.

Kellen nodded.

"Stay with me a little longer," Vee murmured.

But Kellen shook his head, already pulling away. "I have to go."

Vee didn't try to stop him, sighing with disappointment. "I'll see you tomorrow, then."

Kellen nodded again, hair in his eyes, not looking at Vee. "Tomorrow."

<hr>

THE SUBDROP WAS BRUTAL, although hiding it from Jacob was the hardest part. Kellen kept his arms around his ribs, counting the stars as they appeared in the Seattle sky, struggling to breathe deeply and evenly and not let the tears fall.

Tomorrow, tomorrow, tomorrow.

8

MELISSA WAS NICE, if a little terrifying, Kellen decided. Senna was about as fierce as a teddy bear, with her wild hair trapped behind a headband and hair net and flour on her nose. Kellen liked her immediately.

He was there on a trial basis. "Let's give it two weeks," Melissa had suggested. "If you're a good fit, we'll move you to a permanent position."

Vee couldn't stop smiling when he looked at him, which made Kellen heat all the way to his scalp and drop his eyes.

"Kellen, can you get me the bag of flour from the stockroom?" Senna asked.

Kellen made questioning eye contact with Vee, who pointed at the door behind them and to the left of the kitchen proper. He shot him a grateful glance and headed that direction.

The stockroom was large, well-lit, and full of ingredients Kellen didn't even recognize. The fifty pound bags of flour at the far end were easy to spot, though.

The door opened and Vee slipped inside. He stalked toward Kellen with intensity in his eyes, and Kellen gulped.

"What are you—"

Vee caught his mouth in a searing hot kiss, and Kellen forgot what he was going to say as Vee walked him backward until his shoulders hit the wall, lips and tongue hungry and insistent.

Kellen couldn't help the moan as he kissed back with reckless abandon. He was addicted to Vee, he thought wildly, to the way Vee pulled reactions from him, knew what he needed and gave it to him, and kissed like a drowning man in sight of land.

Vee slid a hand down and cupped Kellen's crotch. Kellen couldn't stop himself from bucking into his touch as Vee pulled away, eyes dark and intent.

"I'm going to fuck you until you scream tonight," he whispered, and walked away, leaving Kellen sagging against a sack of flour, aching with restless want.

***

KISSING VEE WAS EASY. Effortless, even. Baking, Kellen discovered, was not. He couldn't get the dough to form, no matter how many times Vee showed him when to add more liquid or flour to help the ingredients come together.

"Bread is pretty forgiving," Vee said as Kellen scowled at the shaggy mass of sticky goop in the bowl. "But even so, you can't just dump it all together and expect it to work. And if you mix it for too long, you'll exhaust the gluten and it'll lose its elasticity."

"I don't know what that *means*," Kellen muttered.

Vee laughed and wiped flour off Kellen's cheek. "Just—watch, okay? This isn't wet enough. Did you add the eggs?"

"Eggs?" Kellen said blankly.

Vee paused. "Okay, so we'll start over." He put a hand on Kellen's shoulder when he saw the look on his face. "Learning curve, Kell, it's okay. You'll figure it out. So first we add the yeast to room-temperature water with a little sugar—"

Kellen did his best to listen, distracted by Vee's proximity, the way his lean figure was showcased by the simple black T-shirt and jeans. Even with the hairnet crushing his perfect hair, Kellen had never seen anyone so beautiful, and he wanted desperately to touch him.

"—the butter," Vee was saying. "Kell?"

"Sorry," Kellen said, shaking himself. "I—um. What?"

There was sympathy and amusement in Vee's eyes. "I've got a muffin batter waiting to mix over there." He pointed. "Can you stir it for me?"

"Yeah, okay," Kellen said.

But he stirred it too much, he discovered when Senna came to check on him and exclaimed about the lack of lumps.

"I thought that was a good thing?" he said.

"Muffin batter has to be lumpy," Senna said, grabbing the bowl and dumping the contents in the trash. "The air bubbles help make them more tender."

Kellen sighed. "I'm sorry." He was no good at this.

"Hey, it's okay," Senna said. She almost touched him and hesitated at the last minute, giving him a smile instead. "My first day was worse."

"Yeah?" Kellen said.

Senna rolled her eyes. "I was a *mess*. At one point I added cumin instead of cinnamon to the apple muffins." Kellen made a face and Senna laughed. "Yeah, exactly. Why don't you run the register for awhile? I can show you how if you want."

"I—" Kellen shook his head. "I'm not—I'm not good with people. I'm not friendly enough."

"Okay, then how about you sweep the floor and wash the bowls Vee and I use?" Senna suggested. "We always need clean stuff."

"I can do that," Kellen agreed.

When the day was over, his arms to his elbows were reddened from the scalding water, and his back ached from leaning over the sink, but Vee kept his promise, taking him home and fucking Kellen on his hands and knees until Kellen was begging to come, and Kellen forgot the frustrations of the day in the bliss that rolled over him.

NEARLY A MONTH WENT by like that. Jacob wasn't happy, but he didn't outright forbid Kellen from working at the bakery, and the day Kellen was able to hand him his first paycheck, Jacob smiled for the first time in far too long.

Still, Kellen couldn't get the hang of baking, no matter how he practiced. He either stirred too much or not enough, resulting in misshapen masses that stuck to teeth and tasted like chalk. Kellen set his jaw and kept trying, until Vee developed a worried frown that lingered whenever Kellen was at the counter, rolling out dough or stirring creations.

<hr>

ONE AFTERNOON AFTER WORK, Vee rolled over in the bed and prodded Kellen gently in the ribs. "So hey."

Kellen twitched, still coming down from the orgasmic high, and made a protesting noise.

"Day off tomorrow," Vee persisted. "I have something I want to do."

Kellen nodded. "Okay. I'll see you at work day after?"

"What? No!" Vee reared back, astonishment on his face. "No, I meant… I have something I want to do *with* you."

Kellen eyed him warily. "Something other than sex?"

Vee's grin flashed. "I mean, I always want to do that. But yeah, something other than. Are you allergic to horses?"

"How would I know?" Kellen asked, bewildered, and Vee laughed, pressing his forehead to Kellen's shoulder.

"I don't suppose I can get you to spend the night?"

Kellen stiffened and pulled away. "You know I can't."

"I know," Vee said, letting him go. His eyes were sad, and Kellen steeled his heart and slid off the bed to find his clothes. "Don't go yet," Vee said.

"I have to," Kellen said, groping for his pants. "Ja—I have things to take care of." He glanced over his shoulder at Vee, lying in the bed watching him. "Are you sure you want me to go with you tomorrow?"

"Yeah, of course," Vee said.

"This still isn't a relationship," Kellen warned.

"I know," Vee said. "I just thought it'd be fun. If you'd rather not…."

Kellen sighed and gave in. "What time, then?"

"Eight," Vee said. He stretched a hand across the bed but Kellen didn't take it. Instead he leaned over and pressed their mouths together, lingering and sweet. He never wanted to stop kissing Vee, he thought, but finally he made himself pull away.

"I'll see you in the morning then."

HE WAS at Vee's house at 7:55 a.m., huddling in the thin hoodie that did nothing to cut the cool wind. He wasn't looking forward to winter, but maybe he'd make enough at the bakery to buy himself a heavier coat, although he could hear Jacob's disapproving voice in his head even as he had the thought.

Vee appeared before Kellen could ring the bell, looking delighted to see him. He caught Kellen around the waist and kissed him hard, tasting like peppermint toothpaste, and then shoved something into his hand.

"Good morning, I saved you some breakfast."

Kellen blinked and looked at the pastry in his hand.

"Apple turnover," Vee said.

"You didn't make it this morning, did you?"

Vee took Kellen's hand and set off, heading down the sidewalk. "Nope. Last night after you left. I even wore that apron you hate."

"It's *dumb*," Kellen protested. "It says 'Kiss the Cook'. You're not a cook, you're a *baker*." He took a bite of turnover as Vee laughed and turned the corner. "Where are we going, anyway?"

"So about six weeks ago, I was out running," Vee said. They came to a gate leading to the trails behind Vee's house, and Vee unlatched and opened it for Kellen. "You know people run and bike and ride on these trails?"

Kellen nodded. "You mentioned horses."

"Yep. I sort of… caught one. She'd dumped her rider and was belting along the trail, and I managed to grab her bridle or rein or whatever it's called as she went by."

"Were you okay? Horses are *big*."

"Yeah, nearly yanked my arm out of socket, but I was fine and so was she. Anyway, her owner invited me out for a riding lesson. It took me awhile to get around to it because certain other things happened at the same time—" Vee slanted a grin at Kellen, who snorted a laugh. "But that's where we're going. I thought you'd enjoy a day out."

"I like staying in," Kellen said, bumping their shoulders together just to see Vee's grin. "But this is okay too, I guess."

"Well, with any luck, you can watch me make a fool of myself, because I know absolutely nothing about horses." Vee's grin turned wicked. "Maybe I'll blow you in the tack room when no one's around."

Kellen tripped over his feet and Vee steadied him, laughing. Kellen managed a return smile, but he couldn't stop thinking about it—Vee on his knees, looking up at him with a gleam in his eyes, maybe his hands on Kellen's hips as he breathed warm air over his groin.

God, Kellen still wanted it. When was the last time he'd gotten a decent blowjob? He couldn't even remember. Most Doms, especially the ones he sought out, weren't the giving sort.

Vee squeezed Kellen's hand. "Earth to gorgeous. What are you thinking about?"

"Nothing," Kellen said hastily. "How far is this place?"

"Just up ahead."

Kellen followed him through the gate onto the property, looking around him with interest. Even in the middle of the forest, there was a surprising amount of open space, the grass green, lush, and almost knee-high in places. Several horses grazed in a nearby pasture, one lifting its head to survey them with interest as he and Vee walked down the wide path toward the red and white barn at the far end of the trail.

"It's pretty," Kellen commented. "Peaceful."

Vee pointed to a horse and rider circling the arena. "That's Star and Kitt."

Kellen froze, pulling Vee to a stop. "Who?"

"Star," Vee said, brow furrowing. "Why?"

Kellen took a step back. He couldn't be there. Star would recognize him immediately and—he didn't even know what she'd do, but he couldn't face it.

"Whoa, hey, *stop*," Vee said, grabbing at Kellen's sleeve. "What's going on?"

Kellen shook his head mutely, panic and shame churning in his stomach.

"Talk to me," Vee said, and there was that note of command in his voice that Kellen was helpless to resist.

He dropped his gaze to where their hands were joined. "Star—I think I met her once."

"Met her… what do you mean?"

Kellen couldn't look up, unable to face the judgment that was surely in Vee's eyes. "I… before you… there was this Dom. He, um—" He swallowed the stone in his throat. "I woke up in the park."

"*What?*" Vee sounded horrified.

"I was okay," Kellen said, managing to get his eyes up to Vee's jawline. "It wasn't that big a deal. But Star… she found me. Called an ambulance."

Vee made a choked noise and the next thing Kellen knew, he was in Vee's arms, folded tight to his chest. "I'm so sorry," Vee whispered, and Kellen pushed back to look at him, startled.

"Why? It was stupid of me. I put myself in that position, you know I did."

"That doesn't mean you deserved it," Vee said fiercely, cupping Kellen's jaw. "Anyway, Star is great. I'll make sure she doesn't say anything about it, okay?"

Kellen closed his eyes briefly, soaking up strength from Vee's touch, and nodded. Nothing for it. He followed on Vee's heels as he headed for the arena.

Star turned the big brown horse toward them when she saw Vee waving. A helmet tamed her hair, but nothing could hide the huge smile that broke out.

"You came!" She swung a leg over the horse's rump and kicked her foot free of the stirrup to slide to the ground, landing with a thump. "Who's this?" She stepped forward, hand out, and then faltered as she recognized Kellen. "Hey—"

"Star, this is my friend Kellen," Vee interrupted. "And this is the first time you two have met."

Star blinked and looked between them several times, but then the smile returned full force and she put her hand out to Kellen again. "It's absolutely lovely to meet you, Kellen. Are you here to take a lesson too?"

Kellen took her hand but shook his head. "I don't know anything about horses. Vee just wanted moral support, I guess."

"Oh, like I *do* know about horses?" Vee said, elbowing him. "I just agreed because I wanted to say I'd done it. Hi Kitt, any runaway escapades lately?" He put his hand out and the horse sniffed it, ears flicking back and forth.

"She's been on her best behavior," Star said,

stroking Kitt's cheek affectionately. "Kellen, would you like to pet her?"

"Oh, um—"

Vee put a hand between Kellen's shoulder blades and pushed him forward. Kellen shot him a dirty look and turned back to find himself face to face with a large and curious horse. She was *huge*, he thought, and reached a hesitant hand up to touch her nose.

Kitt lowered her head to his hands and blew softly across his palms and Kellen didn't move, struck suddenly by her beauty and size. She was entrancing, unpredictable and chaotic and fascinating, and Kellen lifted a hand to cautiously stroke her velvety muzzle.

"Oh… it's so soft," he said, stroking her skin as Kitt blew warm air against his skin. "I didn't know they were so *soft*."

Star smiled at him. "She likes her ears rubbed, where the headstall goes—it gets itchy when she sweats."

Kellen lifted his hand and Kitt immediately dropped her head so he could rub behind her ears, the skin warm and sweaty. When he stepped back, he had tiny brown and black hairs all over his palm, and he looked at them in bemusement.

Star laughed. "You get used to it. Come on, Monica's probably ready for you."

They followed her to the barn, keeping a respectful distance from Kitt's hind end, to discover Monica in the barn aisle, grooming a gray horse that appeared to be sound asleep.

Vee introduced Monica to Kellen. She looked him over with sharp, faded blue eyes, tucking a strand of wispy blonde hair behind her ear, but seemed to be satisfied with what she saw.

"This is Jupiter," she said, indicating the horse. "Jupe's my schoolmaster."

Vee eyed the horse doubtfully. "Is he even conscious?"

"This horse has been around longer than you have, sonny," Monica said. "He'll teach you a thing or two, you wait and see."

"What's a schoolmaster?" Kellen asked, unable to help himself.

"A rare and special kind of horse," Star piped up.

"Is it a breed?" Vee wanted to know.

That made Star and Monica laugh.

"No," Monica said. "It's more of a personality. Old Jupiter here, he'll make you work for every inch of progress you make. If you know how to ask him, he'll give you two tempis down the centerline every time, but if you don't, you'll be lucky to get him to walk in a circle."

"He sounds fun," Vee said, looking alarmed.

Kellen stepped forward and cupped his hands in front of Jupiter's nose. The gray horse opened his eyes and blew softly on his palms, ears pricking in interest, and Kellen rubbed his forehead.

"You're beautiful," he told him, and Jupiter snorted quietly as if he agreed. Kellen couldn't help the smile that spread across his face. When he looked back at the others, they were all watching him. Vee looked thoughtful. "What?" Kellen asked.

"Monica, is there any chance Kellen could take the lesson instead of me?" Vee said.

"Wait, *what?*" Kellen spluttered.

Vee ignored him as Monica nodded, smile lines creasing her sun-weathered face.

"Don't see why not. Kellen, why don't you come over here and I'll show you how to groom ol' Jupe and get him tacked up?"

"But—" Kellen threw a wild look at Vee, who just raised an eyebrow. "I'm not—it's *Vee* who—"

"You don't want to?" Vee said, sounding disappointed suddenly, and Kellen floundered.

"I'm—I do, but—"

"Then shut up and let Monica teach you," Vee said, grinning at him.

"Don't leave?" Kellen said, hating the suddenly unsure note in his voice.

Vee's eyes softened. "Of course not."

THE HOUR PASSED FAR TOO QUICKLY as Kellen absorbed everything Monica taught him. It took about thirty minutes to get the saddle and bridle on Jupiter—"Tacking up," Monica called it. Kellen kept getting distracted by the way Jupiter pushed his nose into his hand, begging for pets.

"And treats," Monica said, a twinkle in her eye. "Don't fall for his game, he's a con artist from way back."

"Can I give him one?" Kellen asked.

"Not until after we take his bridle off," Monica said.

Kellen deflated and Monica patted his arm. "After the lesson. Now come on," she said. "Let's get you on him."

She showed Kellen how to untie him and he led the big gray out to the arena and the mounting block in the center of it. Jupiter stood calmly as Monica positioned the block and gestured Kellen up onto it.

"Handful of mane in your left hand," she said, demonstrating from the ground, and Kellen followed suit. "Cantle of the saddle in your right. This is the cantle. Don't pull on it when you put your foot in the stirrup. Now, foot in—good—bounce on your right foot and spring *lightly* into the saddle, do *not* flop on his back."

Kellen did his best to follow the orders. Jupiter stood still as Kellen got his leg over and settled gracelessly but without thumping into the saddle. Then he shifted his weight and Kellen caught his breath as the world shifted.

"He's just squaring up," Monica said. "Lean down and get your other foot into the stirrup."

Kellen had to fumble for it, swearing under his breath, but he finally got it on.

"Stand up in the stirrups, let's see how long they are."

VEE STAYED CLOSE, watching but saying very little as Kellen listened to Monica's instructions, showing more animation than he ever did except when Vee had him in restraints. Star, who'd taken Kitt's tack off and turned her out, appeared next to him, leaning her elbows against the arena railing.

"So," she said.

"Yep," Vee replied, eyes on Kellen as he settled

into Jupiter's saddle and Monica helped him adjust the stirrups.

"Are you guys dating?"

"Not—sort of," Vee said. Kellen had an actual smile on his face, smoothing a hand across Jupiter's shoulder as Monica spoke.

"You know we've met?" Star said.

"Yeah, he told me." Vee glanced at her. She looked troubled, mouth pursed and brow furrowed. "He's… doing better now."

"He'd been beat to *hell* and back," Star said. "He was covered in blood, I thought he was *dead*. Was it a partner or a mugging or what?"

"Or what," Vee said, wincing. "Look, I can't give you the details. If Kellen wants you to know, he'll tell you himself."

"Fine," Star said. She scowled as she watched. "Shit, he's a natural."

"What do you mean?"

"Look at his hands," Star said.

Vee spent a fair amount of time looking at Kellen's hands in general, but he couldn't see anything unusual about them at the moment. He said as much.

Star rolled her eyes. "They're so *soft*."

"Well… yeah."

"No, I mean he doesn't yank on Jupiter's mouth. Like, at all. Most beginners are all over the place, bouncing in the saddle and basically hanging on the bit like it's their lifeline. Kellen's not doing that."

Vee looked more closely. Kellen's back was straight, his hands steady as Jupiter walked in a wide circle around half the arena.

"He looks… comfortable," he finally said.

"*Yeah*," Star said. She looked faintly envious. "Fuck, I wish I could see what he was like after six months of lessons."

Kellen laughed out loud at something Jupiter did and Vee's heart clutched.

"Oh, you have it bad," Star said, grinning.

"Shut up," Vee muttered, and she snickered.

WHEN THE LESSON WAS OVER, Kellen took Jupiter's saddle and bridle off, talking to him in a low voice and rubbing behind his ears to get at the sweaty spots.

"He goes out with Kitt," Star said. "I'll show you where."

Once they were gone, Monica looked at Vee. "Give me a year and I'll have him winning ribbons up and down the west coast."

Vee blinked. "Seriously?"

"Haven't seen empathy or a seat like that since Star walked into this stable," Monica said, hefting Jupiter's saddle. "Don't suppose you can get him to sign up for regular lessons?"

"He can't afford it, and I doubt he'd let me pay for them," Vee said regretfully.

Monica disappeared into the tack room with the saddle and came out again a minute later, looking thoughtful. "Does he need a job?"

Vee hesitated. "He—I mean, he *has* one, but—"

Kellen appeared around the corner of the barn

and lit up at the sight of Vee. "That was fun," he said, joining them.

Monica glanced between them and raised an eyebrow at Vee, who cleared his throat.

"We should go. Thanks for the lesson, Monica."

"Anytime," she said.

They waved goodbye to both women and headed back the way they'd came. As they walked, Vee captured Kellen's hand, lacing their fingers together.

Kellen looked sideways at him but couldn't seem to help the smile. "Not a relationship," he said.

"Of course not," Vee agreed. "I'm just holding your hand so you don't run away and leave me stranded."

"I don't think I could if I wanted to," Kellen said ruefully. "I'm sore in places I didn't realize had muscles."

"How about we go home and I make you sore in a few other places as well?" Vee suggested.

In answer, Kellen quickened his pace, pulling Vee along as he laughed.

———

But when they got back to the apartment, Vee pushed Kellen up against the wall, an arm across his throat, and kissed the air from his lungs, until there was a faint wheeze in his breath and his eyes were huge and dilated.

Then he dropped to his knees.

Kellen's mouth fell open and he put out an arm as if to stop Vee from getting closer. Vee frowned and he batted the hand away. Kellen pushed at him again, ineffective and weak but not stopping, and Vee tilted his head to look up at him.

"*What?*"

"You shouldn't—" Kellen sounded scared, unsure of himself, and worry replaced the lust in Vee's veins.

He rocked to his feet. "Who's the Dom here?"

Kellen's voice was very small. "You are."

"So I do what *I* want to do, is that right?"

Kellen nodded fractionally, and Vee leaned in and nipped at his chin.

"Well, what I want to do right now is suck your cock, because it's beautiful and I want to put it in my mouth. Is that a problem?"

Kellen hunched forward, forehead resting against Vee's shoulder. "I can't—"

"Can't or don't want to?" Vee took Kellen's arms and eased him away. "You've done this before, right?"

Kellen nodded. "Long time ago. Before—"

"Before the BDSM?"

Kellen nodded again and pressed his forehead back against Vee's shoulder. "I'm supposed to give *you* pleasure," he whispered.

Vee rolled his eyes. "Don't even tell me you subscribe to that bullshit. Just because you sub, *or* bottom, doesn't mean you don't deserve my mouth on your cock."

"But—"

Vee put a hand over Kellen's mouth, silencing him. "Shut up and let me suck your dick."

He dropped to his knees again, letting his hand drag down Kellen's chest until he got to his pants. Kellen's eyes rolled back and his head thumped against the door as Vee fumbled with the belt and finally got it open and the zipper down. He dragged the jeans down to Kellen's thighs and freed his cock from his underwear, wrapping a fist around the base.

Kellen made a strangled noise and Vee looked up to see him staring at him, his hand pressed to his mouth. Vee grinned wickedly at him and swallowed him down, dropping his head until the tip was hitting his soft palate. He opened his throat and sank farther, swallowing around Kellen's shaft convulsively as he adjusted to the intrusion.

Kellen scrabbled for purchase, catching at Vee's shoulders, his hair, fingers harsh and desperate as he writhed, and Vee growled, pulled off, and grabbed Kellen's wrists, slamming them against the wall.

"*Keep* them there," he ordered.

Kellen was panting, eyes huge, but he flattened his palms against the wall. Vee smiled up at him and nuzzled along the crease of his hip, flicking his tongue out to taste the salt. Kellen smelled like sweat and Vee's soap, and Vee couldn't get enough of it. He clasped Kellen's cock in one hand as he explored his body with his mouth, until Kellen was shaking, half-formed pleas falling from his lips.

"I could do this all day," Vee murmured, licking a wet stripe just above the hair at Kellen's groin.

"Oh, please no," Kellen blurted.

Vee couldn't help his laugh. "Well, now you're just giving me ideas." He sucked Kellen's cock back into his mouth, running his tongue along the underside.

"*Vee.*" Kellen sounded wrecked, his voice cracked and hoarse but his palms still flat on the wall even as his hips bucked. "*Please*, Vee—"

"You taste so good," Vee told him, pulling off and pumping him with his fist. "Do you want me to fuck you or do you want to come in my mouth?"

"*Yes*," Kellen said frantically, hips twisting. "Please, I just—I need—"

"Come in my mouth first," Vee said, "and *then* I'll fuck you."

Kellen sobbed and Vee took him deep again, bobbing his head in a steady rhythm as Kellen's back arched and he begged in thick, halting noises that weren't quite words.

Vee snaked his free hand between Kellen's legs, up behind his balls to press against the puckered opening. One quick push and he was knuckle-deep in Kellen's heat and Kellen let go of the wall to curl forward, grabbing desperately at Vee's shoulders.

"I'm going to—*Vee*—"

Vee slapped his hand away and Kellen hunched over and came, thick and salty and bitter in Vee's mouth, his cock throbbing in time with his pulse.

Vee swallowed it all, gentling his touch until Kellen twitched and moaned, knees nearly buckling.

Finally he stood up, wiping his mouth. Kellen

couldn't quite meet his eyes, so Vee tipped his chin up and kissed him, letting Kellen taste himself on his tongue.

When he pulled away, he trailed a thumb down Kellen's jaw. "Facedown on the coffee table," he said.

Kellen nearly tripped over his pants as he struggled to comply, and Vee huffed a laugh as he helped him strip completely and then watched as he settled into place, pale ass gleaming against the dark wood.

He reached into the couch cushions for the lube he'd left there several nights before and squirted a liberal amount on Kellen's hole, using a thumb to rub it in, dipping inside several times until Kellen was squirming again. Only then did he take off his own clothes, kicking his boots into the corner and stepping out of his jeans.

"No prep," Kellen said, cheek to the wood and eyes closed.

"Are you sure?" Vee asked, tracing a light pattern over Kellen's buttock.

Kellen opened his eyes just enough to glare at him over his shoulder. "*No prep*," he repeated.

"Alright," Vee murmured. He took hold of Kellen's hip with one hand and guided himself into position with the other, teasing them both with pressing in and then pulling out before breaching the muscle.

"Come on, come *on*," Kellen chanted, squirming back against him until the table creaked beneath them. "Fuck me, Vee, *please*—"

Vee drove home in one hard thrust, catching himself with his hands as Kellen's spine arched and he flung his head back. He was silken heat, flexing and spasming around Vee's cock until he had to grit his teeth to keep from coming on the spot. Instead he bent over, bracing himself on the table and finding a good angle.

He pulled back and slammed in again, a steady rhythm that had sparks dancing up his spine and igniting behind his eyes. He gritted his teeth to keep the orgasm at bay, driving in harder and faster, chasing his pleasure in Kellen's body as Kellen gripped the table and hung on, encouraging him with half-heard moans of ecstasy.

He was so close, bliss hovering just out of reach—Vee shifted his angle and thrust deep, harder than ever. The sharp *crack* of breaking wood was the only warning he had as the table collapsed and he and Kellen went down in a sprawl of tangled limbs, breath driven from their lungs.

"*What the fuck*," Vee gasped, all thought of coming wiped from his mind as he tried to lever himself up out of the wreckage.

Kellen's shoulders were shaking, and Vee bent, briefly worried, only to realize he was laughing, eyes squeezed shut as he heaved for air.

"It's not *funny*," Vee protested, but he could feel his own lips twitching. "Goddammit, I didn't even come!"

Kellen's laughter only doubled at that, feet drumming the floor and tears on his face as he slapped weakly at Vee's hand. "You—I can't believe —oh my God—"

"Shut up," Vee suggested, fighting amusement, and sat back on his heels. Kellen turned over to look at him, still snorting with laughter, took one look at Vee's cock bobbing forlorn and forgotten between his thighs, and dissolved into helpless giggles again.

"You're the *worst*," Vee told him, and Kellen hiccuped, wiping his face.

"I'm sorry," he managed. "I just—the look on your face—" He caught Vee's hand and pulled himself upright, then pushed Vee backward until he was sitting on the floor, shoulders against the base of the couch. "How's that?"

"Getting better," Vee said as Kellen straddled him. He gripped his thighs as Kellen reached between his legs and sank down onto his cock in one smooth, agonizing slide. "Ah—*fuck*—"

Kellen looped his arms around Vee's neck and smiled down at him. "How about now?"

In answer, Vee caught Kellen's face and dragged him down into a kiss, searching and desperate. Kellen moaned into it, rising and falling rhythmically, their mouths never losing contact. Just like that, Vee could feel it swelling again, and this time he didn't fight it, letting the pleasure roll up from his toes and swallow him whole, coming with a choked moan even as Kellen deepened the kiss.

Even after the aftershocks had subsided, Kellen kept kissing him, hips rolling as he squeezed Vee inside him, until Vee jerked and groaned, over-stimulated.

Only then did Kellen pull away and slide off Vee's lap to sit beside him.

They stared at the ruined coffee table in silence for a few minutes in a post-orgasmic haze, and finally Vee poked Kellen in the ribs.

"You owe me a coffee table," he said, and took it as a personal triumph when Kellen laughed.

"How've you been handling his subdrops?" Farid asked the next day when Vee delivered the now-customary basket of pastries.

"His what?"

Farid looked up, coffee halfway to his mouth. "Subdrops. You *have* been helping him through them, right?"

Vee squirmed in his seat. "I don't... what are they?"

"Oh *Jesus*," Farid said, setting his coffee down. "You mean to tell me you've just... let him go through them alone?"

"*Through what?*" Vee demanded, fury chasing worry through his chest. He'd fucked up, that much was obvious, but *how?*

"Subspace comes at a price, Vee," Farid said. "Newton's third law."

"Equal and opposite reaction?" Vee said, and then straightened, horrified, as the meaning sank in. "Oh, *fuck.*"

Farid sipped his coffee. "Yeah."

"He's been—fuck, he's been dropping like that every time?"

"Maybe not every time," Farid said. "It usually hits after a really intense scene. What happens, once you're done?"

Vee shrugged helplessly. "He... it takes him awhile to come down sometimes. I help him ground himself, and once he can talk without slurring and prove he's not going to fall over when he stands up, he usually says he has to go. I've *asked* him to stay, but he won't—he never stays after a scene." He folded forward, a hand over his mouth. "How bad do they get?"

"Different for everyone," Farid said. There was sympathy in his eyes. "But usually the higher they go...."

"The harder they fall," Vee finished. "Fuck. I have to—"

"Yeah, go," Farid said, waving him off, and Vee scrambled for the door.

———

DOWNSTAIRS IN THE BAKERY, he went straight through into the kitchen to where Kellen was trying to knead some bread dough and not having much success.

"I need to talk to you," Vee said.

Kellen blinked and straightened. "What's wrong?"

"*Now.*"

Kellen's expression shuttered, shoulders rounding, and he scraped dough off his fingers as he followed Vee into the store room.

Vee closed the door and turned to face him. "Have you been dropping?"

"Dropping what?" Kellen asked, clearly bewildered.

"*Sub*dropping," Vee said impatiently. "After we scene and you leave, have you...." He wrapped his arms around his ribs. "God, Kell, have you been dealing with the fallout on your own?"

"Of course I have," Kellen said, and he sounded so confused that Vee wanted to weep. "That isn't—you didn't sign up for that. It's not a big deal, Vee, why—"

Vee grabbed him by the shoulders and pushed him backward to pin him against the wall. "I signed up for *all of it*," he hissed, face close to Kellen's. "You *hid* this from me because—why, you thought I wouldn't want to deal with it?"

Kellen shoved him away and Vee stumbled, caught off-guard. There was anger in Kellen's eyes and clenched fists. Vee opened his mouth but Kellen got there first.

"This is *not a relationship*," he snarled.

Vee absorbed the words and the unexpected pain of them, but Kellen wasn't done.

"I don't have to tell you *anything* I don't want," he continued. "You're not my fucking *boyfriend*, why do you keep acting like you *are*?"

Vee shook his head. "It's not—it's not about that. It's about… you needing help and… you didn't *tell* me, Kell, you didn't let me help, you didn't *trust* me!"

"Because we're not dating!" Kellen shouted, and Vee took a step back, stunned. He'd never heard Kellen raise his voice before. Kellen met his eyes, fury in his own. "You keep trying to make me your—your boyfriend, your… *partner*. I'm *not*. I'm your sub. You fuck me. Beat me. *Hurt* me and I beg for more. But that doesn't make me part of your life, Vee. I'm not your friend, I'm not your *lover*. So stop trying to take care of me and give me what I'm here for, or I swear to God I'll find it somewhere else."

He fell silent, chest heaving, and Vee stared at him. The only noise in the room was their breathing, Kellen's harsh and rattling in his lungs.

"Kell," Vee whispered.

"No." Kellen shook his head hard. "No, fuck this. I'm out. I'm done." He yanked the apron off and wadded it into a ball. Throwing it on the floor, he met Vee's eyes, defiant and angry. "Tear up the contract."

"*No*," Vee said, heart squeezing in his chest until he couldn't breathe. "No, Kellen, please, just—why won't you just let me take care of you?"

Kellen's chin went up. "I can take care of myself," he said, his voice icy cold, and stepped around Vee to open the door.

He went to Melissa's office and dropped his name tag on the desk, looking her in the eyes.

"It's not working out and we both know it."

Melissa picked up his name tag, looking sad. "I'd be willing to let you stay longer—"

"No," Kellen said. He took a deep breath and gentled his voice. "Sorry. But no. Thanks for… giving me a chance."

He walked out without looking back and went to Jacob, finding him under his favorite overpass. Jacob frowned at the sight of him.

"What are you doing here so early? Thought you had a *job*."

"I did," Kellen said. "I quit."

Jacob's face darkened. "You *quit*?"

"It wasn't right for me," Kellen said, bracing himself.

It didn't do any good—Jacob's punch still knocked him off his feet.

"You gave up a *steady paycheck* because it wasn't 'right for you'?" he demanded, towering over him. "You think you can just pick and choose, you spoiled brat? After I let you take this job in the first place, against my better judgment, now you think you can just throw it away?"

Kellen cupped his aching jaw, unable to come up with a defense.

"You'll find another job," Jacob said, voice as hard as his fists.

Kellen nodded silently.

BUT HE DIDN'T HAVE a resume, or a phone, and he couldn't borrow Vee's suit for interviews. Everywhere he went, he met with the same regretful shrug and spread hands. *Nothing we can do if we don't even have a way to get in touch with you.*

He dragged himself back to where Jacob had pitched camp one night, exhausted and defeated, to discover Jacob talking to a man in his forties, hair touched with gray at his temples and narrow, pinched eyes. They both turned to look at Kellen.

"This is him," Jacob said. "Kellen, this is Steven. Go with him and do what he says."

"Why?" Kellen said warily.

"You going to argue with me now, boy?" Jacob growled.

Steven stepped forward, a smile on his face that didn't quite reach his eyes. "Hungry?"

"Not really," Kellen said.

Jacob backhanded him. Kellen staggered backward, heat and pain blooming in his cheek, and Steven made a gesture for him to follow.

Kellen did, too rattled to argue. Steven led him down the sidewalk and through city streets without saying a word. Just as Kellen was regaining his equilibrium and opening his mouth to ask what they were doing, Steven ushered him into a small motel.

Alarm flashed through Kellen but he allowed Steven to take his arm and pull him into the elevator. He didn't touch him once in there and Kellen huddled in the corner, praying his worst fears wouldn't come to pass as Steven watched him with hungry eyes. It hadn't happened in so long; surely Jacob hadn't sold him again.

But he had. Inside the room, Steven caught his arm again and pushed him onto the bed. Kellen bounced and rolled off the side, landing on his feet in a defensive crouch.

"No," he said.

Steven's lip curled in a sneer. "Jacob said you liked it rough. I can do rough."

"*Satin*," Kellen said, looking around him for a weapon as Steven advanced.

Steven hesitated, frowning. "What?"

"I didn't agree to this. Don't touch me," Kellen managed through a throat tight with fear.

Steven's laugh was harsh and his hands were like brands, burning Kellen's arms when he grabbed him.

9

———

He woke up on the floor, voices raised over his head. Someone was banging on the door. Steven let go, swearing, and Kellen slipped under again.

When he woke up again, the room was quiet. He lay very still for a few minutes, assessing the damage. His ribs ached and it hurt to swallow—he had a vague memory of Steven cutting off his air until he'd passed out, bringing him around, and then doing it again. Several times, going by how tender his throat was.

His ankle throbbed mercilessly, a sharp, piercing ache that refused to fade. Kellen tried and failed to wiggle his toes, gasping at the pain.

Someone said something, but Kellen didn't try to lift his head. He didn't think he'd be able to focus anyway, with one eye swollen shut and the other a slit.

"911?" a man said. It wasn't Steven. "I need an ambulance."

THE HOSPITAL ROUTINE was much the same as last time he'd been there. Kellen thought it might even be the same nurse who gently cut his clothes off and dressed his wounds, tsking softly under her breath as she applied butterfly bandages to the smaller cuts.

"Some of these will need actual stitching," she told him.

Kellen nodded silently.

"Is there someone we can call?" she asked. Her eyes were brown, big and friendly and full of sympathy, and Kellen swallowed past the bruises.

"Yes," he rasped.

TWENTY MINUTES LATER, Vee burst into his room, blowing past the nurses and arrowing straight for where Kellen lay in the bed.

"*Kell,*" he said, hands out and hovering as though he was afraid to touch. "Baby, what happened? Who did this to you?"

Kellen blinked back tears. "Vee—"

"I'm here," Vee said. He took the hand Kellen held out as tears spilled down his own face. "I'm here, sweetheart, what can I do?"

"Stay with me," Kellen slurred, throat so tight he could barely speak. "Vee, I—"

"Don't," Vee interrupted. He sat down beside the bed, still holding Kellen's hand. "It was the dumbest fucking argument. I'm sorry, I'm so sorry, I was just so *worried* about you."

"I know," Kellen whispered. He could barely see Vee's face through the eye not swollen shut, so he rubbed Vee's knuckles, grounding himself. Vee was there. He was with him, he wasn't angry. "I safeworded," he managed.

Vee's grip tightened. "You what?"

"I tried to stop him," Kellen said. "I didn't want—in the first place, I *didn't*, I told him no, but—" More tears slid down his face, hot and stinging. "When he wouldn't stop, I said satin, I tried—"

"Oh, *Kell*," Vee said, and bent over, pressing his forehead to the back of Kellen's hand. "I'm so sorry. I'm so *proud* of you and I'm *so fucking sorry*."

"Not your fault," Kellen whispered.

"No, I—" Vee's eyes were sheened with tears. "I never should have—"

Kellen squeezed his hand. "I should have told you about the drops. I'm sorry… sorry I didn't trust you."

"We were both stupid," Vee murmured, and brought Kellen's hand to his mouth to kiss it.

THE DOOR OPENED and a tall woman in a white coat walked in as Vee struggled to keep the tears from falling. She picked up the clipboard at the end of Kellen's bed and examined his chart. Her hair was honey-blonde with pale streaks through it, a pair of severe glasses perched on the end of a button nose and her lips pursed.

"Mr.…" She looked closer. "Smith?" She sounded doubtful.

Kellen's grip on Vee's hand tightened but he just nodded.

"I'm Dr. Bellamy, the attending physician. You've been through the wringer a bit, haven't you?" She flipped a page on the chart. "Who's this with you?"

"I'm his boyfriend," Vee said immediately, dividing a look between Kellen and the doctor that dared them to argue.

Kellen hesitated and finally nodded. "You can talk in front of him."

Dr. Bellamy shrugged. "The worst damage is your ankle. It's broken pretty badly. You may need some pins in it. Other than that, you have cracked ribs—three of them—a sprained wrist, and multiple lacerations and hematomas. Bruises," she clarified. "Also you have a bruised kidney, so you may see blood in your urine for a little while."

Nausea swam inside Vee's stomach and he clutched Kellen's hand.

"Where were you when your boyfriend was getting beaten to a pulp?" Dr. Bellamy asked Vee, and her voice was suddenly cold.

Vee jerked his head up but Kellen answered.

"This is *not his fault*. He had no idea. Don't you dare blame him."

Dr. Bellamy narrowed her eyes but her tone softened. "The police want to talk to you."

Kellen tensed. "No, I can't—"

"I'll be with you," Vee said, rubbing circles on the back of his hand. "I'll be right here. Do you think you can tell them what happened if I'm here?"

Kellen's breathing was short and choppy and it

took him a few minutes to answer, but finally he nodded again.

<hr />

THE POLICE OFFICER was stocky and unimposing, her round face flushed and wisps of nondescript brown hair escaping the bun she'd scraped most of it into.

"Kathleen Orbison," she said. "No relation. Kellen, is it? And who are you?" That last was directed at Vee.

"Boyfriend," Vee said flatly. "*Not leaving* boyfriend, so whatever you need to ask him, you'll have to do it in front of me."

Kathleen inspected him, pale gray eyes sharp and assessing. "Were you there when it happened?"

Vee shook his head.

"Were you involved in any way? Witness any part of it?"

Vee shook his head again, shame and guilt an endless ouroboros in his stomach. He *should* have been there. Should have protected Kellen. Kept this from happening.

But Kathleen just pulled out a notebook. "Then you can stay, but don't talk. Alright, Kellen, start from the top. What happened?"

Vee listened as Kellen told the sordid story, feeling ever more sick to his stomach.

"Who's this Jacob?" Kathleen interrupted, early on.

Kellen shot a glance at Vee. "My… friend. He —he protects me. Takes care of me."

"Is it a sexual relationship?" Kathleen asked briskly, and Vee's chest eased when Kellen shook his head vehemently.

"No. *No.* He—it's not like that. He just… looks out for me."

Kathleen made a motion for him to keep going, still writing busily. "And Steven? Last name? Do you know him?"

Kellen's hand tightened convulsively on Vee's. "I—no. I'd never met him. Don't know his last name. He just—was there, and Jacob said I was t-to go w-with him."

Vee fought the impulse to crawl into the bed with him as rage welled. He would *happily* smash Jacob's *and* Steven's face in, he thought.

"Did he rape you?" Kathleen asked, and despite the matter-of-fact words, her tone was gentle and eyes sympathetic.

Kellen tucked his chin to his chest. "I don't th-think so," he whispered. "He just hit me. A l-lot. I fought him. He was angry. I d-don't remember… everything." Vee wanted to weep for the resignation in Kellen's voice, but he kept his chin up, hand steady on Kellen's. He could fall apart later, once he knew Kellen would be alright.

"The hospital agrees, from the evidence. They did a rape kit," Kathleen said. "He did a number on you, but the man who heard you and kicked open the door stopped him before he went any further."

Kellen said nothing.

"Are you going to catch him?" Vee demanded.

Kathleen switched her steady focus to him. "We'll do everything in our power. We got a description from the witness, and we'll need you to sit down with a sketch artist at some point."

"Is there anything else?" Vee asked.

Kathleen shook her head and closed her notebook. "I think I've got all I need for now. I may have some follow-up questions, Mr. Smith." She rose, tucking the notebook into her boxy jacket and giving them both a nod of farewell.

Alone, Vee stood. "Scoot over," he ordered.

Kellen inched his painful way a foot across the mattress, his teeth clenched, and as soon as there was room, Vee kicked his shoes off and slid onto the bed beside him. He gathered Kellen into his arms, careful not to disturb the lines trailing to the IVs. Kellen made a pained noise and Vee stroked his hair.

"I'm sorry," he whispered. "Can you rest now?"

Kellen nodded against Vee's chest. "Vee, I—" He hesitated.

"What is it?" Vee murmured.

"Nothing," Kellen said.

"Do you want to tell me about Jacob?" Vee asked.

"Yes," Kellen said, pressing his face into Vee's shirt. "But not now?"

"Alright, sweetheart," Vee said. "It can wait."

THE HOSPITAL RELEASED Kellen three days later, with a plaster cast on his ankle and crutches for daily use until it had healed. He sat in the wheelchair as Vee pushed him down the hallway, feeling like an idiot.

Out front was a gleaming black car, long and low and expensive, and a man got out and smiled at them, holding the door. He looked Pakistani or Indian, with dark eyes, a bold nose, and a haircut that had probably cost more than Kellen's clothing budget for the year.

"Kell, this is Farid," Vee said. There was affection and something like relief in his voice at the sight of Farid, and Kellen twisted to look up at him before turning back to Farid, who had one hand extended.

"I've heard a lot about you," he said, voice husky and soft. "It's great to finally meet you."

"You sent Vee the sex toys!" Kellen said suddenly.

Farid laughed out loud, his eyes sparkling. "I did indeed. Let's get you into the car. It's chilly out here."

Kellen managed to lever himself upright with Vee's help. Hopping hurt his ankle, but thankfully the car was close. He sank down onto the leather seats with a sigh of relief, Vee taking his crutches from him to store in the trunk.

Farid got in on the other side of the car, eyes searching Kellen's face.

Kellen looked away, wishing for Vee, but he was talking to one of the hospital employees outside the car, wind ruffling his hair.

"I think I saw you at the club once or twice," Farid said, startling Kellen into lifting his eyes.

"You—you're...."

"A Dom?" Farid nodded. "I've been training Vee, helping him when he makes mistakes."

Protective fury surged through Kellen. "Vee doesn't make mistakes. Vee is *perfect*."

Farid's eyebrows went up and his eyes narrowed. "Like that, is it?"

Kellen hunched his shoulders and turned his face away. "It's not like anything."

"Does he know you love him?"

Kellen whipped back around, mouth opening, but the door opened and Vee slid into the car, hair wind-tossed and cheeks rosy.

"Ready to go?"

Kellen snapped his mouth shut. Farid's eyes were far too knowing, but he gave Kellen the courtesy of looking away.

Vee took Kellen's hand. "You okay?"

Kellen forced a smile. "Yes."

Does he know you love him?

Vee smiled back as the car rolled out of the parking lot.

"So," Farid said, and Kellen shot him a dirty look. "Vee, Kellen is going to stay with you while he recuperates?"

"That's the plan," Vee said. He took Kellen's hand, fingers warm and comforting. "I took some time off work for the first couple of weeks, so he's got help getting around."

"I'm capable of functioning on my own," Kellen said, but he didn't pull away from Vee's touch.

FARID DIDN'T COME up when they got to the apartment. "Let me or Dom know if you need anything at all," he told Vee. "Kellen, I wish we'd met under better circumstances but I'm glad to know you."

Getting up the stairs was a chore, but inside the apartment, Kellen took a deep breath of the familiar air and his nerves eased. Vee tossed his keys in the bowl and fussed around the couch, getting it ready for Kellen to sit.

"Do you want more pillows? Fewer pillows? How do you feel about the pillow situation in general?"

Kellen huffed a laugh and held out his hand. "Vee, stop."

Vee took Kellen's hand and stepped in close, running his palms up and down Kellen's arms. "You should sit down, get off that ankle."

"In a minute," Kellen said. He rested his forehead against Vee's shoulder and closed his eyes. He'd fucked up so much, but here and now, at least he had this.

Finally, he allowed Vee to maneuver him gently to the couch and ease him down onto it.

"Are you thirsty? Hungry? Want to watch a movie? I can get my laptop and we can just chill—"

"That sounds nice," Kellen said, "but first, I —" He swallowed hard. "We need to talk."

Vee's eyebrows lifted. "Oh—Jacob?"

Kellen nodded, feeling faintly sick.

Vee sat beside him, crossing his legs on the seat, and then tried to get up. "Wait. Are you thirsty? Do you want a drink? I can make you cocoa or tea or—"

"*Vee*," Kellen said despairingly. His courage was going to vanish if he had to delay any longer.

"You're right, I'm sorry," Vee said, settling back. "Talk to me, baby."

Kellen took a deep breath, itching to touch him but not sure—Vee's hand closed over his, thumb rubbing reassuring circles on Kellen's knuckles.

"Nothing you say will make me feel any differently," he said quietly.

Kellen suddenly couldn't speak past the stone in his throat. He didn't deserve this man. It took a few tries to get his voice working.

"I left home when I was 16," he said finally. "My parents… my father is a pastor. My mother leads the youth services. They weren't—they didn't—"

Vee said nothing, but his grip was strong and his eyes steady on Kellen's.

"I knew they wouldn't accept… so I left."

"Are they in Seattle?" Vee asked quietly.

Kellen nodded. "Have you heard of the Church on the Hill?"

Vee's eyes widened. "That—*those* are your parents?"

Kellen shrugged. "You see why I left."

"Yeah, of course. God, Kell, that had to be so hard on you. Were you an only child?"

"Thankfully. Anyway, I left a note and I walked away. Jacob found me that first week. I was… I'd been caught stealing an apple from another homeless guy; I didn't *want* to but I was just so hungry…." He shivered, remembering the man's anger. "Jacob faced him down. Got up in his personal space and basically dared the guy to take him on instead. He backed off pretty fast, and Jacob paid him for the apple I stole."

Vee watched him intently.

"He told me I was too young to be out on my own. That I needed a protector."

"Did he ever… touch you?" Vee asked, his voice very careful. "I know you told the cop no, but…."

Kellen shook his head. "I swear, Vee, he didn't. It wasn't… he didn't do that. Ever."

"But he gave you to people who did." It wasn't a question, but Kellen nodded anyway.

"Only when things were really bad though. I—I wanted to help. I went willingly. It wasn't rape."

"Did they do things to you that you didn't want?" Vee asked.

Kellen hesitated and then nodded. "Sometimes."

"Then it was rape," Vee said. His voice was choked and he pulled away briefly to swipe at his eyes. "God, Kell. How long… how old are you?"

"I'm twenty-two. Almost twenty-three, I guess."

"Almost seven years," Vee managed, more tears spilling down his cheeks.

"It wasn't always bad," Kellen said, searching desperately for a way to reassure him. "It—there was one guy… he was how I figured out I like…. Anyway, after him, I started trying to find… more. Jacob hated it. Told me to stop, hit me when I couldn't."

Vee took an uneven breath.

"I *couldn't* stop," Kellen said miserably. "I tried. I really did, I sometimes made it months, even. But I needed—"

"You're addicted, sweetheart," Vee said. "It's not your fault."

"I shouldn't have—" Kellen dragged in air. "I should have tried harder. Not let it rule me."

"That's not how addiction works," Vee said. "That one guy—was he the one who taught you how to ground yourself?"

Kellen nodded. "He was… he took care of me. But then he had to relocate for his job—somewhere on the east coast, I think."

"I'm glad he was good to you, but he still…." Vee's mouth twisted.

"He didn't know," Kellen said, suddenly desperate for him to understand. "He thought I was a hooker, yeah, but he didn't know about—Jacob, or… any of the rest of it."

"Okay," Vee said, blinking rapidly. "Okay." He brought Kellen's hand to his mouth, his lips warm and gentle. Kellen fought back sudden tears.

"You're so good to me," he whispered.

"Because you deserve it," Vee said, leaning in and brushing a kiss across Kellen's mouth. "I want to give you all good things."

"You *do*," Kellen said. He grabbed Vee's shirt when he would have pulled away and dragged him in for another kiss. Vee breathed warmth and amusement into Kellen's mouth and kissed him back. "Vee, I—"

He wouldn't say it. *Couldn't.* Vee deserved better, someone who wasn't fucked up in every possible way. Someone who wasn't addicted to pain, who could give him a happy life and not drag him into his messy issues.

"Make love to me," he said instead.

Vee pulled away enough to meet his eyes, surprise and concern painting his face. "Are you sure you're—"

Kellen caught and hauled him in again, crushing their mouths together. This time it was hungry and desperate, lips and teeth and tongue clashing and colliding, and Vee gasped into it.

"*Please*," Kellen said.

"Okay," Vee breathed against his mouth. He withdrew briefly. "I—we need condoms."

"I know," Kellen said, nodding. "It's okay, I understand, I just… need you."

Vee drew a thumb down his jaw. "How do you want me, baby?"

Kellen considered his options. "I guess we can't really get too athletic. Um."

"Here, scoot down," Vee said, catching Kellen's hips and pulling until his ass was balanced on the edge of the couch.

Already half-hard, Kellen's breath hitched as Vee pulled down the scrubs he'd been given, leaving him bare from the waist down. Vee sighed, sounding somehow both wondering and satisfied.

"God, you're beautiful," he murmured. "Is your ankle okay?"

Kellen hadn't even thought of his ankle in awhile. He nodded, aching to reach for himself but not sure it was allowed.

Vee petted Kellen's inner thigh, drawing tiny circles through the soft hair there, and then inched lower.

Kellen spread his legs, wordlessly encouraging him.

"I need to apologize to you," Vee said, and Kellen's eyes snapped up, startled.

"What?"

Vee hunched his shoulders. "You were right." His eyes were on the floor, but there was shame on his face. "When we—I didn't do it on purpose, but I was treating you like my boyfriend. I—" He looked up. "I think about you all the time."

Kellen froze as Vee met his eyes, raw honesty on his face.

"When I'm not with you, I think, 'I wonder what Kellen's doing'," Vee continued. "Or I'll eat something delicious and wish you were there to share it with me. The other day I walked by the theater and that new movie with Ryan Reynolds was playing, and I wanted to take you to see it."

"Ryan Reynolds is really hot," Kellen agreed, making a desperate stab at levity.

Vee bent and kissed him. "I love you, Kell."

Kellen squeezed his eyes shut. "No," he whispered. "No, Vee, don't—"

"I'm sorry," Vee said. He cradled Kellen's jaw in one hand as he kissed down his throat. "I didn't mean to fall in love with you, or push you into anything. I didn't mean to make this anything you didn't want. It just sort of happened."

"It's too soon," Kellen said helplessly. "It's only been two months, how can you—"

Vee drew back and traced around Kellen's hard shaft, flicking the head briefly and grinning as Kellen jerked. "Domination and submission, with or without pain, is so much more intense than a regular relationship. Farid explained it to me. Because we bare ourselves to each other in such intimate ways so quickly, it's not uncommon to develop feelings just as quickly."

"H-how do you know," Kellen managed, Vee's hand distracting as he slid it lower, behind Kellen's balls. "How do you know it's *r-real*, Vee, it could just be—"

Vee cut him off with a quick, hard kiss. "It's real, baby," he whispered. "And it's okay if you don't feel the same way. But I do want more than sex. I want *you*. All of you. I want you when you wake up in the morning and when you're grumpy because you forgot to eat and when you're laughing at me because I did something dumb."

Tears stung Kellen's eyes. "I w-want that too," he managed, and joy lit Vee's eyes.

"Then shut up and let me fuck you."

Kellen whimpered. Vee kept a grounding hand on Kellen's thigh as he retrieved the lube from under the couch cushions and then leaned over to pull a condom out of the drawer.

The lube was cold but warmed quickly and Vee took his time rubbing it in and around Kellen's hole, whispering encouragement to him.

"You're gonna feel so good on my dick," he murmured.

Kellen squirmed. "No prep."

Vee hesitated. "Are you *sure?*"

Kellen glared at him. "I know what I want, and what I want is for you to fuck me hard, goddammit. Make me *feel it*."

"*God*." Vee rolled the condom on and adjusted until he was in position, on his knees between

Kellen's spread thighs. "You sure your ankle's okay?"

Truthfully, it was aching, a slow, steady beat in time with his heart, but Kellen barely felt it, numbed as it was by the pain meds and the arousal careening through his veins.

"Stop fussing and *fuck me*," he said.

Vee's eyebrows went up. "Who's the Dom here?"

Kellen hissed in frustration, grabbing for any part of him he could find, but Vee leaned back so he was just out of range, lips twitching. Finally Kellen gave up.

"You are," he said. "I'm sorry, Vee, I shouldn't have—"

Vee grabbed Kellen's thigh, lined himself up, and forced his way inside so quickly it felt like one continuous motion.

Kellen arched up off the cushions as his body protested the intrusion, Vee stretching him wide and giving him no time to adjust as he slid deeper. Kellen panted, breath sharp and short in his chest as Vee bottomed out, his eyes distant and ribs heaving.

Silence fell, broken by their harsh breaths, until Vee focused on Kellen's face and his lips curved.

"Hey," he whispered.

Kellen dragged in air through his nose, clutching the cushions. He could feel his body slowly relaxing around Vee's cock, pain morphing into pleasure, and he groaned as Vee gently picked his legs up and slung them over his arms.

"Is that okay?" he asked.

Kellen managed a nod. The cast kept his ankle immobile, something he was grateful for as Vee pulled out and then pushed back in, sensation sharp and lethal as a blade. Vee's thrusts were steady and his rhythm didn't falter, withdrawing until only the tip was inside, and then slamming home over and over. The angle was perfect, Vee's size and shape filling Kellen until his senses were overwhelmed and all he could feel was Vee, in him, around him, brushing his prostate with every tantalizing pass until Kellen thought he might cry from sheer sensation.

He hadn't even been *touched* but he could feel his orgasm building slowly, gathering in his groin, and he caught at Vee's arms, struggling to pull him closer.

"More," he gasped.

Vee's grin was wolfish. "Happily." He sped up, still driving deep each time, until sweat broke out on his collarbones and forehead, his eyes unfocused as he chased his pleasure inside Kellen's body. "You feel—so good," he managed, bending to press their foreheads together.

"'M close," Kellen panted. "Vee, I'm—"

"Gonna come for me, baby?" Vee asked between thrusts. "Let me see it. I want—I want to see your face when—"

"*Touch me*," Kellen begged.

Vee caught his breath and fisted Kellen's cock. Kellen's orgasm burst free on the third pump, a cry ripping from his chest as every muscle in his body locked up and bliss seized him.

"*Christ*," Vee said, slammed deep, and froze, head dropping until their foreheads were pressed together again as he came, breath almost like a sob in his lungs.

Kellen's arms felt heavy as lead, but he managed to get one up to stroke Vee's hair. *I love you so much.* "I'm so glad you found me," he whispered.

"Stay with me," Vee said.

Kellen stopped breathing, and Vee lifted his head.

"Please," he said. "Don't go back to the streets, don't go back to Jacob. Stay with me."

"Vee, you don't—" *You don't mean that. You'll regret offering. You'll change your mind.* "I can't just freeload off you."

"Of course not," Vee said. He pushed himself upright, sliding down until he was on his knees between Kellen's spread thighs. "That's why when you're healed, you can get a job. You can even get your own place if you don't want to live with me."

Kellen couldn't breathe. He struggled to push himself more vertical, grimacing at the pain in his ribs, and Vee helped him sit up.

"You—" Kellen dragged in air. "You don't know what you're asking for."

"Yes I do," Vee said steadily.

Kellen pulled his hands free and covered his face. "*Vee*—"

"How about this?" Vee said, resting his palms on Kellen's bare thighs. "Stay awhile. As long as *you* want. And when you want to go, you can go. I won't stop you. You don't belong to me, baby. But if you'll consider staying… even just for a month or two…." He trailed off and Kellen lowered his hands.

"This is a mistake," he whispered.

Vee's face lit up. "Does that mean you'll stay?"

Kellen nodded, biting his lip. "For now."

Vee leaned up and kissed him, keeping his weight off Kellen's abused ribs. "Thank you," he murmured against Kellen's mouth, and Kellen closed his eyes and wound his arms around Vee's neck, holding on tightly.

10

VEE STAYED with him for the first two weeks, but then he had to go back to work. He made up for his absence by bringing delicious pastries home every afternoon—Kellen had already gained at least five pounds and his chest wasn't as concave anymore.

But that still left most of the day with Kellen alone and bored. Vee loaned him his Kindle and Kellen read every book on it, some of them more than once. Vee liked gothic mysteries and spy thrillers, and Kellen curled up on the couch every day and immersed himself in improbable heroics.

A month into his stay, though, Kellen put the Kindle away and glared at the wallpaper. He was going mad with boredom and he was *sick* of looking at the walls of Vee's apartment. If he had to do it for one more day, he thought he might scream.

He wanted to taste fresh air, feel sunlight on his skin.

"Fuck it," he said, the sound of his voice startling him in the empty room. He stepped into his boots, glad the cast had been removed and he was reduced to a crepe bandage around his ankle, and stood carefully, testing his weight. It was tender, but he could walk. He'd take a crutch in case he got tired, he decided. He grabbed one from its resting place, pulled on his favorite of Vee's hoodies, and swung the door open to the sight of a pretty Indian girl on the other side, her hand raised to knock.

"You're not Vee," she said.

"Um."

"Who *are* you?" the girl said, her eyes narrowing with suspicion. "And why are you wearing Vee's clothes?" Her mouth fell open. "Are you *robbing* him? Oh my god, you—"

"*No!*" Kellen said desperately. "I'm not, I *swear* I'm not, don't call the cops, *please*." Inspiration struck. "Call Vee. He'll tell you I'm—a friend."

The girl regarded him suspiciously, phone half out of her pocket, but finally pulled it the rest of the way out and dialed a number. "Vee, it's me," she said, and rolled her eyes. "Who else would it be from this number? Listen, do you know a skinny blond kid, looks about seventeen, needs a haircut and twenty pounds?"

Kellen straightened, offended. "He *likes* my hair." The girl snapped her eyes up and understanding dawned across her face.

"Why didn't you tell me you had a boyfriend, bhai?" she demanded into the phone. Kellen could hear Vee's voice, sounding frantic, but the girl grinned and hung up on him. "You and me, we need to have a *chat*. I'm Lily, by the way. Vee's cousin."

Kellen hesitantly accepted the hand she thrust at him. "Kellen. I, um—"

"Vee hasn't told me anything," Lily said. "Which means *you* are lucky contestant number seven. Tell me everything."

Kellen looked around him. Even with Lily standing there, promising a diversion from boredom at the very least, he couldn't bear the thought of going back in the apartment.

"I need… fresh air," he said. "Can we maybe walk a bit?"

Lily shrugged elegantly and tossed her heavy black braid over one slim shoulder. She was wearing motorcycle leathers and a T-shirt that said *BAD BITCH* on it in faded, spray-painted letters. Looking closer, Kellen could see the resemblance —her eyes were the same shape as Vee's, nose a near carbon copy of his, and her mouth was wide and smiled easily, just like Vee's.

She followed Kellen down the stairs, which he took slowly and carefully.

"Something happen?" she asked as they reached the bottom.

"Broke my ankle a month ago," Kellen said tersely. Cousin or not, he wasn't telling her his life story.

"Sure you should be walking on it already?" Lily said.

"It's that or go insane in that tiny fucking place," Kellen snapped.

Lily held up her hands. "No skin off my nose. Where are we going?"

Kellen headed for the trails behind the house. He wasn't sure he could walk all the way to Monica's, but he wanted to see the horses. He stepped in under the trees, leaves dappling shade across the path, and felt peace stealing through his soul on kitten-soft paws.

"*Nature?*" Lily asked, in the same tone one might use for the words 'bubonic plague'.

Kellen glared at her. "It's nice here. Quiet, *usually.*"

Lily shuddered but didn't challenge that. "So, how'd you meet my cousin?"

"At a… club," Kellen said. He set out walking at a slow pace, relieved to find his ankle wasn't hurting. "He, um… hit on me."

"Vee went to a club and didn't invite me?" Lily clicked her tongue. "So what do you do, Kellen? And why are you living with Vee? *Are* you living with Vee? Did he tell you why his last relationship didn't work out?"

Kellen stared at her and she grinned, unrepentant.

"I'm… between jobs right now," he finally said. "I was working at the bakery but turns out I'm a terrible baker so I did everyone a favor and quit."

Lily lit up. "You worked for Melissa!"

"How do *you* know Melissa?"

"Oh, did I forget to mention? I'm a private investigator, contracted with Spectral to provide security and intel in any situation and under any circumstances." She flashed a grin. "That was from the pamphlet. Nice, right?"

"You… work for Dominic," Kellen said slowly.

"Well, technically now I work for Cory," Lily said. "Dom's more a friend. Which is good, he was kind of a terrible boss."

"Which means you know Farid," Kellen continued.

"Of course. Can't have Dom without Farid, can you? He's a good guy. Dom's so much happier these days. Why, do *you* know them?"

"Sort of," Kellen said. "I met Farid, anyway. He seemed… nice."

"You should come to dinner at our place," Lily said suddenly.

Kellen stumbled. "I should *what*?"

"It'll be great! You can meet our family! Vee's parents—Tau will love you. Tai may take some time to warm up to you, unless you like hockey, in which case he'll adopt you immediately."

"Fuck the Racers," Kellen said automatically, and Lily's laugh pealed out.

"Oh, you're *in*, pal."

"Kellen!" It was Vee, sounding out of breath and worried as he came belting around the curve of the path and nearly collided with them. He grabbed Kellen's shoulders, looking him over. "Are you okay?" He rounded on Lily before Kellen could answer. "What the fuck were you thinking? He's still recovering, he shouldn't be out for a *stroll!*"

Lily's eyebrows shot up and Kellen pushed Vee's hands away.

"It was *my* idea," he snapped, suddenly furious. "I'm fucking *sick* of your apartment. I haven't

left in a month. I needed to get *out*. I wanted—"
He hesitated. "I wanted to go see Jupiter and Kitt
and Monica, okay? You can't just keep me locked
up in there and expect—"

Vee caught his hand, looking stricken. "I'm
sorry," he said urgently. "God, Kell, I didn't even
think, I'm so sorry, of course you're going crazy! I
should've taken you out way before now. But are
you sure your ankle is up to walking all the way to
Monica's?"

Lily cleared her throat pointedly and Vee
swung back toward her.

"I like your boyfriend," Lily said demurely, but
Kellen could see the glint in her eye over Vee's
shoulder.

Vee pointed at her. "Not a fucking word to my
parents, you hear me? *I* will handle this. You say
anything and I'll—I'll shave your head in your
sleep."

Lily's eyes narrowed. "Fine," she said after a
minute. "But I want to be there when you introduce him to them."

"Go away, Lily," Vee said, turning back to
Kellen again. His eyes were worried but there was
affection in them as he stepped close. "I'm sorry to
fuss," he murmured. "I just...."

"Bye, Kellen!" Lily said.

"Go *away*, didi," Vee said, eyes on Kellen, and
waited until her footsteps faded before taking
another step closer, bringing their bodies flush.
"Hey," he murmured.

"You don't trust me alone," Kellen said.

Vee shook his head. Despite standing toe-to-

toe, they weren't touching. "Not it at all. I just want to make sure you're safe."

"I survived nearly seven years on the streets," Kellen pointed out.

Vee scowled. "You were also half-dead a month ago, I saw the bruises, so just… humor me a bit, would you?"

Kellen tipped his chin up and glowered at him. They stared at each other for a minute and then Vee's lips twitched.

"God." He reached out and gathered Kellen in, tilting his head back and pressing their mouths together.

Despite everything—his frustration with Vee not understanding, the pain in his ankle beginning to make itself felt, his bewilderment at Lily in general, and his stir-craziness—Kellen couldn't help but kiss him back, melting against his frame as Vee wrapped his arms tight around him.

Vee's mouth was sweet and wet and he tasted like almonds. Kellen hummed into it.

"Almond croissants?"

Vee's smile bloomed across his face. "You're getting better."

"Did you bring me one?"

"Ah… unfortunately I had to run out because I learned certain terrorizing cousins had you in their thrall and I couldn't risk delaying."

Kellen scowled. "Bring me one tomorrow, then."

Vee's smile widened and he bent to kiss him again. "You know what makes me happy?" He took Kellen's hand and tugged him gently along the path.

"What?"

"The fact that you *ask* for stuff now," Vee said. He opened the gate to Monica's property. "Remember how you used to just be… passive?"

Kellen hunched his shoulders but nodded.

"Well, I don't think you've noticed, but you ask me for things all the time now. And you're downright *pushy* during sex."

Kellen could feel the fiery blush creeping up his throat. "I'm sorry—"

"Don't you dare," Vee said, squeezing his hand. "I love it. I *love* when you make demands while we're fucking. I don't think you realize just how hot it is."

"I've noticed you like telling me no," Kellen said grumpily, and Vee laughed out loud.

"So maybe the Dom in me has a bit of a sadistic streak. Hey, there's Kitt."

The big brown mare was grazing in a field bordering the path, and she looked up as Vee and Kellen got closer. Kellen rested his elbows on the fence and called to her. Kitt flicked her ears and ambled over, big, liquid eyes soft and curious.

Kellen petted her nose, murmuring quietly to her, until she got bored and went back to grazing. When he straightened, Vee looked thoughtful.

"I have an idea," he said.

Kellen narrowed his eyes. "It doesn't involve cock cages, does it?"

Vee laughed out loud. "Not this time. Do you think you can walk the rest of the way down to see Monica?"

It turned out they didn't have to, though. Monica met them in her golf cart before they'd gotten halfway there. She smiled at Kellen, eyes sharp as ever.

"Heard what happened to you. How are you feeling?"

"Much better," Kellen said, resisting the impulse to duck his head and avoid her gaze. "I can mostly walk again now."

"Monica," Vee interrupted. "Did you ever find someone to help out here?"

Kellen turned toward him, startled, as Monica shook her head.

"Nope, still looking."

Vee raised his eyebrows at Kellen. "Well?"

"Well what?" Kellen asked.

"Well, do you want a job?" Monica said before Vee could answer.

Kellen gaped at her. "But—I don't know *anything* about horses."

Monica shrugged, resting her forearms on the wheel of the golf cart. "Don't take much horse sense to shovel shit. I'll teach you what you need to know."

Kellen's head spun and he reached for Vee's arm to steady himself. "I—I don't… why?"

"You got a gift for it," Monica said bluntly. "Vee here, he ain't bad but he's got no idea what he's doing."

"None at all," Vee said cheerfully.

"But *you*—you know instinctively how to behave, to keep from spooking the horses, to keep them calm. Do you like being around 'em?"

"More than anything," Kellen said. He snuck a glance at Vee. "Almost anything."

Monica shrugged again. "There you go. Can't

pay you much, but it's a living wage, and riding lessons come with."

"I—" Kellen stopped and swallowed. "My ankle—"

"Give it a few more weeks," Monica said. "Come back when you're healed up."

Vee was nearly bouncing on his toes, looking between Monica and Kellen, who couldn't find words.

"C'mon," Vee finally said. "What do you say, Kell?"

"*Yes*," Kellen said, and a smile spread across his face, stretching his mouth wide. "Yes, I'll work for you, *thank you*, I—you won't regret it, I promise."

Monica smiled at him. "Never thought I would. Now get in, I'll give you boys a ride home. You shouldn't be walking so much on that ankle like it is."

THEY CLIMBED the stairs back to Vee's apartment slowly, Kellen favoring his sore ankle and Vee hovering close by. Kellen tried to be annoyed by the helicoptering but he couldn't stop smiling. He was going to work with the horses. Learn to ride. He couldn't *wait*.

Inside, he grabbed Vee's shirt and dragged him toward the bedroom, where he pushed him onto the bed. Vee bounced, laughing, and Kellen flung himself on top of him, landing with a grunt. Vee rolled them, trying to end up on top, and they scuffled and flailed across the bed until Vee nearly fell off the edge.

"Pax," he said, laughing so hard he could breathe, "truce, uncle, whatever, *stop—*"

Kellen tickled him and Vee squawked and jackknifed, falling right over the edge and landing on the hardwood floor with a thud.

Kellen froze and then very slowly peeked over the side of the mattress to see Vee flat on his back, arms around his ribs as he laughed so hard he couldn't breathe.

"You… little *shit*," he gasped, and Kellen relaxed, grinning down at him.

The grin disappeared with a startled squeak when Vee lunged upward, bearing Kellen over backward and landing on top of him with a crow of triumph.

Kellen writhed, bubbles of laughter still escaping, as Vee grabbed his wrists and pinned them to the bed.

"You're gonna pay," he promised, a glint in his eye. He was sitting on Kellen's chest, knees keeping Kellen's arms mostly immobile, and Kellen gave him a sultry look from under his lashes.

"Does it involve my mouth on your cock?" he asked, and didn't miss Vee's startled intake of breath. "Because maybe we can set up a payment arrangement."

Vee stared down at him, eyes wide, and Kellen licked his lips.

"I want to suck your dick, Vee." He waited but Vee didn't move. "*Vee.* Take your goddamned cock out and *let me suck it.*"

Vee swallowed audibly and fumbled for his belt buckle.

"Scoot up," Kellen told him. "You have a big dick but I still can't reach you from there."

Vee choked on a laugh and obeyed, settling on Kellen's collarbones and undoing his belt. He was already hard when he pushed his jeans down enough to pull himself out, leaking at the tip. Kellen wanted to touch, but Vee's knees were still pinning his arms down. He settled for leaning forward and extending his tongue so that he could swipe it through the gathering liquid.

Vee hissed. "Fuck, Kell, your *mouth*—"

Kellen strained forward. He was just able to reach the tip of Vee's cock from his position and it wasn't *enough*.

"Come on," he said, pushing and pulling until he'd managed to free one arm. "Come *on*, Vee, stop torturing me and let me—"

Vee scooted forward and filled Kellen's mouth before he could finish his sentence. Kellen choked briefly, dug his fingers into Vee's thigh, and went to work.

He loved sucking cock. Loved the way it tasted, the salty, bitter musk of it, the silken skin over hard steel, the way the head flared and Kellen could trace the ridges with his tongue, mapping the veins and memorizing the texture and feel and shape.

He especially loved sucking *Vee's* cock, the noises Vee made and the way his hips jerked as if he had no control over them when Kellen took him deep, the smell of his inner thigh, the skin soft and delicate like parchment paper and smelling rich and musky and delectable.

Kellen guided Vee deep, until his cock was

stretching his throat and Kellen's eyes were watering as he fought his gag reflex. He swallowed several times and Vee swore in a throttled voice, garbled and almost unrecognizable.

"Kell, Kell *baby*, god I love it when you suck me, you look so good with my dick in your mouth—"

Kellen hummed encouragingly and slipped his hand under Vee's spread legs and behind his balls to press against his opening.

Vee went stiff, and before Kellen could wonder if he'd done something wrong, his cock thickened and Kellen's mouth was flooded with bitter, salty liquid. Vee swore again, pressing down on Kellen's finger desperately as his hips jolted.

"Fuck, *fuck*," Vee panted, sliding down the bed so he could fall forward and brace an elbow on either side of Kellen's head. "God, Kell—"

Kellen smiled up at him, dopey with endorphins. *I love you.* It almost escaped his mouth that time, and he turned his head and pressed his mouth to Vee's throat instead. But Vee pulled away after a minute, and his smile was wicked.

"Your turn," he said, and slid down the bed even farther.

THE NEXT TWO weeks passed much more quickly. Kellen stayed off his ankle as much as possible to let it heal faster, and Vee distracted him with sex and more sex, and then, when they were too exhausted to go again, with movies on his laptop, curled up in his bed against the pillows. Kellen usually found himself plastered to Vee's side, head on his chest so he could hear Vee's steady heartbeat and the laughs that vibrated through him when something funny happened.

He wondered, sometimes, what Jacob was doing without him. If he was making it alright. If he was angry with Kellen for what had happened. Kellen hoped he wasn't, but he couldn't talk to Vee about it. Vee wouldn't understand, would want to fix the problem, and he *couldn't*. So Kellen kept it to himself, distracting Vee with kisses whenever he looked worried.

THEN ONE DAY, Vee got a phone call. His face fell dramatically when he looked at the caller ID.

"Shit, it's my mom."

"I thought you liked your mom?" Kellen said, trailing an absent finger over Vee's bare abs.

Vee shivered and captured Kellen's finger. "Don't start that—the last thing I need is to talk to my mother with a hard-on. And I *do* like her, but I'm betting Lily's been dropping hints and that's why she's calling." He took a deep breath, pasted a smile on his face, and hit Answer. "Hi, Maa."

His mother's voice was clear even though the phone wasn't on speaker. "Vijay, what do I have to do to get you to call me? Is it so much to pick up the phone, tell me you're not dead in a ditch somewhere? Instead I have to find out from your cousin how you are, that you are *dating* someone?"

Vee rolled his eyes at Kellen, who fought his smile.

"I'm sorry, Maa, I've just been so busy."

His mother scoffed. "With the bakery? Where you are free by 2 in the afternoon? Try another one."

Kellen couldn't help his soft snort of laughter.

"Who was that?" Vee's mother said. "Is that your new partner? You know I never really liked Sean. Is this one nicer? Is he good to you?" Her voice sharpened. "Are you good to *him?*"

"*Maa,*" Vee protested, clearly stung. "Why do you think I wouldn't be good to him? And yes." He pulled Kellen closer, until his head was resting on Vee's chest. "He's much nicer. And he eats carbs."

His mother made a pleased noise. "Let me speak to him, beta."

Vee shot Kellen an alarmed look but Kellen sat up, holding out his hand for the phone.

"Hello, this is Kellen," he said when Vee finally handed it over.

"Kellen, my name is Aruna. When can you come to dinner?"

"I—" Kellen looked at Vee, who was shaking his head and making 'absolutely not' motions with his hands.

"Ignore my son," Aruna said calmly. "I promise neither Alok nor I will eat you. We simply want to know more about you, and perhaps to see Vijay, who has not been home in *months.*"

"*Busy,* Maa," Vee said despairingly.

Aruna harrumphed. "When is good for you, Kellen?"

"Friday?" Kellen suggested, and Vee flopped dramatically back onto the pillows with a groan.

"Friday is perfect," Aruna said, sounding pleased. "Don't worry, it will be a quiet dinner, just family."

She hung up and Kellen looked at Vee, who had an arm over his eyes.

"She said just family."

Vee moved his arm just enough to glare at Kellen from beneath it. "Have you ever *met* an Indian family?" He didn't sound angry, though, so Kellen relaxed and crawled on top of him, straddling Vee's narrow hips. Vee's breath caught and Kellen bent and kissed the bolt of his jaw.

"My parents wanted a large family," he said, trailing kisses down Vee's throat. "My mother felt she'd failed. I think my father thought that too, although he never said it."

Vee was silent, but he lifted a hand and tangled it loosely in Kellen's hair.

"Father insisted on dinner together, 'as a family', but they didn't actually want to talk to me. We'd sit there and the maid would serve us and we'd eat. Sometimes my mother would comment on the food." Kellen closed his eyes and pushed his face against Vee's collarbone. "I tried, a few times, to talk to them. Engage them. You know?"

He could feel Vee's nod.

"I talked about football once. I don't even *like* football, but I was trying...." He went quiet, remembering.

"What happened?" Vee said gently, running his hands up and down Kellen's arms.

"My dad turned it into a lecture about the type of women who are attracted to football players, and how godless and immoral sports were—mostly because of the cheerleaders, I think?"

Vee's hands tightened but he said nothing. Kellen sighed and sat up. Vee looked troubled, and Kellen tried for a reassuring smile.

"All I'm saying is, I've never had a family. Not a real one, that bickers and squabbles and *loves* and are so ride or die for each other."

Vee reached up and pulled Kellen down, rolling them so he was on top. "You have one now," he said fiercely, and kissed him.

Kellen arched into it, winding his arms around Vee's neck. Vee's mouth fit his perfectly, he thought distantly, the perfect shape, size, taste—all of it combining to make Vee a drug Kellen was helpless to resist.

They kissed leisurely for awhile, no urgency to it. Vee was comfortingly heavy on Kellen's skinnier frame, even though he propped himself on his elbows to keep from crushing him.

"So," he murmured, dragging wet kisses across Kellen's jaw. "Now that you're more comfortable asking for what you want… is there anything you *do* want? That we haven't done yet, I mean."

Kellen thought about it as Vee moved down the mattress and pushed Kellen's shirt up to his armpits. He breathed warm air across Kellen's chest, mouth tantalizingly close to a nipple, as he waited for a reply.

After a minute, when Kellen hadn't answered, Vee pinched his nipple sharply.

Kellen curled forward, gasping as he went from half-hard to fully erect.

"I asked a question," Vee said, and there it

was, what Kellen secretly thought of as his Dom voice, strong and commanding and unhesitating. Kellen loved that voice, and he was helpless to resist it.

"I—" He took a deep breath. "I want—" He closed his eyes, trying to figure out how to say it.

Vee waited, propped above him, one hand moving lazily across Kellen's chest while Kellen searched for words.

"The, um… the cock cage?" Kellen said.

Vee hummed encouragingly. "You want to wear that?"

"Y-yes, but not just…." Kellen bit his lip. "I want you to put a plug in me and… the cage." Vee's eyebrows rose and Kellen hurried on. "And I want you to take me out. Somewhere. Anywhere. I don't c-care, I just want—I want to feel you in me and around me with every single step I take, I w-want everyone to look at me and have no idea, but *I'll* know. That my p-pleasure is yours. That *I'm* yours."

"Jesus *fuck*," Vee managed, his voice hoarse.

Emboldened, Kellen turned his head and kissed Vee's bicep. "Don't tell me beforehand," he whispered. "Surprise me."

Vee groaned and caught Kellen's mouth in a searing kiss. "You're gonna kill me, baby."

"Will you tie me up and whip me now?" Kellen asked, leaning up as much as he could to lick Vee's throat. "And then fuck me?"

"Yeah," Vee said thickly. "I can do that."

His riding lesson the next day was exquisite torture, since he was unable to settle in the saddle.

"Sit *deep*," Monica shouted as Kellen squirmed yet again. "Jesus Christ, boy, you got ants in your pants? What's going on with you?"

Vee asked Jupiter to stop without using the reins—something he'd learned recently and loved doing—and shrugged, not meeting Monica's eyes. "I, um… bumped into something yesterday. I have a… bruise." More like thirty of them, but she didn't need to know that.

Monica squinted at him. "Uh-huh," she said abruptly, her tone making it clear she didn't believe him. "In that case, you're doing this entire lesson in two-point."

"What's that?"

"Gather your reins," Monica told him. "Now lift your ass out of the saddle. Keep it there with your knees and thighs only. No, *not* your stirrups —" when Kellen tried to use them for balance. "Start him walking."

Kellen squeezed with his calves and Jupiter swung into a loose, easy walk, head bobbing, and Kellen grabbed at his mane to balance himself, swearing.

"Gather your goddamn reins," Monica said. "Get him on the bit already, he knows how perfectly well—he's being a lazy ass. Grab mane to keep you balanced until you find that sweet spot if you need to."

Kellen shortened the reins some more, until Jupiter grudgingly dropped his head until his nose was pointing at the ground, ears pricked forward.

"Feel that, under you?" Monica asked. "He's

rounding his back, stepping under himself better —nope, get your ass back out of the seat."

Shit. Kellen re-balanced himself and did his best to pay attention as he and Jupiter made a loose circle around Monica, in the center of the arena.

———

HE WAS LIMPING when he got home, and Vee looked up, eyes sharpening when Kellen dragged himself through the door.

"What happened? Did you fall?"

"I think that would have hurt less," Kellen groused. "Do we have Epsom salts?"

"Sure, in the bathroom."

"Excellent. I'm going to take a very long, very hot bath." He bent, muffling a groan at the effort, dropped a kiss on Vee's upturned face, then shuffled off to the bathroom.

11

THEY SPENT the day of the dinner with Vee's parents not doing much of anything. They ate breakfast, then lounged quietly together, talking about the bakery and the horses.

"Monica wants me to enter a show on Jupiter," Kellen told him as they lay on the bed, fingers twined together.

"Already? It's only been what, a month?"

Kellen moved one shoulder. "She says I can handle a beginner class, Jupe will take care of me." His tone was careless but his eyes were uneasy, and he rolled closer to Vee, butting his head against his shoulder. "I don't know what I'm doing," he admitted, voice muffled.

Vee cupped the back of his head. "Monica wouldn't do this if she thought you weren't ready. You're so good at this, baby. The first time you sat on a horse, Star told me you were a natural. She sounded *jealous*."

"Star? Jealous?" Kellen sounded diverted at the thought of that.

"Right? She said you have great balance, and something about your hands. I don't remember exactly, I was mostly just ogling you at the time." Kellen shoved his shoulder and Vee laughed. "Seriously, though. You're gonna be great. When and where is it?"

"Are you going to come?" Kellen asked, sounding genuinely startled.

Vee flinched and Kellen looked ashamed.

"I'm sorry," he said. "I just—it's hard to believe that...."

"Don't be sorry," Vee said gently. "You've been told all your life that you weren't worth much, of course you're having a hard time overcoming that." He lifted Kellen's hand to his mouth and kissed the palm. "You're worth *everything*, Kellen Smith."

Kellen's eyes softened but he ducked his head. "That's not my actual last name."

"I figured," Vee said, smiling.

"It's Abernathy." Kellen looked up, a rueful smile on his face. "I think I'd prefer Smith, honestly."

"Why, what's wrong with it?"

"It's just... *Abernathy*. Isn't that what poncy old Brits with stiff upper lips are called?"

Vee snorted a laugh. "I'm guessing your family tree has more than a few poncy Brits in it." He glanced at the clock. "We should get going."

Kellen groaned but rolled off the bed obediently to find clothes.

THEY TOOK a cab to Vee's parents' house, which was glowing with light in the early Seattle twilight. Strings of fairy lights stretched through the trees that sheltered the small, squat house, more lights cascading from the branches and set into the flagstones under their feet as they walked up the path.

"Maa," Vee said. "She likes light."

"It's so… cheerful," Kellen said. There was wonder in his eyes as he looked around.

"Wait until you see the inside," Vee said, squeezing his hand.

The door opened before they got to it and Aruna bustled out, arms open. She pulled Vee into a hug first, kissing him roundly on both cheeks, and stood back to look him over. Her eyes were sharp as ever, a few more strands of gray in the black ever-present bun, but her mouth was just as ready with its smile.

"You're only a little bit late!" she said, cupping Vee's cheek in one cool, dry hand. "Introduce me, beta."

Vee turned to Kellen, who was standing very still. "Maa, this is Kellen. Kellen, this is my mother. She likes to think she's fierce, but she's really a giant softy."

Aruna smacked his arm, muttering, and then held out both hands to Kellen, who took them hesitantly. "Welcome, Kellen," she told him. "We are so glad you could join us. Come inside, I want to get to know you!"

She hustled them both through the front door and Vee saw it through fresh eyes as Kellen looked around, taking in his surroundings even as he stepped out of his shoes and set them beside Vee's.

Aruna's eyebrows went up and she caught Vee's eye, but he just smiled, watching Kellen's first introduction to where Vee had grown up. The living room was a riot of color, from the hand-worked tapestries on the walls to the blankets on the backs of the chairs and sofa and the rugs on the floor under their feet. Golden light glowed from the lamps in the corners, making the room even more vibrant and warm, and Kellen took a deep breath and let it out slowly.

Vee's father looked up from his paper, bushy eyebrows rising.

"Ah, Vijay." He stood and offered his hand, which Vee took.

"Papa, this is Kellen, my boyfriend."

Kellen shook his hand and Alok looked at him narrowly.

"Tell me, Kellen, do you like hockey?"

"Yes sir," Kellen said. "I'm primarily a Sirens fan, but I'll root for the Wolverines and Seabirds too. Not the Racers, of course."

Alok's eyebrows went up. "I like this one, Vijay. Bring him over more often. Kellen, you come sit with me and tell me who you think shows promise in this year's draft."

Aruna pulled Vee toward the kitchen as Kellen was towed to the couch, casting a helpless look over his shoulder at Vee, who lifted his hands in surrender. *Sorry*, he mouthed.

In the kitchen, Lily was chopping carrots while her mother stirred something on the stove.

"Bhai!" Lily said, looking up. "Is he here? Did you bring him?"

"He's talking hockey with Papa," Vee said,

dropping a kiss on his aunt's cheek. "Tai, how are you more lovely every time I see you?"

His aunt smacked his arm, muttering under her breath about insolent young men, but she couldn't hide the smile.

Lily yanked her apron off. "I'm going to go say hi."

"Lily, the carrots—" But she was already gone. Aruna sighed. "Vee, chop those for me while you tell us about Kellen."

Vee picked up the knife but shrugged. "Not much to tell. I met him when I was out with friends one night. We talked and hit it off."

"How long have you been dating?"

Vee did the math in his head. "Nearly five months, I guess?"

"What does he do?"

"He's the barn manager for the stable up the road from where I live." He realized his mistake when Aruna's eyes sharpened.

"Does he live with you then, beta?"

"I, uh—" Vee nearly sliced his finger and moved the knife away. "He, um. He had a bad time, a few months back. He was beaten really badly and he didn't have anywhere to go, his parents don't approve of him being gay, and I…." He floundered.

"You took him in," Aruna finished. Her face was unreadable.

Vee hunched his shoulders. "He didn't have anyone else, Maa! He needed help, so… I helped him."

Aruna rounded the table and cupped Vee's face in both hands. "My kind, big-hearted son. I am so proud of you. I heard about the thing you do, with the leftover pastries from your bakery."

Vee closed his eyes briefly. "Lily?"

"Of course, who else? She thought it was a good thing you do." Aruna patted his cheek. "So do I. Now go take some tea to Kellen and rescue him from your father. Maybe show him your old bedroom?"

Vee accepted the mug she gave him and escaped into the living room, where Alok and Kellen were still talking. Kellen seemed intensely into the conversation, but he looked up and smiled when he saw Vee, who held out the mug.

"Thirsty?"

Kellen took it and Vee held out his hand.

"I thought I'd show you my bedroom."

"No funny stuff," Alok rumbled.

"Papa, *gross*," Vee said, and tugged Kellen down the hall. His room was the last on the left, opening into a small space at the back of the house, shaped like a triangle. His bed had been tucked into the wide end, now removed to make way for Aruna's sewing supplies.

"It's like a pie slice," Kellen said, looking around and setting the glass on the table by the door.

Vee huffed a laugh. "Yeah. My kid-sized bed was fine, but when I hit six feet—at sixteen years old—things started getting dicey." He pushed Kellen backward, pinning him gently to the wall. "How are you doing?" he murmured, and nipped lightly at his jaw.

Kellen gasped and turned his head away. "Don't—"

"Don't what?"

"Don't turn me on at your *parents'* house," Kellen hissed.

"But I want to," Vee objected. "I want you to imagine me holding you down, fucking you hard, maybe with a hand over your mouth so you don't make a noise."

Kellen's eyes rolled back and his hips jerked. Vee cupped his crotch.

"You like the idea of being gagged?"

Kellen nodded almost helplessly, shivering all over.

"Maybe a ball gag," Vee mused. He stroked a thumb over Kellen's erection. "Stretch your mouth wide open, make you sloppy and sore? God, I like that idea, you not being able to make a noise while I fuck you."

Kellen's head hit the wall with an audible thump, knees giving out, and only Vee's hands on him keeping him upright.

"Kell?"

Kellen didn't answer, head lolling.

"Oh shit," Vee whispered. He hadn't meant to go so far. Kellen deep in subspace *now* was not a good idea. He took a step back, pulling Kellen with him, and guided him to the chair in the corner.

Kellen settled into it and Vee knelt in front of him.

"Come back to me, baby," he ordered.

Kellen's head drooped but he didn't respond.

Vee chewed his lip. Pain would probably just drive Kellen deeper. He needed something to shock him back to awareness without hurting him. He looked around and saw the tea Kellen had set down when they entered the room. Vee put a finger in it—it had cooled off to nearly room temperature. He snatched it up and flung it in Kellen's face before he thought better of the plan.

Kellen reared back, heaving in a great, startled gasp of air, eyes wild. "What, *what*—"

"I'm sorry," Vee said, rubbing Kellen's thighs. "I'm so sorry, I pushed you into subspace but then I couldn't get you back out and I didn't know what else to do, are you okay? Fuck, Kell, I'm so sorry—"

Kellen pulled on his damp shirt and tugged it off over his head, using the back to dry his face. When he emerged from it, his eyes were still dazed but a shadow of amusement was in them. "How exactly are we going to explain this to your parents?"

Vee ignored that, still consumed with worry. He'd heard of bad things happening to subs when they were pulled out of subspace unexpectedly. "Are you sure you're okay?"

Kellen touched his mouth. "I'm fine, Vee. Just… sticky."

Vee bent forward and put his head in Kellen's lap, winding his arms around Kellen's hips. "I could have hurt you. I wasn't careful enough."

Kellen stroked his hair. "I'm not hurt, baby. Just startled and wet. You didn't do any lasting damage. That was actually really quick thinking." Vee lifted his head and Kellen looked briefly worried. "What?"

"That's the first time you've called me anything

besides my name," Vee managed around the boulder in his throat.

"What did I say?"

"Baby," Vee whispered. "You called me—" He pulled Kellen off the chair into his lap, kissing him desperately. Kellen tasted like tea and coming home, and he kissed back just as wildly, mouth plundering as his hands roamed.

There were footsteps outside in the hall and they both froze.

"*Fuck*," Vee whispered. "Think, Vee, think—okay. Here's what we're going to do."

FIVE MINUTES LATER, they went back to the living room and Aruna's eyebrows went into her hairline at the sight of Kellen with damp hair, wearing one of Vee's old T-shirts that he'd left behind.

Alok sighed. "I told you—"

"Kellen spilled his tea," Vee interrupted.

Kellen hung his head, looking abashed. "I tripped on the step going into Vee's room and I tried to save myself and I just… dumped the tea all over me, I'm very sorry, Mrs. Annapurna. But I didn't break the cup?" He held out it, mouth twisting, and Aruna snorted.

"Well, that's something," she said. "At least Vee had a shirt here to give you."

"Vee showed me his room and I saw your crafting supplies. You made the blanket for his bed, didn't you?" Kellen asked as he gave her the empty teacup. "It's really lovely."

Aruna smiled at him. "Keep this one, Vee," she said, eyes on Kellen.

Kellen ducked his head again, blush staining his cheeks, and Vee pulled him close.

"I intend to," he said.

DINNER WAS LOUD AND NOISY, as all good Annapurna dinners were wont to be. Aunt and Uncle had come over, as well as Lily and her sister and her sister's children. Vee kept a close eye on Kellen, making sure he wasn't getting overwhelmed by all the attention, but Kellen had a smile on his face, leaning over to talk to Lily beside him, and his body was loose and relaxed.

After a few minutes, he slipped a hand onto Vee's thigh, still talking earnestly to Lily. Vee gave silent thanks for the huge tablecloths his mother always put down as Kellen's hand inched upward.

"Pass the *dhoti*," Sara asked, and Vee cleared his throat and grabbed it for her. He nearly dropped the glass bowl as Kellen's fingers closed around his dick, setting it down with an audible thump and mumbling an apology.

Kellen and Lily both turned their heads at the noise, Kellen showing nothing but vague interest, and then they were both talking again, Kellen turned half away from Vee, and still his very clever fingers stroked and rubbed until Vee thought faintly that he might die right there, or come in his pants.

Dying would be preferable.

He caught Kellen's wrist and pulled it up into

sight, planting a kiss on his hand and then twining their fingers together and resting them on the table.

Kellen turned and looked at him, eyes sparkling, and Vee shook his head, unable to fight the smile. *Brat.*

Sara asked Vee a question and he turned to answer, still holding Kellen's hand.

———

KELLEN INSISTED on helping to clean up after dinner was over, washing dishes with Lily as Vee and Sara carried them in from the dining room. When the kitchen was clean, Vee raised his eyebrows at Kellen, who nodded.

"Time for us to go," Vee said. He made the circuit of the room, kissing the women and shaking the men's hands, ending up in front of his mother.

She pulled him down into a hug. "Be very careful with him," she whispered in his ear, and Vee froze, surprised.

"What do you mean?"

"He's been hurt. Broken. I can see it in his eyes. Don't let him be broken again."

Vee's throat closed again and he hugged her tighter. "I'm doing my best, Maa."

Aruna turned to Kellen next and hugged him as well. Whatever she whispered in *his* ear was too quiet to be heard, but Kellen's face lit with a smile as he hugged her back.

THE RIDE HOME WAS QUIET, their hands linked between them on the taxi seat.

"I like them," Kellen said finally.

"They like you too," Vee said, squeezing his hand. "Better than me, I think."

Kellen laughed. "Impossible."

"Do you actually like hockey or did you just pull all that out of your ass?" Vee asked.

Kellen hunched his shoulders. "I like hockey," he admitted.

"Why do you sound ashamed?"

"I don't know," Kellen said, looking down at his lap. "I told you my father didn't approve of sports? Said it led to wicked ways, debauchery. I wanted to play hockey in high school but he wouldn't let me. But I've always liked it, so I follow it when I can."

"You're full of surprises," Vee said. "So you follow the Seabirds and Sirens?"

"When I can," Kellen said. "Never been to a game, of course."

"I have a friend on the Seabirds," Vee said offhandedly.

"Wait, really? Who?"

"Embry Rather?"

Kellen stared at him. "You're friends with *Embry Rather*, the second line center for the Portland fucking Seabirds?"

Vee laughed. "I'm gonna have to get us tickets to a game, aren't I?"

"Yeah," Kellen said, grinning at him. "You really are."

The taxi pulled up in front of their building

and Vee paid the driver and followed Kellen out and up the stairs, crowding close behind him.

"Vee," Kellen protested, laughter in his voice.

"Open the door," Vee growled, biting at his shoulder.

"I'm *trying.*" Kellen's hands weren't entirely steady, but he got the key in the lock and the door shoved open after a minute, and Vee pushed him over the threshold. Kellen stumbled and caught himself as Vee kicked the door shut and advanced on him, giving him no time to react, and Kellen fled for the bedroom, trying in vain to stifle his laughter.

12

VEE LEFT the bakery the next day in a good mood. He had a sack of pastries for Kellen and Melissa had just given him a promotion to manager, because Senna had taken a job at another bakery closer to her house. Sad as he was to lose her, Vee was delighted with both his new job title and the raise that came with it. He couldn't wait to tell Kellen.

His steps faltered as he came out of Spectral to the familiar and unwelcome sight of the protestors, back with their posters and banners.

The tall blond man was there, shouting something at the top of his lungs to a crowd that seemed mostly apathetic, although a few people had their phones out and were recording his rant.

Vee stopped and looked closer. The man's hair was so fair it was almost white, with sharply bladed cheekbones, a tight-lipped mouth, and dark brown eyes. This had to be Kellen's father, Vee realized with a jolt of horror.

The man swiveled and caught Vee's gaze. His eyes narrowed and he opened his mouth, but Vee beat him there.

"What happened to your son?"

Abernathy blinked, pulled his head back, and blinked again. "I—what?"

Vee stepped nearer. "Your son. The one who ran away at sixteen years old. What happened to him?"

Abernathy's mouth worked. "H-how do you know about—"

Vee lifted a careless shoulder. "I was curious, after our last encounter. I looked you up, your organization, the one that claims to spread love and light and goodwill and all that jazz? So why did your son feel he had to leave?"

"He chose to go of his own accord," Abernathy snarled. "To consort with wicked men and pay the price. He knew the dangers. He stopped being my son when he walked out the door."

Vee absorbed that. His heart broke for Kellen, imagining him as a gangly teenager, desperate to learn his place in the world and not having the love and guidance of the two people he depended on the most.

"What would you do, to get him back?" he asked. "Would you apologize for hurting him? Tell him you love him and accept him for who he is?"

He saw the answer in Abernathy's face before he spoke. "I would *only* accept him back if he *begged* for my forgiveness and proved he'd changed," he hissed.

Vee spat on the ground at Abernathy's feet. "That for your Christian 'love'." He turned and walked away quickly, ignoring the vitriol Abernathy shouted after him. He had to see Kellen.

HE BOUNDED up the steps into the building and up the stairs, taking them two at a time. The shower was running but it turned off as Vee charged inside and Kellen stepped out onto the bathmat, damp and rosy.

"Hey!" he said, lighting up at the sight of him. "How was your day?"

Vee dropped the bag of pastries and made a beeline into the bathroom. Kellen laughed as Vee grabbed him, winding his arms around Vee's neck and leaning in for a kiss, but Vee shook his head and buried his face in Kellen's throat. He was shaking, he realized distantly, and he saw the moment Kellen noticed it too.

"What happened?" Kellen asked, his voice low and dangerous. "Did someone hurt you?"

Vee shook his head again, the tears in his throat making it impossible for him to speak. He pulled Kellen closer, breathing in the smell of him, grounding himself.

"Vee, you're freaking me out," Kellen said.

Vee loosened his grip but didn't let go. "I'm sorry," he said.

"It's okay, but what happened?"

"No," Vee said, cupping Kellen's face. "I'm *sorry*. I'm sorry no one loved you. I'm sorry you had to figure out all that shit on your own with no one to take care of you and tell you it was okay, I'm sorry—"

Kellen's face shuttered. "What are you talking about."

Vee took a deep breath and let go. "I saw your father today."

Surprise sparked in Kellen's eyes, followed by hope that died stillborn. His shoulders rounded and he took a step away.

"I see."

"It's not your fault," Vee said as Kellen slipped past him to leave the bathroom.

"I *know it's not my fault!*" Kellen shouted, spinning to confront him, fists clenched at his sides. Even naked and rumpled, he was a force to be reckoned with, fury spitting sparks in his eyes. "You think I don't know that? You think I don't know the ten year old boy did nothing wrong when he wanted to kiss his best friend? You think, what, that I blame myself for my father being *evil* and my mother not much better, that I couldn't make them love me?"

"*Yes!*" Vee shouted back. Kellen jerked like he'd been hit. "Yes, I think you blame yourself!" Vee continued as Kellen stared at him. "Yes, I think deep down, you *do* believe that if you were better, or more, or *different*, that they would love you, and because they didn't, that proves you're *not worth loving.*"

Kellen crumpled to the floor, arms going up over his head. Vee scrambled to catch him, pulling him into his lap as Kellen let out an explosive sob and began to weep in earnest. Vee held him, rocking him back and forth, his own tears disappearing into Kellen's wet hair, as Kellen's chest heaved with the force of the grief that wracked his body.

"I j-just wanted—" Kellen dragged in air and keened, a soft, heartbroken noise that made Vee's tears fall faster. "I w-wasn't *enough*." He burrowed deeper into Vee's arms, his face pressed to his chest, and Vee bent over him.

"You *are* enough," he managed, his voice thick. "You are so loved, Kellen. None of what happened to you is your fault. *None of it.*"

Kellen didn't reply, face still hidden in Vee's hoodie, and uneasiness spread through Vee's veins.

"Kell?" he said carefully.

Silence.

Vee rubbed Kellen's shoulder blades. "Hey, sweetheart, can you answer me?"

Kellen said nothing and the uneasiness spun into dread. Vee leaned down and looked into his eyes, but there was nothing of Kell looking back. He was an empty shell, the Kellen Vee loved so much no longer there. It was almost like subspace, Vee thought, but a twisted, *wrong*, version of it. Kellen wasn't flying—he was trapped.

"Come on, baby, get up," Vee said.

Kellen didn't move.

Vee closed his eyes briefly, prayed for forgiveness, and said, "*Get up*," his voice sharp as a slap.

Kellen jerked and clambered to his feet, eyes still empty, and Vee followed him, steadying him before he fell.

"I'm sorry," he said. "Can you hear me?"

Kellen didn't answer.

Vee kept his hands on Kellen's arms, chewing his lip.

"Clothes," he said, turning him toward the bedroom. He wasn't sure, after, how he got Kellen dressed, because he was about as responsive as a china doll, his face as blank as one. He stood swaying once Vee had him dressed, and Vee chewed his lip. He had no idea what to *do*, but he knew he couldn't do this alone. He needed reinforcements. "Come on, sweetheart."

Kellen followed automatically, pressing close to Vee's side but saying nothing. Vee found a taxi and bundled them inside, holding Kellen for the ride across town.

Kellen didn't ask where they were going.

On the way, Vee pulled out his phone.

His mother met them at the gate, eyes pinched with worry as Vee unfolded Kellen out of the cab and guided him up the walk. Kellen went docilely, his eyes still empty.

"What happened?" Aruna asked in a low voice, taking Kellen's other arm.

"It's… like a mental break," Vee said miserably. "We had a… it's not important now. He needs love, Maa. He needs us to love him."

"Of course, beta," Aruna said instantly. "Kellen, love, come inside. I made some masala chai for you, I know how much you like it." She ushered them both into the house and put Vee on the couch with a sharp jerk of her chin, settling Kellen between his legs once Vee had sat down. "Now you stay there while I get you tea and a blanket."

She was back in minutes, handing Vee the cup. He held it awkwardly, hoping the smell would help jog Kellen out of wherever he'd gone, as Aruna disappeared again. This time when she came back, it was with a dark brown afghan. She draped it over Kellen's shoulders and tucked it in, then went to her knees beside the couch, petting his face and crooning to him in Hindi.

Vee could only catch fragments of what she was saying, but it didn't matter. The setting was the important thing, the love that had soaked this house down to its bones, settled into its foundations, so that anyone who stepped through the door had their burdens lifted, at least for a little while.

Alok came in and bent over Kellen, one big hand on Kellen's thin shoulder. "What do you think of the Seabirds' new draft pick?"

Vee blinked back grateful tears as Alok waited for an answer that didn't come, patted Kellen's shoulder clumsily, and settled down in the chair beside them.

Aruna flitted around them, putting out pastries to nibble on and bringing more tea. She talked the whole time in her sweet, soothing voice, describing what she was doing, the projects she was working on, the way Tai cheated dreadfully at bingo night.

Vee lifted his head at that. "You play bingo now?"

"It's good to get out occasionally," Aruna said, lifting her chin. "Besides, it's easy to win against senior citizens, even when you *don't* cheat."

Vee couldn't help the laugh and Kellen stirred.

Vee's amusement cut off and he set the teacup down. "Kell? Baby?"

Kellen blinked several times and looked around. "W-what—"

"Vee called us," Alok rumbled as Aruna took Kellen's hand in both of hers. "He said you needed love, so naturally he brought you here, to us."

Kellen's mouth wobbled and he looked up at Vee, who managed a not-very-firm smile of his own.

"Had me scared," Vee whispered, and Kellen's eyes filled with shame.

"I'm sorry."

"No," Aruna said firmly. "This—" She gestured at the room and everyone in it. "This is what families *do*. We heal each other." She lifted a shoulder. "Sometimes we break little pieces of each other, too, but in the end, we are whole. Together."

Kellen squeezed his eyes shut.

"I'm n-not—"

"Yes you are," Aruna said, voice leaving no room for argument. She smiled suddenly, bright and sunny. "I always wanted another son, although I did not imagine him so blond." She put her hand on Kellen's head, a benediction of sorts. "Rest, beta."

Kellen hiccuped but obeyed, his eyes closing and body relaxing into real sleep. Vee held him until he was deeply under and then Aruna beckoned him into the kitchen. Vee disentangled himself carefully, easing himself free without waking Kellen, and tiptoed that way.

Where he was immediately caught in a hug by

his tiny, sometimes terrifying mother. Vee sagged against her, letting go of the terror that had been gnawing at his insides, and stifled a sob against her neck as she held him.

"I was so s-*scared*," he managed. "I thought—I thought I broke him, I think I *did* break him, just like you told me not to do, what do I *do*, Maa—"

"He was already broken, love," Aruna said gently, wiping his tears away. "Now, we help him heal. Deep breaths. Dry your face." She led him back out to the living room and Vee lifted Kellen's shoulders and slid back onto the couch. Kellen draped himself across Vee's lap with a sleepy mumble, one arm going around his thighs, and fell asleep again.

THEY STAYED FOR DINNER, which was quieter than last time to give Kellen a chance to recover his composure. Vee stuck close, never more than arm's length away, but he relaxed slightly when Lily appeared in the doorway in heavy motorcycle boots and a black leather jacket.

"Kell, my love, when are you going to leave Vee and run away with me?" Lily asked, collapsing on the sofa beside him.

Kellen's laugh was a little shaky, but it was there. "Probably never, sorry. You don't have the right equipment."

Lily clutched her chest dramatically. "I guess I'll be a spinster, living alone with my horde of cats. And when I die, they'll eat my body because no one else loved me enough to check on me more than once a month."

Her mother swatted Lily's boots off the table. "Such nonsense!"

Lily blew her a kiss. "Except you, Maa."

Tai fixed her with a sharp glance. "When are you going to choose a husband?"

"Absolutely fucking never," Lily declared cheerfully, winking at Kellen and ducking the smack her mother tried to deliver.

"*Language!*"

"Hey, you started it with the H-word," Lily complained.

Vee sat back and watched Kellen as Lily and her mother continued to bicker. He was still too pale, his movements slightly uncoordinated, like he couldn't remember quite how his joints fit together, but his eyes were clear. He turned his head and caught Vee's gaze and his lips quirked up.

Hey, he mouthed.

Hi, Vee told him silently. *You okay?*

Kellen nodded. *You?*

Vee *wasn't* okay. Kellen's episode had terrified him, made him realize just how deep Kellen's issues ran, given him a glimpse into the yawning craters of his psyche. He wanted to hold him, protect him from the world, and never let anything bad happen to him again.

But Kellen didn't need to worry about Vee, and he would, if he knew how upset he was. So he smiled at him and Kellen relaxed.

They held hands walking to the cab after saying goodbye to the family. Held hands for the ride across town. Held hands going up the stairs single file.

Vee unlocked the door and Kellen followed him inside. They stepped out of their shoes and Kellen pulled Vee toward the bedroom. Vee went willingly, crawling onto the bed and tucking Kellen's thin frame up against him.

But that wasn't what Kellen wanted. He didn't want tender and caring. He wanted heat and passion and the flare of senses that reminded him he was alive. He wanted *grounding*. He squirmed away from Vee's arms and swung a leg over his hips.

Vee looked up at him, his dark eyes vulnerable in the moonlight, and Kellen swallowed back more shame.

"Fuck me," he said.

Vee touched the hand Kellen had put on his chest. "I don't think that's a good idea."

Kellen tried to hide the flinch. "Do you want me to go?" he asked, barely able to get the words out.

Vee's eyes widened in shock. "What? *No!*"

"Then *fuck* me, Vee, *please*. I need—I need to f-feel something, anything besides this, this—"

Vee rolled them so that he was on top, Kellen pinned beneath his comforting weight, and Kellen swallowed a sob of relief.

"You want it?" Vee asked, and Kellen nodded frantically.

"Please, p-please—"

"Then you'll take it my way," Vee said, his

voice hard and uncompromising. He let Kellen up so they could get undressed, but stopped him when Kellen tried to go to his knees. "On your back."

Kellen swallowed hard and obeyed. Flat on his back, he stared at Vee, kneeling above him, skin silvered by the moonlight. He was stroking himself slowly, getting himself hard, and Kellen reached out to touch, to *feel* something, but Vee slapped his hand away.

"My way," he repeated.

Kellen subsided and Vee leaned over to retrieve the lube. In this position, his eyes were unreadable, watching Kellen intently. Was he angry, Kellen wondered, angry that Kellen had disrupted his life and home and caused so much chaos? He didn't *seem* angry, but then, Kellen didn't think he'd ever seen Vee truly furious about something.

He wasn't hard, but he ached for Vee to touch him, to fill his empty places and soothe the cracks in his soul. *Please*, he thought, and maybe Vee heard him, because he lowered himself and pushed up and in. Kellen arched his back as Vee forced his way inside. He loved unprepped sex, loved that tripwire moment where everything teetered between pain and pleasure. He craved that first hot rush of his body opening and Vee—only Vee now, no one but Vee forever—filling him to overflowing.

Always considerate, even when working through issues in his own mind, Vee paused to give Kellen time to adjust. Kellen didn't *want* time to adjust. He pulled at Vee's arms, wrapped his thighs around his ass and tried to pull him deeper.

Vee made a noise and caught Kellen's wrists in one hand, pinning them to the bed. With his other hand, he grabbed Kellen's chin and forced him to meet his gaze. Trapped in place, Kellen had no choice but to look at him as Vee withdrew and just as slowly slid back in.

He was a butterfly in amber, frozen and on display as Vee took his deliberate pleasure from Kellen's body with no variation of rhythm. Slow and steady, in and out, until Kellen was writhing, nearly in tears.

"*Vee*," he begged, but Vee didn't answer, didn't do anything except continue to fuck him in that maddeningly slow rhythm, staring into his eyes.

Now Kellen was hard, leaking heavy, slick drops onto his abdomen. He was desperate to be touched, taken out of his mind, but Vee would not be budged, his hands inexorable and eyes hooded.

The sensations rolled through Kellen in an overwhelming flood, making his skin tingle and scalp prickle as he gasped for air. He wasn't Kellen anymore, he was a vaguely Kellen-shaped mass of nerve endings, every one of them raw and exposed and being plucked by Vee's merciless fingers.

"I'm sorry," he panted.

Vee paused briefly at that, then resumed.

"I shouldn't have dragged you into this," Kellen managed. He closed his eyes against the tears but Vee's rhythm still didn't falter.

Kellen let go, stopped trying to force Vee into what he wanted, and went limp, sliding over the edge into subspace. Above him, Vee caught his breath and picked up speed. Kellen floated, pleasure coiling at the base of his spine as Vee fucked him harder, faster, picking Kellen's legs up and slinging them over his shoulders so he could drive deeper with every thrust.

Vee went rigid, arms stiffening, and then he slumped forward. He let Kellen's legs slide off his shoulders and pulled out. His hot mouth was on Kellen's cock before Kellen could make a sound, fingers sliding back into his hole, slippery in the mess he'd left behind.

He worked Kellen over fast and ruthless, drawing his orgasm up and out with skilled touches until Kellen clutched his head, crying out as he spilled in Vee's mouth.

Only then did he let go and crawl up the bed. "Do you understand now?" he whispered.

Kellen, still half-floating in subspace, turned his head to look at him but couldn't remember how to speak.

Vee touched his mouth. "I'm just as addicted to you, baby."

Kellen blinked and tried to form words.

"I love you," Vee said, eyes intent on Kellen's face. "I'm with you. And we'll do this together."

Kellen closed his eyes and nodded. He wanted, so much, to say it back, but Vee didn't push him. He just laid a butterfly-soft kiss on the corner of Kellen's mouth and pulled him close.

———

HE WOKE him up early the next morning, rubbing his shoulder as Kellen lay on his stomach in bed.

Kellen twitched, rolled over, and yawned. "Hey," he said, blinking sleep out of his eyes.

Vee bent to kiss him. "How are you feeling?"

Kellen put his hand over his mouth. "Morning-breathy," he said, voice muffled but eyes amused.

Vee sat back with a laugh. "And mentally?"

"Okay, I guess?" Kellen said. "Why?"

Vee took his hand, running his thumb over the knuckles. "I'm afraid what happened yesterday could… happen again. If I'm not around."

Kellen raised his eyebrows. "Ah." He shrugged. "I feel fine, Vee, really." A smile flashed across his face. "Kinda sore, but otherwise fine."

"Where… did you go?" Vee asked haltingly.

Kellen's face clouded.

"Was it like subspace?"

Kellen shook his head. "No. It wasn't… subspace makes me feel safe. Protected, even when I'm flying. This was… empty." He shivered, folding his arms across his ribs.

"Okay," Vee said hastily. "We don't have to talk about it. But do you think you'll be okay alone?"

"Well, I'll be with Monica," Kellen pointed out.

"Can you have her keep an eye on you, make sure she texts me if you start acting funny?"

"*You're* acting funny," Kellen muttered. He rolled his eyes when Vee just waited. "Fine, I'll ask her, okay?"

"Thank you," Vee whispered. He bent to kiss him, catching Kellen's hand when he tried to fend him off again. "Morning breath doesn't scare me," he murmured, and pressed their mouths together.

When he finally raised his head, Kellen was dazed and rumpled. Vee smiled down at him.

"I have to get to work. Have a good day."

Vᴇᴇ ᴡᴀᴛᴄʜᴇᴅ the time impatiently until Dominic and Farid arrived at the office. As soon as they did, he packed a basket, pulled some coffees, and ducked upstairs.

Farid was at his desk and he smiled at the sight of him. "I could get used to this."

Vee hesitated at the sight of Dominic, sitting in one of the chairs.

Farid's eyes sharpened on Vee's form and he frowned. "Something happened. What happened?"

"I can leave," Dominic offered, half out of his chair.

"No, it's okay," Vee said, setting the basket down and collapsing in a chair. "I shared a scene with you, sort of. And you know what's been going on. Kellen and I sort of... it wasn't *really* a fight, but there was yelling, and, um... crying? And then Kellen—" He rubbed his face. "He like, had a break with reality or something. I don't know how else to describe it. He was conscious but nonverbal, he'd respond to cues but it was like he... wasn't there."

"Dissociative episode," Farid said. "How did you get him through it?"

"I sort of panicked," Vee admitted. "We'd been talking about how he didn't deserve what had happened to him, and he *did* deserve a family that loved him, and that's when he… checked out. So I… took him to my parents'."

Farid's eyebrows went up. "Interesting. Why?"

"He needed love," Vee said, clenching his hands on the chair to keep them from shaking. "So I took him to the place that could give him the most love possible. We stayed there all afternoon. He came around fairly quickly but he was shaky and out of it for awhile longer. It scared the fuck out of me, 'Rid."

"I imagine so," Farid said, his eyes sympathetic. "It was an out of the box solution, but it sounds like it worked well. Good instincts."

"I love him," Vee blurted.

"I gathered as much," Farid said calmly. "What does he feel?"

"I—he hasn't said it back." Vee pressed a hand to his sternum, to the bubble of emptiness there. "I think he wants to—there are times when it's like he almost gets up the nerve but then loses it just before he commits. I haven't pushed him."

"So you want to know what to do now?"

"I don't know how to fix him," Vee said miserably.

"You can't," Farid said. He picked up a muffin from the basket and handed it to Dominic. "He's the only one who can fix himself. But you can help him get there faster."

"How?"

Farid held up three fingers and put them down one at a time. "Psychiatrist. Therapist. Medication."

"You think he needs a shrink?" Vee asked, startled.

"I think he's broken in ways we can't even comprehend," Farid said levelly. "Just because the fractures are in his mind and not his body doesn't make them less valid. He went to the hospital for his broken ankle, didn't he?"

"No, of course," Vee said. "I just... I didn't think of it. What do I need to do?"

"You need to find him a therapist to help work through his past trauma and address it properly, and he'll need a psychiatrist who can work with him on medication. Maybe he'll get lucky and won't need the medicine long, just until he levels out. Or maybe he'll need it all his life." Farid pulled out his phone. "I'll give you some names."

"And I'll pay for them," Dominic inserted.

Farid and Vee both turned to look at him, startled.

"You don't have to do that," Vee began.

"He doesn't have insurance, does he?" Dominic said. "I thought not. Then you're not going to be able to afford a decent shrink. 'Rid, find him a good one and a better therapist and get it set up. Have them bill me." He stood. "Gotta get to work. Vee, it was a pleasure. I hope Kellen finds the help he needs soon."

The office was silent after he left and Vee looked at Farid.

"Why would he do that?"

Farid's eyes were warm, fixed on the doorway Dominic had vanished through. "Because he's a good man. And maybe, partly, because he didn't have the chance to help someone else once and he's never forgiven himself for that." His voice dropped. "Even though it was my fault."

Vee waited but Farid didn't elaborate.

"Okay," Vee said after a few minutes. "Would you… thank him for me?"

Farid nodded. "I'll get the appointments set up and text you the details."

"Any afternoon after three p.m.," Vee said, standing. "I'll tell you how he's doing. And 'Rid—thank *you*."

Farid waved him off, smiling. "Go do some actual work."

* * *

HE GOT the text from Farid as he was clocking out for the day. A name and address, with a note.

Appointment is next week, Thursday, 4 p.m. She works with the BDSM community.

Vee texted him back. *That was fast. Thanks again.*

Helps to have connections, was Farid's reply.

* * *

VEE WAS on edge climbing up the stairs. Kellen was getting out of the shower when he walked in, and Vee set the usual bag of pastries down and went into his arms.

"You didn't see him again, did you?" Kellen asked, his voice careful.

Vee shook his head. "Just… glad to see you." He eased back and brushed a quick kiss across Kellen's mouth. "Listen, there's something I want to talk to you about."

"Do I have to be naked for it?"

Vee pretended to consider, and Kellen shoved at his shoulder, fighting a smile, and bent to pick up his clothes.

"Would you be willing to talk to a therapist?" Vee asked, following him into the kitchen. If he hadn't been watching for it, he wouldn't have noticed the slight hesitation in Kellen's stride.

"About what?" Kellen reached for the bag and pulled out a croissant.

"You know what about," Vee said softly. "Kell...."

Kellen didn't look at him, taking a bite of the croissant and sitting down on the couch, his legs tucked under him.

Vee sat down beside him, careful not to touch him, and waited.

Kellen ate his croissant, staring straight ahead.

"You *do* think I'm broken, then," he said after a minute.

"*No*," Vee protested, aching to take his hand, but something in Kellen's posture told him not to try. "It's not—I love you exactly as you are. Your experiences *made* you who you are. But there's...." He scrubbed his hands through his hair, searching for the words. "There's some shit in your past that you *have* to deal with. You can't just hide it and pretend it's not there. Bad stuff happened to you. It wasn't your fault but you still have to *face it*."

"Why?" Kellen whispered, his voice smaller than Vee had ever heard it.

"So you can heal," Vee said, and Kellen's body softened as he leaned toward him. Vee gathered him in with breathless relief, holding him close. "I want you to be the happiest and healthiest version of you there is," he murmured against Kellen's damp hair.

"Therapists cost money. I don't have insurance."

"It's taken care of," Vee said.

Kellen pulled back, eyes narrowing. "You?"

"No," Vee said.

If anything, that made Kellen look *more* suspicious. "Who else knows or cares about me?"

"More than just me," Vee said, his heart twisting. "But it was Dom. Farid's boyfriend. Do you have any idea how rich he is?"

Kellen shook his head.

"Pretty sure he doesn't know either," Vee said. "He won't even notice the cost, and I think… I think it's helping him, too. To be *able* to help someone."

"You want this?" Kellen asked, his eyes carefully considering.

"Yes," Vee said. "I do, Kell, I think… it's important."

"Then I'll do it."

"Good, because it's next week," Vee said, and ducked the mock-punch Kellen threw at him, tugging him close again. "I love you," he said against the top of his head.

Kellen sighed. "You're a manipulative bastard." The squeeze of his hand on Vee's bicep took any sting out of the words.

Vee's phone buzzed and he twisted to pull it out of his pocket. "Oh, it's for you."

Kellen took it and a smile spread over his face. "Star wants to hang out."

"Yeah? You should go!"

Kellen blinked and looked up at him. "You wouldn't mind?"

"Of course not, why would I?"

Kellen ducked his head, looking back at the phone. "No reason."

Jacob, Vee was willing to wager, and he was careful not to let the spike of fury show.

"You should go," he repeated.

"I wouldn't be out late," Kellen said, texting as he spoke.

"It'd be fine if you were."

"And I'll tell you where we're going."

Vee caught his chin and turned his head. "I'm not your nanny. Stay out as long as you want, go wherever you feel like going, drink as much as you want, just don't drive if you're drunk."

Kellen opened and closed his mouth. "You don't mind being left by yourself?"

Vee grinned. "A night on my own? I'm gonna watch shitty kung-fu movies in my underwear all night. I can't wait."

Kellen wrinkled his nose but couldn't fight the smile as he returned his attention to the phone. "I'm meeting her in an hour."

"I'll text her if I need you while you're gone, but you need your own phone. Wanna go with me this weekend to look at options?"

"Sure, but I'm paying for it," Kellen said, handing Vee's phone back.

"Duh," Vee said, and tickled him until Kellen was squirming and begging for mercy.

"Did you know tickling is an actual kink?" Kellen asked once they'd stopped the horseplay and he was draped idly across Vee's lap. "Like, people pay to be tickled."

"I'm learning that the BDSM world is vast and full of weird corners that are probably best to avoid," Vee said. "I found out about sounding cages when I was researching cock cages and I'm not sure my balls will ever crawl back out of my body." He shivered and Kellen laughed.

"They're not so bad. Well… no, they are. But some people like it, you know? They need it." His eyes shuttered briefly. "It sucks to need something so badly that you're willing to do anything to get it."

Vee brushed Kellen's hair off his forehead. "It's better, for you. Right? It hasn't been as bad?"

Kellen bumped Vee's hand with his head. "It's so much better," he said, and something in Vee's chest relaxed. "It's still there—I can feel it, the urge, the… need, I guess, to feel the pain and let go? But it's like I can push it aside now, focus on other stuff. Before, all I could think about was when I could get to the club and find a Dom. Now I think about all kinds of things. Monica made me ride two-point *without stirrups* today." He sounded outraged and Vee couldn't help his laugh. Kellen glared at him. "It was *torture*."

"You *just* got done saying you liked torture," Vee pointed out, and Kellen pinched him. "Ow! Watch it, I'm not the painslut!"

"Fuck you," Kellen said, laughing.

"Okay," Vee agreed, and Kellen's laughter cut off. Vee watched his face, the suspicion and confusion forming. "What is it about topping that bothers you so much?" he finally asked.

Kellen sighed and dropped his head back into Vee's lap. "It—I don't take control. I don't *want* to take control. If I'm in control, I can't fly. You don't hit subspace, do you?"

Vee shook his head, stroking Kellen's hair. "Honestly, it feels more like a runner's high. Everything's heightened, my senses are sharpened, and it's like I have a good buzz, but I don't *fly*. Not the way you do. And I did, once. I ever tell you about that?"

"You subbed?" Kellen looked stunned.

"Farid introduced me to friends of his, a professional Dom and his sub. The Dom—Sanyam—said before I could safely take on a sub, I needed to know what it was like to submit. So… I did."

Kellen rolled his head to look up at him. "What did you think?"

"I hated it, mostly," Vee admitted. "The feeling of being exposed and vulnerable—" He grimaced. "Not for me. But I did eventually let go and hit subspace, and yeah…." He stroked Kellen's cheek. "I see why you like it so much. But that's why, huh? You just don't want to be the one in control. You know I can top you from the bottom, right?"

"Yeah, but—" Kellen shrugged. "Not for me," he parroted, and Vee laughed.

"You should get dressed, unless you're wearing ratty sweats out for drinks."

"Shit, Star!" Kellen scrambled to his feet, nearly tripping over his pant legs, and fled for the bedroom.

13

———

Kellen met Star at her favorite club, The Orange Robin. She was dressed in a spangly outfit that draped off one shoulder and made her dark skin glow, her hair pulled up into a perfect mohawk.

"They specialize in alcoholic citrus drinks," she said, giving Kellen a kiss on the cheek. "You're not leaving here *not* drunk. Come tell me about all the horrible things Monica's been doing to you."

"Two-point," Kellen groaned. "*Without stirrups.*"

"We're gonna need a lot of alcohol," Star said.

———

Four hours later, Star poured him out of the taxi onto the sidewalk in front of Vee's apartment.

"You… sure y'don't need help?" she slurred.

Kellen waved her off, vague and uncoordinated. "Be fine. G'home. Thanks… for, y'know."

Star hiccuped, giggled, and slid back into the taxi.

Truthfully, worry was threading its way through the alcohol mist in Kellen's brain. Vee hadn't texted Star about him once. He'd been gone for *hours* and Vee hadn't asked where he was or what they were doing.

He was angry Kellen had gone out after all and was punishing him. That was all there was to it. Kellen blinked muzzily and firmed his jaw. He'd just tell him—he'd explain, and apologize, until Vee understood and forgave him.

He made his way up the stairs as quickly as he dared as the world tilted around him dangerously. Halfway up, something crashed from Vee's apartment and dread lanced through Kellen's stomach. He was *breaking* things, he was so angry.

Run away, a tiny part of his alcohol-soaked brain urged him.

No. Kellen started climbing again. This was Vee. He'd understand, eventually, and if he had to hurt Kellen a little bit before forgiving him, well… he'd accepted more from worse people. Even welcomed it, once.

He got to the door and managed to push it open just as another crash came, shaking the walls. The door swung wide to reveal Vee in his boxers, standing stock-still in the middle of the tiny living room, arms up in some sort of defensive pose, his foot—Kellen's brain snagged and stuck. He went back over the details, very carefully. Vee. Boxers. Arms. Foot—yep, still through the lampshade. Kellen looked up slowly.

Vee looked ashamed. Embarrassed. But not angry. "Uh… hi," he said.

Kellen glanced past him to the laptop still playing a movie on the couch. A *kung fu* movie.

Crashing noises. Kung fu movies. Vee's defensive pose. The penny dropped.

Kellen couldn't stop the laugh and didn't try as Vee blushed bright red under his olive skin.

"You—" Kellen clung to the doorknob to keep his balance. "You were—"

"I was practicing my kung fu moves, yes, shut up," Vee said. He very carefully disentangled the lampshade from his foot, hopping on the other to remove it, and Kellen gave up on being upright.

He let the delight peal out as he slid down the door and onto the floor, holding his ribs and laughing until there were tears rolling down his cheeks and his stomach ached. At some point, Vee sat down on the floor next to him, but Kellen couldn't get his breath. Every time he looked at Vee's face, it sent him off into another fit of giggles.

Vee's mouth twitched and he rubbed it, trying to hide the smile. "It's not that funny," he complained.

"It's *hilarious*," Kellen gasped, wiping his eyes. "You—I can't breathe—the *poor lamp*—" He flopped onto his back, still clutching his ribs, and howled.

Then Vee was laughing too, on the floor beside him, his shoulders shaking. "I looked like an idiot, didn't I?" he managed.

"I have never—" Kellen dragged in air and

hiccuped a giggle. "Never seen anything so dumb in my *life*. Oh my *god*, I love you *so much!*"

Vee went very still, beside him, his eyes suddenly dark and unreadable. "What?"

Kellen tried to muffle the laughter and remember what he'd said. "I said… oh." He looked up, into Vee's face as he propped himself on one elbow above him. There were tears gathering in his eyes.

"Say it again," he begged.

"I love you," Kellen managed, and the first tear slid shining down Vee's cheek.

Vee dashed a hand across his eyes and leaned in to kiss him. "Am I going to have to put my foot through another lamp to hear it again? Because I'll do it. I'll buy out a lamp *warehouse*, just clean them out, you won't be able to *walk*—"

"Shut up," Kellen interrupted, laughing. He reached up and pulled Vee down against him. "I love you, I love you, I love you. Okay? No more lamp carnage."

"The neighbors must be *pissed*," Vee murmured against his mouth.

Kellen giggled again. "Take me to bed, you idiot."

* * *

Vee's phone beeped one morning and he rolled over to look at it, blinking at the screen.

Sorry for delay, the text read. *Tickets for u at Will Call. See u after game tonight?*

Vee punched the air in delight as Kellen emerged from the bathroom, toweling his hair dry.

"What are you so happy about?"

"Got plans tonight?"

Kellen shook his head. "Did you want to go out?"

"Embry got back to me. They're playing the Sirens tonight and he's left tickets for us at the stadium." Vee grinned as Kellen's face lit up. "Wanna go to a hockey game with me?"

"*Hell* yeah," Kellen said. He dropped the towel and jumped on the bed. Vee grabbed him and rolled so Kellen was underneath him, then nosed his way down his chest, slowly filling out and adding muscle, kissing and licking the soft skin, until he came to Kellen's dick, rapidly hardening against his thigh. Vee hummed, wrapping his lips around the head.

Kellen's abs tensed and one hand came up to tangle in Vee's hair, and Vee smiled and went to work in earnest.

It didn't take long at all—rarely did, when Vee put his mind to it. Within minutes, Kellen curled forward with a helpless noise and his cock thickened as he came in heavy spurts down Vee's throat.

Vee swallowed it, easing Kellen through it and then planting small kisses all over the crown and down the shaft as Kellen did his best puddle impression on the mattress.

"Your turn?" Kellen slurred.

Vee shook his head, smiling, and crawled up his body to kiss him. "Good morning."

Kellen sighed against his mouth, wrapping his arms around Vee's neck. He did that a lot, Vee had noticed, like he needed the connection, maybe a reminder that he was safe, or just something to hold onto. Whatever his reason, Vee didn't care—he loved it.

They made out leisurely for a few minutes, Vee exploring Kellen's mouth in languid, slow sweeps of his tongue as the sun crept across the bed.

When he pulled away and glanced down, Kellen was soft again. *Perfect.* Vee reached for the cock cage he'd stashed in the drawer the night before and held it up.

Kellen went rigid, eyes wide. "Vee—"

Vee put a finger to his lips and scooted down the bed. He'd practiced with the contraption a few times, so it was relatively easy to feed Kellen's cock into the cage and lock the ring behind his balls. He reached up again and grabbed the lube, smearing a little around the metal to keep it from chafing, and then looked up.

Kellen was very still, but every muscle was tense.

"How does it feel?" Vee asked.

"It's... f-fine," Kellen managed.

"Good. Roll over."

If possible, Kellen's eyes got even wider. "V-Vee—"

Vee paused in retrieving the plug from the drawer. "Hm?"

"You just said—we're doing this now? You're taking me to a *hockey game* like this?"

"Am I?" Vee said, as if the thought hadn't occurred to him. "How interesting." He patted Kellen's thigh. "Roll over."

"Oh *god.*" Kellen rolled over and buried his face in the pillow, knuckles white on the bedspread as Vee took his time coating the plug with lube. Then he gently spread Kellen's cheeks and pressed the plug inside. It had a flared base to keep it securely seated, and was just long enough to brush against Kellen's prostate if he bent too deeply at the waist, but otherwise would simply keep him open, reminding him of Vee's presence without a hand on him.

Kellen stifled a noise against the pillow as his hips jerked and Vee soothed him with a hand on his back.

"Relax and take it, baby." He pushed it in the rest of the way and stroked the skin around it, making sure it was settled in place. "Comfortable?"

"*No*," Kellen said, glaring over his shoulder at him.

Vee couldn't help his laugh. "Hey, I did you a favor—I made you come *before* I put it on, didn't I? Or would you rather I let you dangle?"

"I'd rather you didn't do this to me the day I'm going to see my first hockey game," Kellen gritted.

Vee bent and kissed the wing of his shoulder blade, the scars rough under his lips.

"Your first?"

Kellen made a noise against his forearm.

Vee kissed his shoulder again. "You know what to say," he murmured. "We don't have to do this at all. If you'd rather take it out and we'll just enjoy the game—"

Kellen was very still for a minute and then rolled over. There were nerves in his eyes and in the set of his mouth, but he shook his head.

Vee sat back on his knees, narrowing his eyes. "I don't want you doing this because you feel you have to. Kell, you have to promise me—if it's too much, you *will* safeword. I won't punish you, baby. I have to know you're okay with this."

Kellen sat up and caught Vee's face, pressing their mouths together in a hot, urgent kiss. "I want this," he whispered when they broke apart. "I hate you a bit right now but I do, I want this."

Vee relaxed and kissed him back. "Okay then. Are you hungry? I'll make us breakfast."

<hr>

THE GAME WAS in the afternoon, something Kellen was grateful for. If he'd had to go through an entire day with the plug rubbing against his rim and the cage keeping him soft, he thought he might lose his mind.

They spent the morning quietly, going out for a short walk to see how Kellen handled movement. He was awkward at first, moving hesitantly, but it didn't take long before he was able to take longer steps. Finally he nodded, and Vee squeezed his hand.

"Sure?"

"Yeah," Kellen said. "It's—I can do it."

They went home for lunch, Kellen practicing sitting as Vee made grilled cheese sandwiches with bread from the bakery, humming to himself.

"How ya doing, champ?" he called as Kellen shifted his weight again.

Kellen shot him a glare that had absolutely no effect. "Uncomfortable," he said through his teeth. "You're an asshole."

Vee laughed, sliding a sandwich onto a plate.

"You wanted this, remember? I'm just trying to be a good boyfriend and give you what you want."

"Ugh." Kellen shifted his weight, and Vee came to stand over him.

"Hey." He tipped Kellen's chin up. "Think about tonight." His eyes were warm with affection. "Think about how it's going to feel, out with thousands of people who have no idea what's going on, but *you'll* know. Every little movement, every time you turn or shift or bend, you're going to feel me around you. Inside you, filling you—"

Kellen shoved him away hard enough to make Vee stumble, hunching forward. Arousal made his head spin, careening through his veins, and he sucked in air in desperate gasps as Vee rubbed his shoulder.

"Deep breaths," Vee said, and he sounded amused but also sympathetic. "Deep, slow breaths, there you go."

It took a few minutes for Kellen to recover his bearings and lift his head. Vee smiled down at him.

"Hungry?"

"God, you really are a sadist," Kellen said, and Vee laughed, bending to kiss him.

"I never used to think I was, but the way you react—it's addictive. You're so beautiful."

Kellen grumbled but kissed him back.

THEY TOOK the train to the stadium and Kellen almost forgot his body's conflicted signals in his surprise at the size of the crowd when they arrived.

"I didn't realize it was such a big deal," he said wonderingly as they joined the streams of people heading for the entrance.

"Hockey's finally picking up a following in the Pacific Northwest," Vee said. His hands were shoved in his pockets, watching everything around them, but somehow Kellen had the feeling he was fully focused on him. It was comforting, knowing he was so close. They could stop anytime. He moved closer so their shoulders were brushing, and was rewarded with a quick, brilliant smile.

Tickets retrieved from Will Call, Vee inspected them as they headed for the huge doors.

"Holy shit," he mumbled, looking closer. "How the fuck did he swing that?"

"What?" Kellen asked, leaning in to look.

"We're right behind the visiting players' bench," Vee told him. "Close enough to touch, practically."

Kellen was nearly vibrating. "You never told me how you know him."

They made their way through the huge concrete stadium as Vee explained.

"We were good friends in high school. Kind of drifted apart after, but he came to my college graduation ceremony, and I try to go see his games every chance I get. He's a great guy, you're gonna really like him."

Kellen jerked to a stop. "I'm going to *meet him?*"

"Well… yeah," Vee said, guiding them out of the path of the crowd. "I want to see him again, it's been awhile. You don't have to if you—"

"No, I *do*," Kellen interrupted. "Just—" He gestured vaguely and Vee's eyes crinkled.

"Should be fun," he said, and dodged Kellen's half-hearted shove, laughing.

***

THEY FOUND their seats and sat through the warmups, the flashing lights, the mascot getting the crowd in on the action, the music so loud it thudded through Kellen's bones. Every time he moved, the plug reminded him of its presence, but he was only half-aware of it, too focused on the swirling flow of the players in white and teal on one end and purple and gold on the other.

Vee took his hand and Kellen flashed him a grin. Vee pointed to a tall figure near the goalie.

"That's Embry," he said. "Do you have a favorite player on the Birds?"

"Saint, but he's everyone's favorite, isn't he?"

"You're *my* favorite," Vee said.

Kellen wrinkled his nose at him. "Disgusting."

Vee laughed, and then leaned forward to bang on the glass as Embry stepped onto the bench. Embry was even more imposing up close in his pads and skates, keen blue-gray eyes lighting up at the sight of Vee. He waved and Vee pointed at Kellen, who waved back weakly, feeling stupid. Embry's smile widened and then the lights dimmed and a young girl came out to sing the national anthem.

THE GAME WAS A BLUR. Kellen was proud of himself for being able to keep up with most of it, although half the time he didn't understand the refs' whistles or why a fight had started. Vee wasn't much help, shrugging when Kellen turned to ask why someone was fighting yet again.

"Embry's said they've had a problem with the captain—Saint—taking a lot of hits. Maybe that's what it is?"

Whatever the reason, there seemed to be a fight happening every time Kellen got his bearings. The Seabirds scored, then the Sirens. Saint seemed to be everywhere on the ice, a blur of movement always two steps ahead of his opponents. He sank a puck and his team collided with him in a joyous celebration. Kellen cheered, breaking off with a gasp as the movement reminded him of the plug.

Beside him, Vee smiled and Kellen glared at him. Vee's smile just widened and he took Kellen's hand. *Mine*, his eyes said, and Kellen swallowed, the game forgotten in the heat of Vee's gaze.

THE SEABIRDS LOST by a slim margin, the Sirens scoring just before the final buzzer to pull ahead by one. Vee patted Kellen's hand and stood.

"Probably for the best," he said as Kellen gathered himself. "If they'd won, they'd want to go out and celebrate, and Embry would invite us along, and I kind of just want to take you home already."

"But we're still meeting the team?" Kellen asked as he followed him from the row.

Vee laughed at him over his shoulder, leading

the way up the steps. "Yes, we're still meeting them. If you think you can handle it."

THEY HAD to wait in the hallway as the team showered and dealt with the press. Embry had sent word they were to be allowed in, so other than a few curious glances from staff, they were left alone. Finally, Embry himself came out into the hall. He was smaller without all his gear on but still strikingly handsome, a friendly smile on his face as he hugged Vee and then turned to Kellen, hand out.

"Embry Rather," he said.

"Yeah, I know," Kellen said, shaking his hand. "That was a really close game."

Embry shrugged. "Can't win 'em all. 'Specially not when Saint's out there getting dirty hits put on him all the time. Speaking of, you wanna come in and meet him and the rest of them?"

MEETING the team was a confusing mishmash of loud voices and half-naked men towering over Kellen. Saint was the only one close to his size, brown eyes intense but his smile friendly, if somewhat distant. He asked if Kellen liked the game and Kellen said something—he wasn't even sure what, but it seemed to do the trick. Saint's smile widened and then Embry was pulling them away, to a corner where they could talk without having to shout.

"We're heading back tonight but not until

later," Embry said. "You guys wanna hang out, grab some dinner with us?"

Out with the team. Under any other circumstances, Kellen would have leapt at the chance. He moved and the plug shifted, making him catch his breath. He slanted a look at Vee, who got the hint immediately.

"I'm not feeling a hundred percent," he said easily. "Probably something I ate. Next time you're in town, yeah?"

"For sure," Embry agreed. He held out a hand to Kellen and then pulled Vee into a hug. "It was great seeing you. Text me more often, eh?"

THE RIDE HOME was somehow worse than the trip to the stadium. Every nerve in Kellen's body seemed to be overloaded, making him jittery and unable to hold still, which of course just made it worse, the plug grinding against his prostate until Kellen thought he'd lose his mind.

Vee put a hand on his thigh as Kellen squirmed. "Be still," he said, soft but with that note of command in his voice.

Kellen took a shuddery breath and let it out slowly. It took a few minutes to relax his muscles, and his leg still wanted to bounce with nervous anticipation, but Vee's hand pressing down helped. When he was finally still, Vee smiled at him, sweet as a sunrise.

"You're doing so well," he said, and the pride in his voice made warmth expand in Kellen's chest. "Almost there."

He crowded close to Kellen all the way up the stairs to their front door, pushing it open and Kellen through in almost the same motion. Socks and shoes went flying and then he was advancing on Kellen with fierce intent in his eyes.

Kellen backed up fast, through the living room and into the bedroom, where he hit the bed and fell backward onto it, grunting as the plug shifted inside him. Vee was on him before Kellen could rearrange himself, mouth hot and needy on Kellen's as he pushed up his shirt and tugged at his belt buckle. Kellen helped as much as he could, lifting his hips so Vee could shove his jeans down.

"I've been going crazy," Vee panted, yanking Kellen's shirt off. His hands seemed to be everywhere, mapping out Kellen's skin under his fingers as if he'd never felt it before, memorizing every inch of him, and Kellen arched into it with a moan.

"*You've* been going crazy?" he managed as Vee pushed him farther up the bed and settled himself between his knees. He spread his legs and Vee laughed, ducking his head to blow warm air across Kellen's trapped cock. "*Don't*," Kellen gasped, but Vee just looked up at him, eyes dark with promise, and went back to it. His fingers were warm as they traced his flesh through the thin metal bars and Kellen stifled a groan with a hand stuffed in his mouth as his body responded.

"You know I could make you come with this on?" Vee asked, stroking the skin of Kellen's inner thigh. "I've been doing some reading. I could milk your prostate for *hours* and make you come while you're soft."

Horror turned Kellen's bones to ice. He couldn't do that. Surely Vee wouldn't do that *to* him. But Vee was removing the plug, smiling wickedly up at him, and then two fingers probed his hole.

Kellen clutched at the bedspread as Vee pushed inside. His cock was trying desperately to respond, trying to harden, but it couldn't, trapped as it was in the cage. It was agony, Vee's fingers sliding deep, stretching him open. Vee took his time pressing idly in and out, too random for Kellen to predict.

Kellen's ears were roaring, his mouth dry, every atom of his being focused on Vee's movements.

Vee added some more lube, expression serene as if he had all the time in the world, and pushed back in with three fingers. He twisted his hand, knuckle catching on Kellen's rim and making him jerk and cry out. Vee soothed him with his free hand on Kellen's thigh, stroking it gently even as he drove deeper. He found his prostate and rubbed, and Kellen came up off the bed with a wild shout. Vee caught him, pinned him down, held him there as Kellen shook, fingers still probing deep inside, finding and nailing that bundle of nerves with every pass.

It was too much. He'd been worked up all day, on a roller coaster of emotions, and Vee had settled in between his legs with an expression Kellen knew very well—it said he was focused on his task and he wasn't going to stop until he was satisfied, and Kellen... couldn't do it. He couldn't face the torture of an hour or more of Vee milking his prostate and not letting him come properly, he *couldn't*.

He choked on a sob. "*Satin*," he said, and Vee froze as Kellen burst into tears.

Then he was pulling out, scrambling up Kellen's body and gathering him into his arms. Kellen clutched at him, babbling incoherently.

"Shh, breathe," Vee said, rocking him gently. "Deep breaths, sweetheart."

"I'm s-sorry," Kellen managed through his tears, "I'm sorry, I didn't m-mean to—"

"Yes you did, and I'm glad you did," Vee interrupted. "Can you tell me why?"

"It—" Kellen hiccuped. "Too much. I couldn't—"

"You were too overstimulated already?" Vee translated, and Kellen nodded, rubbing his wet face against Vee's chest. Vee tipped his chin up and kissed him. "I'm so proud of you," he whispered, and pressed their lips together again, exploring Kellen's mouth with slow, gentle sweeps.

Kellen couldn't kiss back very well, thoughts muzzy and indistinct, but Vee didn't seem to mind. Kellen felt almost like he was sliding into subspace, his world fraying around the edges, and Vee hadn't even touched him yet, not really.

"Earth to gorgeous," Vee said, sounding affectionate. "I'm not ready for you to check out on me just yet."

Kellen made a mighty effort to concentrate. "Why—why do you call me that?"

Vee looked puzzled. "Because you are, and I'm not very creative with pet names?"

"B-but—" Kellen motioned toward his back. "I'm… broken. You've seen—"

"You're *not*," Vee said, and set him back on the bed. His hands were quick and careful as he removed the cock cage, checking for any chafing, and then he helped him upright, turning him so they both faced the mirror that hung over the bed, Vee's chest pressed to Kellen's back. "Look at yourself," Vee ordered.

Kellen looked. His hair was longer, falling into his eyes even more, but every time he mentioned getting it cut, Vee ran his fingers through it and Kellen decided to wait a little longer. His face wasn't as lean as it had been when they'd met, but the scars still covered his chest and back, thick and ropy and ugly.

He said as much, and Vee shook his head.

"You've got it all backwards. They're not ugly. They're proof of life." He touched one over Kellen's rib and Kellen caught his breath. "They're beautiful, because they show me that you're here. With me. Can't you see that? Can't you see what a miracle you are?"

Kellen squeezed his eyes shut but the tears escaped anyway, scalding his cheeks, and Vee gathered him closer.

"Look in the mirror," he said, and Kellen opened his eyes. Blunt pressure nudged his hole and Kellen's mouth fell open as Vee slid inside, a slow, steady push until he was buried to the hilt. Kellen was stretched and spread, every nerve lighting up like fireflies under his skin. His head dropped back but Vee caught his hair and pulled him upright again. "*Look*," he said, slipped out, and slammed home.

Kellen was helpless against it, held in place with an arm around his waist and the other in his hair, sensations drowning him as Vee pounded in ruthlessly and Kellen watched them in the mirror.

Vee looked almost angry, as if determined to show Kellen what he saw. He bit down on Kellen's shoulder and then he shifted his angle and Kellen lost his grip on reality as Vee found his prostate. He let go, falling through the endless black, stars cascading behind his eyes, safe in Vee's arms.

"Mine," Vee said from a thousand miles away and right next to his ear as his hand found Kellen's cock. "Mine, and *beautiful*. Come for me, Kellen. Come *now*."

Kellen's head fell back again and this time Vee let it happen, stroking Kellen through his ecstasy in quick, short pumps of his fist. Kellen finally collapsed against him, head heavy, and Vee's hips sped up.

"Fuck, *fuck*," he muttered under his breath, slammed deep, and pulsed thick and heavy in Kellen's core. It took forever and no time at all for him to shudder through the dregs of the orgasm, shaking as he held Kellen upright.

Finally, he eased out and helped Kellen lie down on his side. Kellen, still spaced and out of it, lay quietly as Vee padded to the bathroom and came back with a warm cloth.

Kellen reached for him with an unsteady hand. "Vee—"

Vee knelt beside the bed, taking his hand. "What is it, sweetheart?"

Kellen opened his mouth. Closed it on the words. He couldn't say them. It wasn't right.

"Stay," he said instead, tightening his grip.

"Wild horses and all that," Vee said, climbing into the bed behind him and kissing the nape of his neck.

Kellen sighed and fell off the edge into oblivion.

"Nervous?" Vee asked.

Kellen let Jupiter's saddle flap drop and shook his head.

"Liar," Vee said, affection in his voice.

It was early, the sun barely up, but already the arena behind the trailer was filling with people warming up their horses, some taking them over the small jumps, others sticking to the edges of the ring.

"Okay, I'm nervous," Kellen said. "Might puke."

Monica stepped out of the trailer and tsked. "It's a schooling show, not Aachen. Chill."

She stomped by as Vee whispered to Kellen, "What's Aachen?"

"Rolex Grand Slam," Kellen whispered back.

Vee gave him an incredulous look. "That's supposed to tell me anything?"

"Really prestigious jumping show," Star volunteered from Jupiter's other side, where she was tacking up Kitt.

"Are *you* nervous?" Vee asked.

Star laughed. "Nah, I've done a bunch of these. See you out there, K."

She led Kitt away as Vee raised his eyebrows at Kellen.

"K?"

Kellen shrugged. "She likes it."

"Well, I have to say I'm liking *you* in that getup," Vee said, leering at him.

Kellen laughed as he smoothed a palm across his new jodhpurs, brand-new and tight fitting. The tall boots were torture to get into and he suspected they'd be worse to get out of, but he secretly liked the way they looked, the gleam of the shiny black leather against the fawn of the pants.

"Seriously," Vee said. He stepped in close behind him and pressed a kiss to Kellen's shoulder. "Tell me you'll wear this to bed sometime. I'm going to be hard every second you're out there."

Kellen glanced around, made sure no one was looking at them, and surreptitiously reached between them to cup Vee's crotch. Sure enough, he was hot and hard in his jeans, and Kellen's breath caught in his throat.

Vee nipped his earlobe. "You're hot as fuck," he breathed. "I can't believe I get to touch you."

Kellen groaned and spun, chests pressed together and arms around Vee's neck to kiss him.

"Riders in the ring!" someone shouted.

Kellen pulled away and Vee made a disappointed noise but let him go. Kellen smiled as a tall man walked by in the opposite direction, face turned away to survey the riders. There was something familiar in the set of his shoulders, he thought, but Vee was handing him his reins and Kellen's stomach swooped and dipped.

Time to go out and prove he wasn't worthless.

GOD, he loved riding. He'd learned that fact the very first day he sat on Jupiter and learned that simply shifting his weight in the saddle would get the big gray horse stopping, speeding up, or turning. Monica had promised him that bridleless lessons were in his future, but for now, Kellen was just as glad to have the sense of security as Jupiter trotted serenely around the ring, seemingly unconcerned by the other entrants jostling past them.

Kellen kept his focus on posting Jupiter's trot, making sure he was on the right diagonal as he rose and fell with Jupiter's springy steps. This was where he was comfortable. The world made sense to him in two places—on a horse and in Vee's arms.

Maybe he could get Vee to ride Jupiter double with him someday, he mused, smiling to himself at the thought. Blond hair in the crowd caught his eye but it was gone when he looked again. *What is wrong with you? Pay attention!*

"Extended trot!" the announcer called, voice tinny through the loudspeaker.

Kellen asked Jupiter to lengthen his stride and they made several more circuits of the arena. There were eight of them in the class, the majority beginners like Kellen. Most of them were sloppy, even he could tell that much—their posting uneven and hands awkward on the reins—but there were two that Kellen was watching. One was a young white woman on a palomino mare, her seat solid as a rock, eyes calm and thoughtful and hands featherlight on the reins.

The other was an older Black man, his clothes somewhat shabby and his horse a rangy brown gelding of no discernible breed, but Kellen had been watching him since the beginning of the class and he had yet to actually see the man give his horse a cue. It was as if he thought it and the horse did it, flowing from walk to trot to canter and back again as smoothly as breathing.

Ahead of them, the palomino spooked at a shadow or a flapping pennant, making her rider grab mane just as the announcer said, "Canter, left lead."

Kellen shortened his reins and cued Jupiter forward into an easy canter. In front of them, the girl had recovered her equilibrium and was cantering as well. Kellen wanted to look for the man but didn't dare take his focus off what Jupiter was doing.

"Working walk, please. Working walk."

Kellen sat deep and Jupiter slammed on the brakes, going from his rocking-horse lope to a medium-speed walk, ears forward and head bobbing as they continued. Gratitude swelled inside Kellen. *Bless you, you beautiful old soul*, he thought. They might not win, but at least he hadn't embarrassed himself.

He placed second, the black man getting first and bending down to hug his lanky gelding, who seemed bored, and the girl on the palomino coming in third.

Kellen's face hurt from his smile as he rode out of the arena and swung a leg over Jupiter's shoulder to slide off. Vee was at the gate to meet him, his grin matching Kellen's.

"I had absolutely no idea what was happening but you looked *great*!"

Kellen laughed and Vee scooped him up into a jubilant hug.

"Congratulations, baby," he said against Kellen's neck. "I'm so proud of you."

"Kellen?"

Kellen turned to stone in Vee's arms, staring fixedly over his shoulder into the distance. He knew that voice, but if he didn't look, he wouldn't be there. This would be a bad dream, a hallucination or waking nightmare. *He's not here. He's not, he's not, he's not—*

Vee stiffened and sucked in air. "*You.*" Kellen tried to step back but Vee held onto him, glaring at the man Kellen knew was standing behind him.

"Let me go," Kellen said.

Vee's grip didn't loosen, fury already sparking fierce and wild in his eyes.

"*Vee.* Let me *go.*" Kellen put his hands on Vee's shoulders and shoved, breaking his embrace. He stumbled back a pace and turned, bunching Jupiter's reins in hands that were suddenly sweaty. "Hello, Father," he said, distantly grateful his voice didn't shake.

Abernathy—they'd only ever called him that, at the church. Pastor Abernathy in formal situations, but in relaxed settings, with friends and peers, he was just Abernathy. Kellen hadn't known he *had* a first name until he was nearly eight years old—was standing a few yards away, dressed in his usual black suit. His hair was thinning, the blond fading into silver, and there were more lines around his eyes and mouth. His shoulders were rounded and hunched in the jacket of his suit, his hands clutched together in front of his stooped frame.

"What are you doing here?" Vee said, the loathing thick in his voice.

Abernathy shot him a poisonous look and refocused on Kellen. "I need to speak to you, son."

"Vee, take Jupiter to the trailer."

"Oh, fuck that," Vee snapped. "I'm not leaving you alone with this man."

Kellen gave him a look that was equal parts frustration and gratitude just as Monica stalked up.

"I'll take 'im," she said, holding out her hand for the reins. "Good job out there, kiddo." She turned, looked Abernathy up and down slowly, then harrumphed disparagingly under her breath and led Jupiter away.

"Kellen—"

"Not here," Kellen interrupted. He turned away, refusing to let the trembling show, and stalked across the showgrounds until they were away from the spectators. Vee was right on his heels, eyes worried and solicitation in every line of his frame. Kellen loved him and wanted to punch him. No, that wasn't right. He wanted to punch something—someone—but it wasn't Vee. Finally he stopped and faced his father. "How did you find me?"

Abernathy's mouth twisted. "Your… friend,

Jacob. He's been keeping tabs on you, said you had a job, that you'd be here."

Vee's fists clenched and he took a step forward. "Where is he?"

"I told him it was better if I came alone," Abernathy said to Kellen, as if Vee wasn't there. "But he explained your situation and how he never touched you sexually. I'm glad you had a father figure. That you weren't completely alone."

Vee made a horrible choking noise. "That *father figure* sold him as a *prostitute* to make ends meet. That father figure used him as a *punching bag* when he had a bad day or any time Kellen did something he didn't like. He's a manipulative, evil, crawling sack of *shit*, just like you." Kellen touched his arm and Vee swung around. "You can't seriously be willing to talk to him," he said.

Kellen met his eyes. *Please understand*, he begged silently. Vee stared at him for a long moment, his mouth tight and eyes red, but finally he took an abrupt step sideways, removing himself from between Kellen and his father.

"Why are you here?" Kellen asked, knowing his voice was slightly unsteady. "I don't want you."

"I had to see you," Abernathy said. "To see for myself what you… had become."

Kellen tipped his chin up. "And?" he challenged.

"It's not too late." Abernathy took a quick step forward, and Vee tensed. "Come home, son. Renounce this wicked lifestyle. Ask forgiveness. It will be given, I promise. Ask God to take away the sinful urges. We'll find you a good Christian girl.

Take you back into the fold. You don't have to be like this. Just… come home."

Kellen stared at him. His senses were dulled, ears ringing and breath thundering in his head. Every second that ticked by seemed to pass with unbearable speed and aching slowness.

"I used to think about what I'd say to you if you found me, on the streets," he finally said. "I'd daydream about you finding me, usually after Jacob had given me to a rough john. You'd be horrified at what you'd driven me to, the bruises on my face and bloody nose, and you'd beg my forgiveness for caring more for your god than you do for your *own child*." He snapped his mouth shut abruptly as Abernathy stared at him. Kellen took a careful breath. "I stopped thinking about you before I was seventeen years old. I knew you weren't even looking for me. Do you remember, Father? Do you remember what you said the night I left?"

Abernathy looked confused. "I didn't—"

"It wasn't to me," Kellen interrupted. "You and Mother were in the den and I was going into the kitchen for a drink and I heard you. She'd said something about someone—some famous actor or singer, I don't know—coming out as gay. And you said… you said, 'I would kill him myself before I let our son be gay.'"

Vee made a small, wounded noise, but Kellen couldn't take his eyes off Abernathy's face.

"Do you remember?" he asked again. "Because I do. That first year, it was the only thing I heard in my head. *I would kill him myself.* You said that. You. My *father*. And my mother didn't argue, didn't say anything, and I knew—" He sucked in air that sliced like a knife. "I knew I didn't have a home. I didn't have a family. That I had to leave."

Abernathy opened his mouth and Kellen shook his head violently.

"*No.* Jacob was—*is*—an evil son of a bitch, but I would still take living with him over living with you in a *fucking heartbeat.*"

Abernathy flinched but Kellen wasn't done.

"The good news is, I don't have to." He put out a hand without looking and Vee caught it instantly, his grip warm and comforting. Kellen lifted his chin, daring his father to say something.

Abernathy's mouth pinched, disgust souring in his eyes.

"I love him," Kellen flung at him. He wanted the words to *hurt.* "This man, this man right here? He's a *thousand* times the man you are. He saw at my worst, my most broken and beaten down, and —" He faltered and Vee's grip tightened. "He gave me what I needed. He gave me *solace.*" Kellen shook his head. "Get away from me. Don't *ever* come looking for me again. I don't want you. I don't need you. I'm not wicked or perverted or foul or any of the things you said in my hearing about gay people. Do you know when I knew? Ten years old. *Ten years old* and realizing I liked boys, knowing you'd hate me forever if you knew the truth. Do you know what that did to me? It took me way too long to see that there's nothing wrong with being who I am, and that's *on you.*"

He turned to Vee, heartbeat a mad, racing scramble in his ears.

"Get me out of here," he whispered.

Vee moved immediately, dragging Kellen away from Abernathy—not his father, never his father, only some miserable, crawling, hate-filled slug who oozed poison like breathing. They were heading for the parking lot, Kellen realized dimly, and Vee's parents' small car that he'd borrowed for the day.

Somehow Vee got Kellen into the passenger seat and Kellen fumbled for the belt with shaking hands as Vee ran for the driver's side. He sent gravel flying as he spun the wheel and hurtled them out the gate and onto the road.

About a mile along, Kellen's stomach twisted viciously and he doubled over. "*Stop.*"

Vee stood on the brakes, the tires screeching a protest, and Kellen was out before they'd stopped moving. He just made it to the edge of the road before he vomited, heaving his guts out into the weeds in helpless waves, shaking through the acrid burn that stung his nose and made his eyes run. Vee was there, somehow, hand warm on Kellen's back, saying something Kellen couldn't understand over the roaring in his ears.

When his stomach was empty, Kellen sagged backward onto his knees. After a few minutes, he let Vee help him to his feet. His legs were spaghetti beneath him, and he barely made it to the car before collapsing. Vee tucked his feet inside and buckled him in before going back around and getting behind the wheel again.

Kellen lay against the seat and watched him for a few minutes as they drove back into the city. Then he straightened, an idea catching him. "There's somewhere I need to go."

Vee shot him an incredulous look. "*Now?*"

"Yes, now," Kellen said. "Turn here. Go straight for awhile, and then you're going to turn left on Maclean." He kept sharp watch out the window. Their surroundings crumbled into disrepair around them as Vee took them deeper into the worst part of town.

He could feel Vee's misgivings in the air, but he didn't speak. Kellen wanted to touch him, but he was filthy. Filth. He blinked against the sting of tears and straightened suddenly.

"Pull over," he said.

Vee swung to the curb and Kellen hurled himself out of the car. Dimly, he could hear Vee cursing behind him, fumbling to unbuckle and catch up, but he didn't stop to see, running straight for the familiar silhouette under the bridge, broad-shouldered and forbidding.

"*Jacob!*" he shouted.

Jacob turned. Two steps away. Jacob's mouth fell open in slow motion. Kellen hit him in the face with every ounce of the fury and hatred and grief that had poisoned him from the inside out for the past six years, and Jacob went down hard.

Kellen flung himself on top of him, straddling his chest and punching him again. One. Two. Three—his arm was caught in an iron grip and he was dragged backward, off Jacob's limp form. Vee hauled him upright and Kellen let him. On his feet, he stared down at Jacob, who looked smaller than Kellen had ever seen him, clutching his bruised jaw and moaning.

"Don't ever come near me again," Kellen said,

and kicked him in the ribs, quick and sharp. Then he turned away. "Take me home."

Vee followed him to the car, utterly mute. The silence was fraught as he drove back to the main road and turned them toward his apartment. Kellen spent the drive staring out the window. When would Vee realize he was too much to deal with? When would he tell him it wasn't going to work, and Kellen had to go? He waited, but the words didn't come. Vee drove silently, but as he pulled up in front of their building, he reached out and squeezed Kellen's knee in his torn breeches, filthy with mud and engine grease from the puddle he'd knelt in. Then he got out of the car and came around to open Kellen's door.

Kellen got himself out of the car, shaky and uncoordinated and twitched away when Vee offered him a hand up the stairs. Vee let him go without comment and they climbed in silence.

In the apartment, Vee dropped the keys and stepped out of his shoes as Kellen stood dumbly, still buzzing with adrenaline and rage. His head spun.

"How are you feeling?" Vee asked, voice careful.

"I'm angry," Kellen said baldly.

"I know, honey."

Kellen clenched his fists, knuckles of his right hand stinging. "I'm *so angry*. I want—I want to punch something again. I want to—" He swung away, impotent fury setting his veins aflame, and slammed his fist into the wall. "*I hate him!*" he screamed. He pummeled the wall for a few minutes, letting the rage scour him from the inside out, but then Vee was there, pulling him away.

"Stop, *stop*," he said, voice a warm balm of worry and love. "Kell, sweetheart, you're going to hurt yourself."

Kellen pushed him.

Vee stumbled back, mouth opening.

Kellen stalked forward and this time Vee backed up on his own, through the living room and into the bedroom. His thighs hit the mattress and he sat down hard, staring up at Kellen, who stood over him.

"Do you think I'm going to hurt you?" Kellen asked. His blood was fire and ice, seared and frozen, but his voice was… empty.

Vee would tell him to stop now. That he was too fucked up. He had to go.

But instead, Vee shook his head. "You would never hurt me," he said quietly.

"I could," Kellen said.

"But you won't." Vee's eyes were steady on his.

"I want to fuck you," Kellen said.

Vee's breath stopped. Started. Stuttered. Then he dragged his shirt off over his head and threw it on the floor. His pants joined them a minute later and he scooted up the bed until he could reach the lube.

Kellen followed him on, still fully dressed and hardening in his breeches at the sight of Vee lying beneath him, his golden skin glowing in the late morning light and eyes dark and hungry.

"You need prep." Because Vee was right. No matter how angry Kellen was, he would never hurt

Vee. Not even by accident, if he could help it. He would die first.

But Vee shook his head again, and this time he looked embarrassed. "Actually, ah—" He reached between his legs, making Kellen's dick twitch, begging to be released, and pulled a plug from his hole, lip caught between his white teeth as he tugged it out slowly.

Kellen stared at him. "You're explaining that, later," he said, and shoved his breeches to his thighs. His cock sprang free and he grabbed the lube, slicking himself up with shaking hands. Vee watched, murmuring filthy encouragement until Kellen caught his thigh and pushed his legs up and apart, bending him nearly double. He lined up his cock and drove home in one swift, punishing thrust. The perfect silken heat made him groan even as Vee writhed, pinned in place by Kellen's hands.

Kellen stayed buried deep for a long moment and then began to thrust, watching the expressions that flitted across Vee's face. There was pain, at first, but it was chased away quickly by a burgeoning pleasure that made his eyes droop, his face relaxing as he sighed and hooked his heel around Kellen's hips to pull him in deeper.

Kellen closed his eyes and established a steady rhythm, pulling almost all the way out and then slamming deep, relishing the tiny gasps and bitten off moans that spilled from Vee's mouth in an ever-increasing litany. He fucked him hard, letting the love that poured out of Vee's very existence burrow its way into his soul, soaking the dry, barren ground and nourishing the tiny, tender shoots that Vee had been planting there for months.

He was crying, he realized about halfway through. He wasn't alone anymore. He was loved. He was *worth something*. His life had meaning. He was good at something, something he loved. He loved people, and people loved him. His muscles tightened, scalp prickling, until he felt like a rubber band, stretched almost to breaking, and still he fucked his lover until Vee was thrashing, begging incoherently, tears leaking down his cheeks.

Then Kellen wrapped a hand around his cock, stroking him in hard counterpoint, driving him to the edge without mercy.

Vee flung his head back against the pillow, shouting his bliss as his body locked up punishingly tight around Kellen's cock, squeezing until it was almost impossible to move. Kellen forced his way deep and the rubber band snapped. He emptied himself on a long, shaking groan, the orgasm ripping free as stars went off behind his eyes.

Wrung out, he let Vee's legs drop and fell forward, onto Vee's chest. Vee caught and steadied him, hand stroking Kellen's hair away from his face.

"Okay?" he whispered.

Kellen shook his head and let the tears flow, the sobs forcing themselves out. The grief was a black creature hunched on his back, claws digging into his shoulders, but there was release here too, of a different kind, as he wept the poison from his soul and Vee held him, crooning to him in a voice thick with tears of his own.

He had no idea how long it was before the tears eased and he was able to take a shuddering breath, pressing his face to Vee's throat.

Vee stroked his back, fingers warm and unflinching against the scars, tracing each one he found with a sure, deft touch. *I'm here*, he told Kellen silently. *I'm here, I see you, I love you.*

Kellen fell asleep that way, tall boots still on, pants crumpled around his thighs, and Vee's arms holding him tight, caging him with love.

14

———

THREE DAYS LATER

THE THERAPIST WAS a sienna-skinned woman with dark, calm eyes and a serious face. She smiled at Kellen and introduced herself as Adriel Garcia.

"Your boyfriend can wait out here while we talk, is that alright?"

Kellen gulped and nodded, wiping his sweaty palms on his jeans. He shot a nervous look at Vee, who patted his shoulder.

"I'll be right here."

Dr. Garcia's office was done in ocean hues of blue, grey, and slate. Serene paintings graced the walls and fidget toys lined the shelves next to the chair she pointed him to. Kellen picked one up, just to give his hands something to do.

"Why don't you tell me why you're here?" Dr. Garcia said.

Kellen lifted a shoulder, studying the toy. It

spun between his fingers, the rounded prongs blurring. "Because I'm f—messed up."

"You can swear," Dr. Garcia said, crossing her legs. "Do whatever makes you comfortable. Why do you think you're messed up?"

"I lived on the streets for six years," Kellen said. "My f-friend sold me to people when we didn't have steady money. I left home when I was sixteen because I knew I was gay and my parents would disown me and throw me out, or send me to conversion camp. I wanted it to be my choice, so I walked out in the middle of the night."

Dr. Garcia said nothing, listening intently.

"And because that's not enough, I'm addicted to pain," Kellen said bluntly. "I can show you the scars."

"That's not necessary. What do you mean, addicted to pain? In a BDSM context?"

Kellen nodded, spinning the toy again. It helped to not have to look at her. "I… when I was on the streets, all I could think about was the next time I could fly. I'd sneak off to Cuffs whenever I got the chance. The meaner the Dom, the better. I wanted—" He breathed deeply, conjuring up a memory of Vee, his foot through the lampshade, and was able to relax a fraction. "I wanted to be hurt. I begged for them to do their worst, and if they wouldn't, I'd find someone on the streets to hit me, usually by picking a fight."

"No limits," Dr. Garcia said, writing something down.

"I'd never safeworded in my life before Vee."

"Tell me about Vee."

This Kellen could talk about all day. "He found me at the club. I was blackballed and Vee said he'd help me. He was afraid… of what I'd do to myself, if he didn't."

"And he helped?"

Kellen nodded. "He made me get tested, and we signed a contract to be exclusive for three months." He faltered, realizing their contract had expired and neither had noticed.

"He sounds like he's good for you."

"The best," Kellen said, throat tight. "He didn't really know what he was doing at first, but he's got friends in the community."

"That's good," Dr. Garcia said. "A support network is important. Do you have a support network, Kellen?"

"I—" Kellen shrugged and looked at his hands. "I have Vee. And I guess… Star, and Monica. My friend and boss," he explained, glancing up. "I've met Vee's family and they told me I was one of them now but—"

"You don't feel welcome there?"

"No, I *do*." Kellen struggled to find the right words but she beat him to it.

"You think you don't *deserve* to feel welcome there?"

"Yeah," Kellen whispered, slumping in his chair. He wanted Vee, the warmth of his hand, the sweet-spicy scent of his aftershave, the peace he brought with him wherever he went.

"Why not?" Dr. Garcia asked.

"Because all I do is fuck things up," Kellen said harshly. "I've never gotten it right, not once. Not even with Vee. I've hurt him. Yelled at him. *Left* him."

"He's here now, isn't he?"

"Because I got hurt and he came for me. *He* did that. *He* forgave me."

"How did he know you were hurt?"

Thrown, Kellen blinked. "I—what?"

"Was he your emergency contact?"

"No," Kellen said slowly. "They asked who to call and I gave them his name."

Dr. Garcia tilted her head and smiled. "Sounds to me like you did something right."

Kellen floundered.

"So you and Vee are in a Dom/sub relationship?"

"Yes," Kellen said. "Vee said… you're in the community?"

Dr. Garcia nodded. "I'm a sub in a committed relationship with my Domme. I counsel many people from all walks of life who dabble to varying degrees in the kink scene. But what about you and Vee? How often do you scene?"

"When we first started, it was almost every day. Every day I could get away, anyway. I didn't live with him, and J—" Kellen bit his tongue. "I couldn't always leave. But I tried, because I needed it so much, and Vee would give it to me and after he'd hold me and I could pretend things were… different."

"And now?"

Kellen had to stop and think, which startled him. "Uh… I mean, we've had *sex*…."

Dr. Garcia's lips twitched but she gestured for him to continue.

"But I don't think we've scened since we went to the hockey game, maybe a month ago? I haven't… I haven't asked for it in awhile, I guess? I don't—I don't remember." He wrapped his arms around his ribs, wishing again for Vee.

"When you scene, does Vee respect your limits?"

"Vee helped me *find* my limits," Kellen said. "I never said no, before him."

"But you've said no *to* him?"

"Yeah, the night of that scene, actually. He was, um—I was really overstimulated and I thought he was going to keep me on edge for several more hours and I safeworded."

"What was his reaction?"

"He held me and told me he was proud of me," Kellen said, remembering the way Vee's arms had felt around him.

"Do you understand why that's so important?" Dr. Garcia asked.

Kellen shook his head. "I mean… not really. It's just a word."

"No," Dr. Garcia said, leaning forward. "It's you taking control, Kellen. You ended the scene. Vee immediately stopped what he was doing because of you. *You* took control of yourself, instead of always being the submissive one, the *passive* one. You were active. You said, 'no, I don't want that'. That's *huge*, Kellen."

Kellen lifted a shoulder. "It's Vee," he said feebly. He looked up. "Can I… ask a question?"

"Of course."

"Addiction—" Kellen chewed his lip. "It's bad. I know that. It's dangerous and makes me do stupid things… but I *like* subbing," he blurted. "I don't *want* to stop. It feels so good, it makes me feel safe, Vee takes such good care of me—do I have to stop completely? Cold turkey? Never do it again?"

"I can't really tell you for sure yet, it's too early to say," Dr. Garcia said. "How long have you been with Vee?"

"Four… no, five months."

"And you haven't felt the need to go out and find anyone else in that time? Get your 'fix' elsewhere?"

Kellen shook his head vehemently. "Absolutely not."

"Well, if I had to guess… no, I don't think you have to stop. You just told me you haven't scened in a month. Have you ever known an addict to voluntarily go without their fix for that long, simply because it didn't occur to them?"

Kellen swallowed hope. "Does that mean I'm… *not* addicted?"

Dr. Garcia made a thoughtful noise. "Who's to say what addiction really is? It's a tricky beast, not a one-size-fits-all. Maybe you'll always need the pain. Maybe you'll grow in a different direction. But let me ask *you* something. If you left Vee today, or he left you, would you go back to your old ways? Would you go back to the club and find a Dom to hurt you?"

"No," Kellen said instantly.

A smile spread across Dr. Garcia's face. "Why not?"

"Because… because I don't want it if it's not with Vee," Kellen said, clutching the fidget spinner. "I—it's… he's it. If I can't fly with him, then I don't want to fly at all."

Dr. Garcia sat back. She looked *proud*, Kellen thought. "Tell me, Kellen, did you want to come here today?"

"No," Kellen said immediately.

"And are you willing to come back, now that you've met me and we've talked?"

"I—yeah," he said, surprising himself.

"Good. Because I want to see you once a week for awhile. I have a feeling there's a lot you need to unpack and set down. I can help you do that, if you want me to."

Kellen nodded, gratitude surging. "I think… I do."

"Then I'll see you next week at the same time," Dr. Garcia said. Her smile was gentle. "You did very well. Next time, I want to talk about your father, but I think we're done for now."

"You think… you think I can…."

Dr. Garcia waited but Kellen's throat had closed up and he couldn't get the words out.

"I think you're an incredible young man," Dr. Garcia said quietly, holding his eyes. "And it's my pleasure to help you learn how to see that, and teach you how to heal your scars. My receptionist will help you set up the appointment for next week."

She smiled and somehow Kellen made it to his feet and found his way back out to the lobby, feeling floaty, like his head wasn't quite connected to his body. Vee shot upright and Kellen walked straight into his arms.

"You okay?" Vee whispered against his cheek.

Kellen shook his head, blinking back tears. "No." He kissed Vee's throat. "But I think… maybe I will be. Someday."

EPILOGUE

The sunshine poured in through the window, filling the room with warm, golden light. It lit the dust motes in the air, setting them sparkling, and backlit Vee's black hair with a bright halo.

"You never did explain the plug." Kellen trailed a finger over Vee's arm where it rested on his abdomen.

Vee, facedown beside him, lifted his face from the pillow and blinked muzzily, hair on end and his eyes dazed. "Oh. Ah… well, I was trying to think up ways to convince you to top me, and I thought if I made it easier, and maybe made a joke about riding *you*, that you'd be willing to try it. Didn't really expect it to turn out the way it did, but I'm definitely not complaining."

Kellen didn't try to hold back the laugh. "You are *such* an idiot. Come here."

Keep reading for sneak peeks of more incredible
romances by Michaela Grey!

ACKNOWLEDGMENTS

For Aaliya, who can't spell "noodles", and Sarah, who saves my ass on a near-daily basis.

ABOUT THE AUTHOR

Michaela Grey told stories to put herself to sleep since she was old enough to hold a conversation in her head. When she learned to write, she began putting those stories down on paper. She resides in the Texas Hill Country with her cats, and is perpetually on the hunt for peaceful writing time.

When she's not writing, she's watching hockey or blogging about writing and men on knife shoes chasing a frozen Oreo around the ice while trying to keep her cat off the keyboard.

Tumblr: greymichaela.tumblr.com
Twitter: @GreyMichaela
Facebook: www.facebook.com/GreyMichaela
E-mail: greymichaela@gmail.com

BLINDSIDE HIT

CHAPTER ONE

Etienne Brideau was ugly. He knew this fact, and most of the time he didn't think about it. He tried not to look in the mirror, to not catch a glimpse of his reflection in windows. He was good at what he did and that was what counted. He could out-skate anyone on his team and had the best plus/minus average in his minor league hockey team. The men he picked up in furtive encounters, safely away from the prying eyes of those who wouldn't approve, didn't seem to mind that his nose was too big and bony, his mouth was oddly shaped, and his smile showed too much gum, or maybe it was just that he never gave them the chance to see him in the light.

It didn't matter, he told himself. He'd helped his team win the Kelly Cup last year, for Christ's sakes. Who cared what he looked like? He was destined for the NHL, and nothing was going to get in the way of him getting there.

When he was traded to Toronto's minor league team, he knew in his heart he was on his way. He hugged his teammates, wished them well, and packed his bags for Ontario.

"Cape Breton, huh?" Malcolm Kendricks was a big man, with a wide smile and booming voice. He'd introduced himself as the owner and general manager of the Thunder, his handshake hearty. "Good team. Defense a bit weak this year."

Etienne said nothing.

Malcolm glanced up, grin a flash of white against dark skin. "Relax, son. I've been watching tapes of you. You're a good left winger—potential to be great, I'd say. But you need to learn to play well with others. Your team is there to support you."

Etienne swallowed the retort. "Yes sir."

"You're not a puck hog, I'll give you that," Malcolm mused, looking through papers on his messy desk. "Rudy Wells is your team captain and first line center. He'll decide where he wants you."

"Isn't that usually the coach's decision, sir?"

"Ah well, you'll see," Malcolm said cryptically. "The team's on the ice, come meet them."

Etienne followed him down the hall and up the ramp to the rink. He could hear blades on ice, cheerful voices and the occasional thwack of sticks against pucks. His spirits rose, along with his nerves, as they emerged into the brightly lit space.

Some fifteen players were milling around one end of the ice, a few others on the bench.

"Shootouts," Malcolm said unnecessarily. "Rudy! Over here!"

A figure split off the group and made for them. Rudy was small, barely five foot nine, and lean, with dark skin and darker eyes. His smile was friendly, welcoming as he skidded to a stop beside them.

"Rudy, this is Etienne Brideau," Malcolm said. "He's all yours."

Rudy pulled off a glove and held out a hand. "Good to meet you, Etienne. Looking forward to seeing what you bring to the team. Got your gear?"

Etienne hefted his bag.

"Great. Let's get you a stall and on the ice." He led Etienne down the hall to the locker room, showing him the stall cleaned out and waiting. Etienne unpacked his gear as Rudy leaned against the stall next to him.

"Jackdaws have good things to say about you."

Etienne glanced up, halfway through stripping his clothes off. "They're a good team."

"Got family there?"

"No, actually." Etienne bent to pick up his chest guard. "My dad's in Brampton."

"Nice. I'm guessing we're a pit stop for you, am I right? Or is your dream to play for the ECHL until you retire?"

Etienne couldn't help the snort. "I want to play for the Seabirds, but I'll go to any NHL team that'll take me, to start."

"Fair enough. Well, I'll use you while I have

you. I talked to Malcolm about your contract. Coach Hannity—the Freeze' head coach—may call you up occasionally, if they have a break in their line needing to be filled. Have you played in the AHL before?"

"Once or twice, with the Jackdaws," Etienne said, reaching for his skates.

"The Freeze are a good team. I'm friends with a few of them, like Adam Caron and Li; I can give you some tips on how they operate."

"You know Adam Caron?"

Rudy shrugged. "Sure. Good guy."

"I've seen him skate in a call up for the Wolverines," Etienne said, trying not to sound starstruck. "His puck handling is ridiculous." *And he's hot as fuck. Probably best not to say that part out loud.*

"Taught him everything he knows," Rudy said with a wink.

"So where's *our* coach?"

"In his office, probably," Rudy said. "He spends most of his time there. You have a problem, bring it to me first." Something in Rudy's expression warned Etienne not to pry.

He finished lacing his skates and stood, towering over the much shorter center.

"Let's go meet the team," Rudy said, smiling up at him.

EVERYONE CROWDED around when he and Rudy came back up the tunnel, shaking Etienne's hand

and slapping him on the back in friendly greeting. Most of the names Rudy tossed at him didn't stick, but a few stood out. Liam Thibault was a huge blond defenseman with a sunny smile. His shadow was a right winger named Johnny Girard, six inches shorter and fifty pounds lighter, as dark as Liam was bright. They never seemed far from each other and Etienne watched them curiously out of the corner of his eye as Rudy continued to introduce people. Were they together? Were they out? Did that mean he might have a chance to be out too?

"Logan Martel," Rudy said. "First line goalie. He doesn't speak, but he'll make himself understood."

Logan was tall and lanky, with olive skin and intense brown eyes. He had the goalie stare down cold, but his smile was friendly when he offered his hand.

"Theo Yoong and Robert Broussard," Rudy continued. "Theo's a D-man and Brewski's a left wing like you."

Theo was average height, spiky black hair standing up in sweaty clumps and golden skin gleaming from exertion. Beside him, Broussard scowled and didn't put out a hand. He was rangy and lean, with light brown hair and mistrustful green eyes that measured Etienne and found him wanting.

Etienne didn't offer to shake his hand, giving him a nod instead.

"Jax and Wyatt," Rudy said, pointing to two young men standing together a few feet away. "Wingers, fourth line. Let's do some shootouts!"

he added, clapping his hands to draw attention. "Tenny, how about you go first?"

Tenny. His old teammates had called him Bridey, but Etienne found himself liking the way Tenny sounded. He nodded and gripped his stick as Logan skated for his crease.

He opted for an easy slalom toward the net, getting a feel for the ice—firmer than he was used to, sweet and clean beneath his blades—and watching Logan's reactions. He was going to be tough to get past, Etienne could already tell, keeping his movements to a minimum and not expending too much energy as he waited for Etienne to make his move.

Etienne sent a slapshot at Logan's left shoulder. Logan caught the puck and smacked it to the ice, and Etienne grinned, giving him a quick salute and circling back to the others. He watched as the rest of the team took their turns, cataloging Logan's reactions. When it was his turn again, he scooped up a puck and barreled straight for the goal.

Logan tensed, readying himself. Etienne sent the puck out in front of himself, aiming for Logan's left side, but at the last second he caught it with the tip of his stick, pulled it back as Logan lunged for it and sank it behind his skates.

Logan hit the ice and slid as the puck bounced off the back of the net. Etienne circled the goal and extended a hand to help him up. Logan accepted it, his eyes thoughtful and amused, and Etienne went back to the others.

"Nicely done," Rudy said, smiling at him. "Not often someone gets one over on Logan."

"Probably just lucky," Etienne said.

"Practice is at eleven every day," Rudy told him. "Strategy and planning sessions every Friday. Workout starts at eight—you don't have to be there but it's highly encouraged. Welcome to the team, Tenny."

Blindside Hit is available on
Amazon and Kindle Unlimited now!

ODD MAN RUSH

CHAPTER ONE

When Rune Hedaya walked into the Sirens' locker room, dread crawled inside Eli McKenna's chest and curled up there.

Practice hadn't started yet, everyone still busy getting their gear on, and the room was the usual raucous mess of stick tape and balled up socks being hurled around, chirps and rude comments and bragging blending seamlessly into white noise that Eli effortlessly filtered out. He focused on getting his own gear in place, buckling his pads on and keeping his breathing slow and even.

He was shrugging into his chest protector when William Caron, their head coach, had ushered the tall stranger inside, a hand on his shoulder. It was a measure of the respect Caron commanded that the room immediately quieted, although maybe they were just curious about the newcomer. He was strikingly handsome, dark brown hair shaved close to the sides of his head and left long on top, with olive skin and sharp eyes that surveyed the room.

"Boys, this is Rune Hedaya," Caron announced. "He comes from the Otters. He's a d-man, and we're gonna try out some pairings today."

The captain was the first to greet him, because there was a reason he was captain. "Seth Williams," he said, holding out his hand.

Rune took it as others crowded around.

Eli breathed through his nose, in and out, not looking over. He stood, gave himself a once-over, and then bounced on his skates several times to make sure everything was settled and secure. When he glanced up, Rune was walking toward him.

"Hi," he said, hand out. "Rune."

Eli accepted the hand, hoping his hesitation hadn't shown. "Eli," he said. "Um. Goalie."

Rune's eyes creased with amusement. Up close, they were a striking blue-green. "Is *that* why all the gear?"

He had a faint accent, but Eli couldn't place it. It sharpened the corners of his words, made them crisp and clear. He was grinning, waiting for a response, and Eli just shrugged awkwardly.

"You know what they say about d-men," he said. "Can't read a clue to save their lives, let alone a play. I was just helping you out."

Rune's eyebrows shot up and he burst out laughing. "*Ouch*! Guess I'll just have to prove you wrong, huh?"

Eli found himself smiling back without meaning to, and he ducked his head, breaking eye contact. "Yeah, sure."

"Rune," Seth said, appearing at Rune's elbow. "Come meet Ilya and Josh. Couple of our d-men."

"Nice to meet you, Eli," Rune said. "See you out there."

He let himself be pulled away and Eli took another deep breath, rolling his shoulders and letting the tension flow from him on the exhale.

Daved was watching him when he turned for the door. Sympathy, visible only to Eli who knew him so well, glimmered in his eyes.

Don't, Eli warned him silently, and Daved just nodded and pulled the door open for him.

ON THE ICE, it was better. But then, it was always better on the ice. Here, between his pipes, he knew what was expected of him. *Stop the puck.* That's all he had to know. All the training, all the discipline, all the stretching and exercising—it all came down to that.

He shaved down his crease methodically, breathing loud inside his helmet, as the rest of the team, roughly half in black jerseys and the other half in gold, spilled onto the ice and spun out into broad loops and circles, cheerfully calling abuse at each other. Eli let it wash over him, in it but not of it. He went through his warmup routine, counting each part off in his head, until Coach blew his whistle.

"Eli against Väinö," he said. "Eli, you're gold team. Vinyl, you're black, obviously."

"No, Seth is," Jay pointed out, causing a wave of snickers.

Coach gave him an unimpressed look and Jay grinned, cheeky and unrepentant. "Here are the pairings," Coach continued. "Black with me, gold with Rob."

Rob, the assistant coach, held up the whiteboard by his side and Eli scrutinized it. Rune had been paired with Josh. They were talking quietly off to the side, heads together. Eli didn't try to listen in. He read the rest of the lines and headed back to his crease.

The first few minutes were a burst of frenetic activity, the players all coming off a two day break and more than ready to get back into action. Eli stayed loose and ready in his crease, watching the play like a hawk.

Jay tried a sharp angle shot off him and Eli blockered it away with ease. It was scooped up by Rune and dumped into the far end. Eli watched as they gave chase. Rune was a good skater, fast and balanced, with an agility that belied his size. He crashed the scrum in the far corner and flipped the puck out to Josh, who sent it backward to Seth.

Ilya picked Seth's pocket before Seth could make a move toward goal, though, and then they were all heading back toward Eli, Ilya on a breakaway out in front. Eli floated forward to the edge of his crease, watching Ilya bear down on him. He knew Ilya well enough by now to know when he was going to make his move. He always dropped his right shoulder, *there*—Rune came out of nowhere just as Ilya fired, hurling himself to the ice in front of the puck.

It hit him in the bicep and Rune grunted and slid in a sprawl of long limbs through Eli's crease. Eli caught his arm, stopping his forward motion, as Ilya skidded to a halt in shock and the others caught up.

"Is *practice*," he said accusingly. "Coach is kill me if I hurt new d-man in very first practice! Why you so stupid?"

Rune grinned up at Eli, still flat on his back. "Thanks for catching me. You're not too bad at this goalie thing."

"Yeah well, you're a lot bigger than a puck," Eli said, pulling off his blocker and extending a hand. "Slower, too."

Rune laughed as he took his hand, grip firm, and let him pull him to his feet. "Are you always this mean?"

"I'm honest," Eli countered, but he couldn't fight the smile on his face.

"Whoa, did you just make Reaper smile?" Jay demanded.

Eli rolled his eyes. "I smile, Davo. If I don't smile at you, it's because you're not funny."

"Does that mean I *am*?" Rune asked.

"Jury's still out," Eli retorted.

Coach blew his whistle. Rune winked at Eli and skated away.

So it went for the rest of practice. Every time anyone with the puck got close to Eli, Rune was there first, breaking their shot, spoiling their aim, sometimes straight out slapping the puck off their stick. He was as fast as he was agile, not afraid to use his size but also careful not to make unnecessary contact.

"Why the fuck did the Otters let you go?" Eli overheard Josh demand during a lull.

Rune shrugged easily, his reply inaudible.

After the first ten minutes or so, Coach switched it up, putting Rune with Ilya. Their chemistry was obvious from the beginning, working off each other's passes seamlessly. Rune shot Eli a blinding smile as he swept by him at high speed, gone before Eli could even smile back.

At least he's having fun, Eli thought, but something prickled under his skin at the thought of Rune and Ilya being friends. He shut that thought down before it could really form, turning his focus back to the practice. Daved was barreling down on him with the puck and Eli knew from experience just how hard he was to stop at that speed.

It wasn't that he didn't want Rune to have friends, Eli told himself in the shower. He didn't even *know* Rune, it was ridiculous to be concerning himself with Rune's hypothetical relationships.

Eli turned his face into the spray and closed his eyes.

He'd just found himself watching for Rune's brilliant smile, wanting it turned on him, wanting Rune's attention, his focus. On him.

But he couldn't want that, he reminded himself, and turned the shower off.

He came out of the shower to find the room deserted. Not surprising—he'd taken awhile. He dropped his towel and stepped into his underwear, pulling them up over his hips.

"Why do they call you Reaper?"

Eli spun.

Rune was leaning against the door, ankles crossed, turning his phone over and over between long fingers. He raised an eyebrow when Eli didn't immediately answer.

"Oh, uh—" Eli struggled to marshal his thoughts, reaching for his pants. "It's stupid."

"Try me."

Eli zipped his pants and picked up his shirt. "Because I don't have a sense of humor and I'm lethal between the pipes."

It didn't take Rune long. "So you're the grim reaper. I like it." That bright smile spread across his face, making Eli feel like he'd been punched in the gut. He covered by sitting down to put his socks on, focusing hard on what he was doing.

"What—why are you still here?" he asked without looking up.

"Oh, group of guys wanted to take me out for lunch at some place called Savour? They said it's the team's favorite restaurant. I thought I'd see if you wanted to come with us."

Bad idea bad idea bad idea.

Eli shook the thought away and stood to step into his shoes. Going out to eat once with his team and the new guy wouldn't hurt anything.

There was nothing *to* hurt. Rune was just being friendly.

"Sure," he said, and Rune's smile widened until Eli couldn't breathe.

"Awesome! Well, I don't have a car, so… any chance of a ride?"

Eli had the sinking sensation that he'd bitten off more than he could chew. He was helpless to do more than nod and grab his keys off the shelf.

Rune followed him out of the rink, keeping pace easily. He looked around, taking in the rain-soaked pavement and the trees that crowded above them, forming a lacy, green-shaded cover over their walk to Eli's car.

"Sure is pretty out here," he remarked.

"Could be worse," Eli allowed. "Could be east coast."

"Hey, east coast is gorgeous—oh, you're teasing me. Who says you don't have a sense of humor?"

Eli shrugged, unlocking the car. "People who think fart jokes are funny."

"Ah," Rune said, sliding into the passenger seat. "Jay."

"Among others."

The car fired up smoothly and Eli rubbed the leather steering wheel with one thumb. "So why *did* you get traded?" he asked as he left the parking lot. "If you don't mind saying."

Rune stretched his long legs out as far as they would go, lacing his hands over his belly. "That's classified," he said comfortably.

Eli felt the flush all the way up to his ears. "Right. Never mind."

"Oh hey, no!" Rune said, sitting up. "That was a joke, I'm sorry. A stupid joke. Not funny."

The flush burned hotter. Eli hunched his shoulders, clutching the wheel tighter, and said nothing. Now Rune would see exactly how humorless he was.

The pause was awkward and Eli didn't know how to fill it.

"I, uh… I didn't fit in with the Otters, I guess," Rune said suddenly. He scratched his nose. "I didn't like how they relied on muscle and heavy hits to get the job done. They wanted me to be more aggressive. I just wanted to play."

Silence fell in the car as a pop singer crooned on the radio.

"My first year in juniors," Eli said after a minute, "my coach made me loosen one of my pipes. If anyone bumped into it, it would pop off immediately and I'd get a whistle."

"Oh," Rune said. "That's…."

"Yeah." Eli took a slow breath. "Dirty. Or at least weighting the game in our favor. It made me—it made me sick. I didn't want to cheat to get a win. If I didn't win clean, what was the point?"

"Yeah," Rune said softly. "I'm sorry."

Eli shrugged, turning the corner toward the restaurant and looking for a parking space. "It's over and I survived. So did you."

"Will they let me play hockey here?" Rune asked, and for the first time he didn't sound confident and sure of himself.

Eli parked and took a moment to gather his thoughts. "I think so," he finally said. "Cary— Coach—he may want you to hit someone sometimes, shake 'em up and put a little fear of God and the Sirens into them, but he'll have already seen your talent. You're not just big dumb muscle to him."

Rune was watching him when Eli looked at him. "You like him."

"And respect him," Eli said. "He's a great guy. He'd open a vein for us and every single one of us would do the same for him. You'll see."

Rune's eyebrow went up. "Damn. So what do you like to do for fun?"

Eli blinked at the sudden shift in topic. "I mean, normal stuff," he hedged. "Why?"

"Just curious. You're so quiet. I wanna know what makes you tick."

"We should go inside," Eli said abruptly, and unbuckled.

Rune didn't move, watching him with narrowed eyes. "You like to drink? Party?"

"No," Eli said, startled into truth. "I'm boring. I like to read. I don't go out unless the team drags me out." He fidgeted with the seatbelt. "Why do you *care?*"

"Why do you think?" Rune asked cryptically. He pushed his door open and stepped out before Eli could answer, leaving him to swear and scramble after him.

The guys were already in the back of the restaurant at their favorite booth when they showed up, and they were greeted with cheers and chirping over being late.

They settled in, Rune right next to Eli on the bench, and Eli picked up his menu, determined not to notice how solid and warm Rune's thigh was pressed up against his own. He almost managed it until Rune nudged him with his knee.

"What's good here?" he asked under the chatter of the table.

Eli forced himself to focus. "The beef au jus is nice. Or they have an Italian sub that's not too far off our diet plan, especially if you get it with all the vegetables."

Rune smiled at him and when the server came by, he ordered the beef au jus. "So," he said once she was gone. "What's there to do around here, boys?"

"Webber will show you all the best coffeeshops," Jay said. "'Specially the ones with cute baristas. You got a girl, Runer?"

"No girl," Rune said equably, leaning back against the seat and spreading his arms along the spine. His fingers brushed Eli's shoulder and Eli forced himself not to react. "No guy, either."

The booth went momentarily still.

"That gonna be a problem?" Rune said. His voice was utterly calm.

"We see you play, you fuck anyone you want," Ilya said into the fraught silence. "You're not hit on me though. I have girlfriend. Very beautiful. You want see?" He was digging out his phone before anyone could stop him, thumbing through pictures and then holding it out so Rune could see.

"She *is* beautiful," Rune agreed. "What's she doing with your ugly ass?"

Ilya cackled. "NHL player, baby. Lots of money!"

Eli focused on the air entering his lungs, trapping it there, then letting it out slowly. Rune wasn't straight. Rune had been—possibly, unless Eli's wishful thinking had clouded his vision—hitting on him.

Rune's fingers brushed his shoulder again and Eli turned to look at him. Up close, Rune's smile was somehow even more beautiful, his striking eyes crinkling at the corners.

"We good?" he murmured under whatever Ilya was saying.

Eli took a breath. Another one. Rune waited.

"Yeah," Eli said. He mustered a smile, even though it wasn't very big. "Of course. So where are you from, anyway? I can't quite place your accent."

"Germany by way of Syria," Rune said. "My parents wanted a better life for their kids. Papa's an engineer and Mama's a doctor. Hey." He leaned closer and lowered his voice. "Do you wanna maybe hang out later? Just the two of us?"

Eli froze. Was he asking what Eli *thought* he was asking? The look in Rune's eyes said maybe, just maybe, he was.

He opened his mouth to say something and his phone rang, cutting off his answer. *Shit.*

"Sorry," he muttered, dragging it from his pocket. "I have to get this."

"Is that Noemi?" Jay demanded, and Daved elbowed him in the ribs. "Ow! Tell her I said hi, Reaper. *Ow*, Davvy, stop it!"

"Who's Noemi?" Rune asked.

"Um." Eli slid from the booth, the phone still ringing. He glanced at Rune, looking up at him with nothing but friendly curiosity in his eyes, and back down at the phone. "My wife. Excuse me."

He hit answer and walked away without looking back.

Preorder Odd Man Rush today!